THE OTHER MOTHER

TINA ÅMODT is a writer and translator. Born in 1985 on the West Norwegian island of Askøy, she now lives in Oslo. She made her debut with *Builders' Prose*, which was published to great acclaim. In 2015 she received the Stig Sæterbakken Memorial Prize. *The Other Mother* is the first of her novels to be translated into English.

ALISON MCCULLOUGH is a translator and writer based in Stavanger, Norway. She holds a BA in English Literature from the University of Oxford and an MA in Film Studies from University College London. Her translation of Klara Hveberg's *Lean Your Loneliness Slowly Against Mine* was longlisted for the 2022 PEN America Translation Prize.

THE OTHER MOTHER

TINA ÅMODT

TRANSLATED FROM THE NORWEGIAN BY
ALISON McCULLOUGH

PUSHKIN PRESS

Pushkin Press
Somerset House, Strand
London WC2R 1LA

The Other Mother was first published as *Den andre moren*
by Forlaget Oktober AS in Oslo, 2023

Published in agreement with Oslo Literary Agency

First published by Pushkin Press in 2026

ISBN 13: 978-1-80533-337-1

The authorised representative in the EEA is eucomply OÜ,
Pärnu mnt. 139b-14, 11317, Tallinn, Estonia,
hello@eucompliancepartner.com, +33757690241

Designed and typeset by Tetragon, London
Printed and bound in the United Kingdom by Clays Ltd, Elcograf S.p.A.

This translation has been published with the financial
support of NORLA, Norwegian Literature Abroad.

Pushkin Press is committed to a sustainable future for our
business, our readers and our planet. This book is made from
paper from forests that support responsible forestry.

www.pushkinpress.com

1 3 5 7 9 8 6 4 2

THE OTHER MOTHER

T HE NIGHT BEFORE THEY LEFT, I woke with the feeling that
there was no going back. Now I just had to tell her, I thought,
because I was certain Helene would be able to see it on me. As if I
had been savaged by a dog I had petted without permission during
the night, or woken to find my hair turned completely white. But
the day arrived without Helene saying anything at all. Henry and
I had been up for over an hour when she came down to us, sweet-
smelling and freshly showered. She poured herself a cup of coffee,
grazed my hip as she took a glass from the shelf above the sink, not
stopping to ask why I looked so strange, or to place a hand on my
chest and say: how come your heart's beating so fast?

She lifted Henry from his high chair and sat him on her lap,
asked how the night had been, 'I didn't hear him,' she said, 'did you
both sleep well?' while Henry tugged at her shirt as usual, crazed at
the prospect of finally getting some milk. 'Not too bad,' I replied. I
felt shaky, but that could be down to all sorts of things; I've felt that
way almost every morning after this long year of night weaning
and sleep training and everything else we've had to battle our way
through to get life back on an even keel. 'We should probably wake
Olav, too,' Helene said. I nodded, smiled so she wouldn't assume
I was in a bad mood. Had she really not noticed?

Olav's room was warm, almost pitch dark. It was my mother-in-
law who recommended we get the blackout curtains. I like to keep
them closed, as if to deny the miserable view of the apartment blocks

7

opposite our neighbourhood, and the railway line that divides the suburb's expensive and cheap properties from one another like a poorly camouflaged barrier. 'Good morning,' I said softly. Nothing unusual in my voice. Olav didn't answer. Nothing strange about that, either. I stepped over the mattress on the floor that keeps Helene and me apart at night: we lie there on alternating evenings, one of us with Henry in our bedroom in the so-called marital bed, while the other seeks refuge on the mattress here in his big brother's room, earplugs bestowing a good night's sleep. Nightly separation. The best part of the day.

I crouched down beside the sticker-covered edge of the bed. Olav was lying on his stomach in his Ninjago underpants, the duvet kicked off. I placed my palm on his naked back, between his slender shoulder blades. 'Are you awake, honey?' I said. 'You're going to Grandma and Grandpa's house today.' He shifted slightly, mumbled, but continued to lie there with his eyes closed. I stroked his long hair, the blonde curls that had appeared to our amazement, and which I now can't get enough of. Sticking out from beneath his pillow, something shimmered – it was a little plastic animal he'd been given by an older girl at the kindergarten ages ago and which he had recently rediscovered, some garish piece of pink crap covered in glitter. Oh, my sweet little boy. All I wanted to do was sit there. To watch him in the warm, peaceful darkness, just be us.

Us, us, us. And nobody else.

When I realized I was on the verge of tears I straightened up, put my hands to my face and tapped my knuckles against my cheekbones three times, an idiotic but useful ritual I've performed for as long as I can remember. I had to concentrate. Just see them off, act warmly, look normal, say the kinds of things I usually said.

If I managed that, I thought, there might still be hope. I might still be able to find my way back, like in the Grimms' *Fairy Tales*, a path of small, shining white stones appearing before me the moment moonlight floods the forest.

I WAIT FOR THE NIGHT SKY TO BRIGHTEN. It's an entire day since they left. I stand at the sink in the bathroom and study the woman who looks at me from within the frame of the mottled mirror. Her short hair is not white. Beneath the thin T-shirt she has slept in, there's no weeping wound from teeth sinking through the flesh to the bone. She looks normal. She sucks in her stomach. Tries to avoid looking at her pasty upper arms. It's Monday, the summer holidays, and I'm alone in the house. I can't remember when I last had so much time to myself, the last time I studied myself this way. And this is just the start. The plan is that I'll follow them on Sunday, the day before the Latvian decorators move in – they don't take their holidays at the same time as everyone else, which is why we chose them – when I'm finished with all the preparations. Sorting and tidying up. Stacking heavy boxes in the loft. Emptying the kitchen drawers – the entire kitchen will eventually be replaced with a new one. I have to prise up floorboards and skirting. Fill and paint the walls of what will be both boys' bedroom, and those of our bedroom too, if I have the time. Stick to the budget. Do a decent job. Erase almost every trace of our lives here, so the house can be transformed into a place we won't want to leave. Or give up, without a very good reason.

It's a lot of work, but we set aside ample time when we booked the flights back in the spring – it was Helene who wanted me to come on the Sunday instead of the Friday, 'so you can do something nice once you're done,' she said, 'meet up with friends or go out on the town, whatever you want.' I understood that this was the greatest gift she could give me, additional days and nights to myself. To further liberate me from the physical demands of motherhood, relieve me from having to perform as a wife and daughter-in-law for a few extra days. But I was unsure of her motives. Maybe she quite liked the idea of a couple more days away from my dark mood. Or did she actually hope the person she would drive to pick up from Trondheim airport would meet her with a soft and hopeful gaze – be the same, but changed, like when Gandalf the Grey returns as Gandalf the White after bringing down the Balrog, a virtually immortal demon.

She's always had greater faith than me.

We watched *Lord of the Rings* again during the winter; I was surprised at how fun I found it. As the first images of the landscape of the horse kingdom of Rohan flickered across the screen, Helene had placed a sofa cushion in her lap: 'Here – would you like to lie down?' The tender gesture blindsided me.

I rub the sleep away with cold water. My fringe is greasy, and therefore darker than usual. During the first years of our marriage, I hardly ever allowed myself to be seen without peach-coloured lipstick and black eyeliner; I was trying to be elegant, I think. I can no longer put on make-up like that; I no longer have the face of someone who believes beauty can ensure her happiness, or at the very least a constructive mindset. My eyes – it almost looks as if I have an eye infection. It drives me insane, always having to meet that mournful gaze! But I do remember how I used to laugh so loudly that strangers on the bus would look up from their phones and start to chuckle. At work, one of the auditors who checks the annual report once came over to my desk and said: 'You always cheer me up whenever I see you – I just wanted you to know that.'

Being happy is like being bewitched. But there is nobody here to bewitch me. The tasks I face might be extensive – the house is still overflowing with them – but I have a schedule, a plan, it isn't the house that's the problem. I really don't know how I'm supposed to dissolve this thing that has lodged in my throat. The waves of stomach cramps, like contractions. I recognize the feeling from when I was small, from when I sat at the dinner table or curled up in my hiding place among the ivy at the bottom of the garden. Is everything that seems safe about to collapse? Is my body trying to warn me?

The evening before they left, as I was on my way home from the supermarket with a carrier bag full of squeezy yoghurt pouches and raisins and new colouring supplies for the plane, I spoke to Mayliss on the phone. 'Surely you can understand why I might be feeling a bit put out,' she said. 'One minute you're sitting here in my living room eating cake, and the next you're calling me and talking about DNA tests.'

Then came the accusations, the ugly, invasive allegations. 'Well, I suppose I shouldn't be surprised. You're not exactly overflowing with love for Henry, either.' 'Where on earth did you get that from?' I replied, 'That's totally uncalled for!' 'I'm only repeating what I've heard,' she went on, 'I'm only saying what I've seen. And Mamma completely agrees.' 'Your mother?' I asked. She didn't reply. She tartly rounded off the conversation; I was standing beside the row of garages, where Helene and the children couldn't see me. 'Well, speak soon. Or no – I'm sorry – I suppose we'll speak whenever it next suits *you*.'

I haven't heard from her since.

*

The Sunday arrives. I imagine Helene there in the arrivals hall. The kids aren't with her; they're waiting with their grandparents – we spare them long car journeys whenever we can. Helene stands first beside the kiosk, then the baggage belt. She calls to find out where I am. No answer. She waits, calls again; maybe she sighs loudly, feeling fed up. She checks the online newspapers to confirm that the airport express train hasn't derailed, that the queues at Oslo airport are normal. The messages stream into my phone, irritated at first, perhaps accompanied by a little joke – *Have you barricaded yourself in the toilets, or what?* – then anxious, full of confusion: *Did you get the day wrong?* But not angry, because the idea that I would fail to keep our agreement still hasn't occurred to her.

But it wouldn't have happened like that. I never would have given Olav false hope. I would have given them plenty of notice.

What constitutes plenty of notice? A day before? Two?

This isn't something I need to consider, because I'm not going to do anything of the sort. I'm going to stick to the plan. Everything will proceed as normal. I'm not going to see Mayliss again, no matter what she says – I'll say no, it isn't appropriate, this has gone too far, I'm sorry I wasn't clearer from the start, I'm sure you understand. She has to respect my decision. Surely she'll respect it? But I don't know where her boundaries lie, whether she's the type of person who throws all propriety out the window when she feels affronted.

I think I crossed that line.

'All this ruminating,' Janne would have said, had I shared this with her. 'You can just press pause now and continue with it after the holiday, or how about waiting even longer, until the redecorating is finished, or maybe even until next summer?' She's only too happy to share the techniques she's learnt at couples counselling: 'Try to think of your ruminating as self-sabotage.'

But I haven't shared this with Janne. She's just as unsuspecting as Helene. They don't even know that Mayliss exists, or, well, of course Helene has picked up on the fact that there's a Mayliss who I've spent a lot of time with while on maternity leave, but she has no idea who she is. Why we ended up spending time together. Neither of them has seen the photo Mayliss sent me of her son and Henry playing in the sandpit: turned slightly away from the camera, they squat on their haunches, each holding a spade, the sun shining on their skinny little-boy necks; their ears look a tad oversized because they both have so little hair. They are so small. They have no idea just how alike they are. As I stared at the screen, a jolt of terror shot through me. Even though I deleted the image, I felt its reverberations all that evening; there was something almost sexual about the intensity of the aftershock, as if an orgasm had surged through a cadaver. And still I didn't stop. Still I met up with them again the following week.

E verybody knows I'm the kind of person who gets things done. That I'm the kind of person who works systematically, who never delivers anything that hasn't been checked through one final time. So I've got down to business, made a start on my tasks. I've emptied all the wardrobes – Helene's clothes fit in four transparent refuse sacks, mine in three; the boys' clothes I've sorted by season. Many of Henry's have long since become too small. He's big for his age, taller than his brother was at this stage in his development. I don't like to see the clothes in bags like this – there's something vulgar about it. But it's just a feeling. I'm doing it this way because it's practical. I've also cleared out quite a few of the boys' things, have thrown away piles of drawings and put the baby toys Henry has grown out of into a separate cardboard box, along with the least-used toy cars and bits of plastic rubbish that came free with the magazines Olav pesters us for every now and then. All this I'm going to give away. The boys won't even notice.

But the work is slow going. The house is silent, I am silent; I haven't spoken to anyone other than Helene and a couple of the neighbours who haven't gone away on holiday. And I've texted Joachim to tell him I'll call him soon. I have to, because soon I might need him in a way I've never needed him before. I really ought to call Janne, too – all my friends, the ones I have left. I ought to write them letters and send gifts, strengthen those connections, cultivate their sense of loyalty.

Or is it already too late for that?

Yesterday I didn't get to bed until the early hours, and this morning I lazed about until after eight. I've eaten a family-size bag of cheese puffs and haven't bothered to change my underwear. Long-awaited pleasures. But they fail to soothe the heaviness that moves deep in my chest.

I feel lost. Not just because I don't know what I'll do if Mayliss refuses to let this go. And not just because I'm unsure whether I can keep it up any more, this role I've been assigned and which I have to play as if my life depends on it. It's also that I now have time to sit around and think. Think, without being interrupted by crying, or shouts of *Mamma, Henry bit me!*, or a dirty nappy that needs changing, or questions like whether I forgot to buy washing powder. All the details I've divulged to Mayliss are one thing. But that I have the time to think – that's much more far-reaching. And it disturbs me. Like lone, young male wolves, my thoughts roam further and further, until all at once I find myself in a place I never imagined I'd end up, having believed I'd never again manage to think anything more advanced than: If Henry doesn't fall asleep this instant, I am going to go insane.

It probably shouldn't surprise me, the fact that this reunion with free thought feels so overwhelming. They've always known it, those who have kept women occupied with caring for children, with scrubbing and peeling, with lacing up their corsets nice and tight. There's also a kind of grief in it. But if I continue to think without restraint, I have no idea who I'll find staring back at me from the mirror by the end of the week.

THE HOUSE WITHOUT MY FAMILY. It's bigger. The silence pushes the ugly Anaglypta-covered walls further apart. Our furniture and all the toys almost seem like stage props. The children's toothbrushes, crusted with blue toothpaste, sit on the bottom shelf of the bookcase – we forgot to both brush their teeth and pack their toothbrushes before we hurried out to the car and headed for the airport yesterday morning. Their mess is scattered, floating flotsam and jetsam. Henry's sticker book full of diggers, a gift from Helene's brother. Olav's many hair elastics and Kinder Surprise figurines and sticks. Helene's dirty socks. An over-washed and faded bra slung over the back of the sofa.

I drink coffee at the kitchen table, dip a spoon into a bowl filled with sugary cereal and whole milk. Fat and sugar are what's keeping me going. The stapled booklet that contains the architect's drawings and vision for the house lies next to the little vase filled with the clover Olav picked as a parting gift, 'For you, Mamma.' Darling Olav. Since he was born, I've hardly been able to distinguish love from grief, have been plagued by the recurring thought: I'm going to have to bury my child. I don't know whether Helene has similar thoughts about Henry – she may well do, of course – but we're not alike in this. She doesn't cry at the news of abortion bans or people searching in vain for their relatives among the rubble of destroyed buildings; she doesn't devour the Amnesty International newsletter about how many gay people were hanged in Iran over the past week. She doesn't have this brutally intense urge to flee every time she feels offended or afraid. If she did, she probably never would have taken me back.

As young as he is, it's already clear that Henry takes after Helene, after members of her family – he's so jovial, has such a spring in his step. He's going to be just fine. Despite growing up with me.

With me, in this patchwork of a so-called family.

As I lay there tossing and turning in bed two nights ago, I suddenly heard him pulling himself to standing in his cot, his breathing focused and rapid. The evening sunlight forced its way between the gap in the curtains to cut straight across my forehead. First his tiny hand stuck up over the bumper, followed by his chubby arm in his sheep-patterned pyjamas, then his face, his full lips, his beautiful but slightly protruding brown eyes. Helene's eyes are brown. Mine and Olav's are blue. I thought he was going to start screaming, to demand milk. But the moment he realized that it was me lying there, he smiled, as if he'd caught sight of himself in a mirror.

'You have to go to sleep now, it's night-time,' I said. I felt sickly and feeble, as if I'd been trying to hide but had been discovered. Then I picked him up, laid him down beside me and pulled him close.

I don't think Henry can have been more than three weeks old when he began to smile, much earlier than Olav. But it took time for me to give myself over to those smiles, to interpret them as being down to anything other than tummy aches or reflexes – the smile, the infant's ancient survival strategy. 'I don't think he recognizes me,' I said, as I sat next to Helene on the sofa, my feet on the coffee table and using my thighs to support the tiny baby in the too-big woollen bodysuit I was cradling so he was facing us. 'He probably thinks I'm just some random woman.' 'Of course he recognizes you,' Helene exclaimed, 'don't be so ridiculous.' I fell silent. Shame always makes me hot and red in the cheeks, it's so easy to see it on me. I smiled at Henry, allowing him to grip both my thumbs, sticking out my tongue to get him to copy me. Then, in my most pathetic, manipulative voice, I said: 'You know how great it makes me feel when you sound just like my mother.'

OUT ON THE PATIO IT'S POURING WITH RAIN. The garden furniture's cushions have turned dark with it – I should have brought them inside to prevent them growing mouldy, it's rained constantly since Helene and the boys left. The flowerbeds that line the garden are beautiful, flowers I don't know the names of growing in an attractively arranged and sopping-wet tangle. The people who lived here before us planted them. The apple trees are young and wispy. At the entrance to the garden stands a yellow bag I'm supposed to fill with building waste once I finally make a start on pulling up the laminate flooring. I'm cold, still wearing only my underwear and the top I've slept in, but there's nobody here to see my rolls of flab and cellulite.

The dining table is teak, taken from my grandmother's house after her death. Helene thinks it's ugly, she wants to replace it with something in Valchromat or untreated oak, 'Something that doesn't feel so 2009, I don't think the teak will really go with anything once we've redecorated.' She's probably right. She's binge-watched every episode of all the Scandinavian versions of *Architects' Homes* and feels a deep sense of joy at being surrounded by beautiful, solid objects. I like it too, and I trust her taste; she and the architect had hit it off, they were on the same wavelength. But I don't know when she became like this, yet another middle-class woman with an interest in interior design. When we met, all she owned was a few IKEA chairs and a lamp she'd been given by a friend. And she knows how I feel about the table. She doesn't listen. She doesn't want to listen. Which children's book is that from? *Karius and Bactus*, maybe?

I've never slept alone in this house. I've been a stay-at-home parent for almost an entire year now, since last summer, when Henry had just learnt to wriggle along on his tummy and I offered my colleagues a pack of cheap ice lollies before leaving the office and taking over the parental leave. The co-mother's quota. Just after we moved here.

I'm alone, yes, but my wild and ever-expanding mental land-scape is crammed with people. Not just Helene and the boys. Not just Mayliss. Not just friends I have or once had. When I opened the door to the laundry room yesterday evening, it was as if I was looking straight at Fitness Guri. It was Helene who nicknamed her that, and out of loyalty and in an attempt to shake a private joke out of the catastrophe, and probably also as a kind of defence mechanism, I've kept using the name ever since.

A little way off, under a tree, or whatever it might have been, stood my mother. I started. It isn't that I haven't thought about Fitness Guri and my mother and my sister over the past year – of course I have, time and time again – but the thoughts have been automatic and lifeless, like a collection of old Barbie dolls I've occasionally picked up and looked at and not known what to do with. Now the dolls have started moving. They shift their positions, recreating scenes I thought I was long since done with. All at once I feel a small hand touch the thin skin just behind my earlobe. I stiffen, as if waking to someone parting my thighs and telling me to stay silent.

'YOU CAN THINK of your relationship as a bank account,' Janne once said when we met up for coffee and a debrief after she and Peter had been to the family welfare office. 'Right,' I replied, 'how interesting!' 'It explains everything,' Janne went on, 'just listen to this! As a couple, you have to constantly put money into your account and keep an eye on the balance. A kiss goodbye might be fifty kroner in; some kind words in the middle of an argument might increase your available funds by a thousand. The aim is to have the greatest safety margin possible, because then you're prepared for the crises. With a million kroner in the bank, having to take out fifty thousand might not feel great, but it isn't actually a problem. But if you're scraping the bottom of the barrel, poor as shit and with only ten kroner left, taking out even a single kroner is going to hurt like hell. Does that make sense?' 'Of course,' I replied, nodding, 'of course it does.' 'But that's not all,' Janne continued, her eyes shining with a-ha moment glossiness, and I was buoyed by her enthusiasm, how she truly seemed to believe that couples counselling and its metaphors were going to get her and Peter over the hump, 'because then there are the things that instantly put you in the red. Anything from events or memories to a triggering type of behaviour, which can cause your account to slide from, say, a million in the plus to three hundred thousand in the minus, no matter how much you might keep up the loving gestures or make your deposits. It's fucking unfair. But for some of us, these huge outgoings crop up all the time, almost out of the blue – everything from your partner responding to you in a way that reminds you of a childhood trauma to open wounds in the relationship's history. And when you come up against any of this stuff you simply don't have a chance, because that's when your cerebellum takes over. All you can do is accept that your savings are gone and start the whole fucking process of building up your balance all over again. Do you get what I'm trying to say? Can you relate to any of this?' She looked at me. 'Not in the slightest,' I said, and then we both burst out laughing, a long, raw wave of laughter crashing over us, as if we were two broke, drunken bums who knew each other's dirtiest tricks and ugliest secrets.

U s, us, us. And nobody else. We live as a modern nuclear family. Without anyone to help us with the babysitting, without grandparents next door. Among friends and neighbours who avoid interacting with the children to any significant extent, either because they aren't interested or because they have enough on their plates with their own families and busy lives. It's just Helene and me. Here in the house we are the adults, we make the rules and control the narrative. Only we know how Olav likes to have the crusts cut off his bread, that both he and Henry refuse to wear anything made of denim, or smart trousers with pressed creases. No one else is alert to how Henry's left big toenail grows into his skin if it isn't clipped in a special way. The trick that makes him forget just how much he dislikes being covered in sun cream, by singing 'Head, Shoulders, Knees and Toes', is something only we know how to do. Presumably we're the only ones who understand that Olav doesn't want to taste the pear-flavoured ice lolly because he's convinced it's made of cucumber. We are their mothers. If they catch a stomach bug, we wipe up their vomit. When they learn something new, we clap for them or ask them to show us again. We're the ones who take their temperatures, cut their fringes, google *how to teach boys to pee standing up*, build things out of Lego, read aloud cheap picture books with sound effects even when the batteries have run out. Only we think Olav's paintings of castles and bluebells are breathtakingly beautiful. We're the ones who sing lullabies for them at bedtime, and we're the only ones who get to enjoy the sight of them in the morning, when Henry is allowed to climb up into his big brother's bed and they hide beneath the duvet, tittering. Their thrashing legs, the never-failing, gleeful excitement when we pretend we can't see them: 'Where are they?' Helene says, 'Have they gone out?'

Us, us, us. And nobody else. That's how it feels, and yet it isn't true.

When Helene became pregnant with Henry, it didn't bother us that the boys wouldn't be genetically related. We said: They'll be brothers no matter what. We said: They'll never doubt that they belong together. That there were probably many other children, many other mothers – of course I knew this, but until I met Mayliss, I didn't understand it. It was abstract theory, something we some-times threw into conversation as if in passing – 'Do you ever wonder if they have any half-siblings out there?' – but without ever really believing it, or thinking that it might apply to us.

It isn't just the fact that Mayliss and Nicolai exist that makes me so restless. The thing that's dangerous isn't just stumbling into a jumble of biological ties.

It was so easy. Not to say anything to Helene.

As if I'd pressed play on a song that had been paused for almost two years: that was how I demolished everything we had rebuilt after my indiscretion – *poof!* Suddenly I was at it again, with my double life, with my lies and cock-and-bull stories, as the old people back home on Sotra would say.

What does it mean? I don't know. Only: I can't live like this any more.

But what do I want? To tell all, to lance the abscess, so I can at least purify myself? Or to simply leave her sooner rather than later, to be alone, to rip our children's lives to shreds, but in return be spared further accusations, be spared the risk of hearing that I'm a fucking hypocrite, once and for all? A hypocrite of a wife. And a fake mother. The latter she would never forgive.

I've only really got to know Mayliss since the winter, but I've known of her and Nicolai for over a year. That first meeting was pure chance. It was last year, before the terrorist attack, before we moved, at the very start of my maternity leave. We were due to travel to Spain the following week; I had taken Henry into the city to buy UV-protection swimsuits and sandals when all at once I found myself outside Pride in the Park. At the entrance I bumped into an acquaintance from Helene's old choir, a doctor who works in sex ed; she was stationed at a stall featuring condom balloons and huge bowls of lube. 'You should check out the kids' area,' she suggested, 'it's really nice!' Henry was hot and tired, we should have been heading back to pick up Olav from kindergarten, but surely a quick look wouldn't hurt, we couldn't not go in now that we were right there. Maybe I would even bump into someone I knew, perhaps someone I couldn't admit I was hoping to see.

I steered the pushchair past the many food trucks decorated with rainbows, the empty stage, the tables in the baking heat where several groups of young friends wearing matching vest tops and rainbow socks were sitting, along with the odd poor country homo with an aura of loneliness so intense I had to pretend I was looking for somewhere to change the baby's nappy. Henry was grizzling, we had just made the transition from the pushchair's carrycot to the seat and it was too big for him, he sort of slithered around in it. 'Do you want to come out?' I asked, unbuckling the harness and picking him up. He looked about him, squinting in the sunlight. The park had just opened, the crowds were sparse as yet. Where was the children's area? I had no idea, and it didn't really matter. I just sat down on a bench. On which a woman with a pushchair was already sitting; a small child stood beside her, practising keeping its balance by holding onto the bench's seat. The woman smiled at me. I smiled back. Because that's what you do, at Pride in the Park, you smile at strangers, it's safe, you're happy, happy for the park, happy for Pride, happy to belong to the minority that has suddenly become the majority. I held Henry under the arms; his short, stiff legs pushed against my thighs. 'How old is he?' I heard the woman say. 'He's a boy, right?' 'Almost six months,' I replied. I had no time to say anything further because her child toppled backwards towards me, and before I knew it he had crashed into my legs. 'Oopsy!' I cried. 'Careful!'

It was so random, the whole thing. The fact that I just happened to sit right there. That the boy looked up at me – and I down at him. I stared into his little face. A distortion – that's what it was. There must have been several months between them, but I recognized almost everything. The childhood photos of Helene, against which we had been constantly comparing Henry's features, it was as if they were instantly erased and I saw nothing but this new likeness. There was the shape of the eyes, large and somewhat protruding; both were almost completely bald. Two little copies of each other. Or no, not copies. This strange boy had slightly odd ears, and his face was both narrower and longer than Henry's face, and yes, weren't they actually quite different, when it came down to it? And don't young children all look alike, isn't it true that there's a limit to how different such small children can be, and why should I care at all, why did I feel queasy, as if I had just been caught doing something terrible?

I reacted not rationally, but on instinct. I had to get away, extricate myself from the situation, just as I've fled Oslo City shopping centre several times because I think the two men ahead of me on the escalator are each wearing an explosive vest under their down jackets, or got up from my table outside a café after just a couple of sips of my coffee because a white van is slowly reversing up onto the pavement. But I saw the look in her eyes. The other mother. She had seen what I had seen, of course she had, it was as vivid as the colours in all the flags that had been raised around us, and I felt it in my entire body, just as you can sense when you're about to be locked in somewhere: she was about to say something, and the castle in the air I had built for our family was now about to go up in smoke.

It could have been an insignificant encounter. It could have been no more than an exchanged glance, perhaps a knowing smile, followed by a discreet retreat, a shuffling back to our respective lives, perhaps with our hearts beating a little faster than usual, the unease like a vague pressure in our heads, but also with the possibility that things were not as we feared, that there was still hope we'd get to live in peace for at least the next fourteen years, until the children turned fifteen and would be able to decide for themselves whether they wished to seek each other out. We might still have been able to think: Maybe there are no other children except mine. Because that's what we want to imagine, Helene and me. Even with friends who have had children in the same way, we never speak about the wishes we expressed at the clinic. We hardly even talk about it with each other. When I read interviews with celebrity lesbian couples who declare how thankful they are to their donor, how they constantly tell their children about that kind Danish man, I never quite believe them – of course they're grateful that their children exist, of course both they and we know that this is one of the few opportunities afforded to people like us, and, moreover, that we're blessed to have this right enshrined in law, but who wouldn't prefer that he didn't exist, that the children were created in us entirely of their own accord? That they are ours, and no one else's. That we know all there is to know. That we have control.

'Shit,' I said. 'Isn't my kid the spitting image of yours?'

Did I actually say that? Apparently so. I could have got up, I could have walked away, I could have left well alone, but oh no, there I was, in the searing heat at Pride in the Park, smiling as I faced this stranger who sat there with her boy in her lap and her huge breasts and her big beer belly stuffed into her black denim shirt. The bottom half of her face appeared to have sort of melted; the ears seemed smaller and lower than was normal, her mouth hung too far down towards her chin. Her bare arms were covered in black tattoos. Among the throng of shapes, among the poppies and topless women, I glimpsed the face of a cat.

She laughed. 'Holy shit, he really is!'

What now? What now? Why did I say anything at all? What a fucking idiot! I wanted to leave. To bundle Henry back into the pushchair, to strap him in and vanish into thin air. But it was too late. 'They're so alike,' she continued. 'I guess you must have used Dandy too?' 'I must have done what?' My voice was harsh, she should have taken the hint, but the hint only glanced off her, she smiled as if she had asked me the time and then she said it again, the donor alias, one of these peculiar, made-up names that are listed alphabetically on the sperm-bank's website, along with information about the donor's ethnicity, height, eye colour. 'Dandy,' she said. 'The donor. You must have used him too?'

I was stunned. Not just at the fact that I had started this conversation. But that she could take it all with such… good humour? As if she had helped herself to a dish I had served, and just managed to identify the secret ingredient. But I didn't even have an answer for her, it felt as if I were being forced to stand before a meeting room full of people and explain a set of accounts I had never seen. 'Actually, I don't know,' I said. It was a confession. An intimate, crude confession to a stranger. She laughed a little, a stupid, bumpkin-esque laugh – where was she from, Toten? 'You don't know?' I shook my head. Now I really had to leave! But of course I kept speaking. 'No, you're not allowed to choose your donor in Norway,' I said didactically. 'Not any more.' 'You're not?' she said. 'Well, that's pretty crazy.' I felt something repulsive and damp swelling within me, like a dirty nappy left out in the rain, this unpleasant feeling that she had a point. Henry mewled and squirmed, he was so hot. 'But maybe you didn't have your treatment in Norway?' I continued. Anything to ease the discomfort. 'No,' she said. 'Stork Fertility – Denmark! And he stuck on the first try. So that made it cheap!' She laughed again, patted her stomach. I thought I had never seen anything so vulgar.

What came afterwards? How did I end up giving her my number? Was it because she told me she had been living in Oslo for no more than a few months, that she knew so few people? Was it the fact that she gave Nicolai her phone as we spoke, and later, when I heard an ad jingle, I realized she had opened YouTube – *YouTube* – for a little boy who wasn't even a year old, Jesus, how I hated seeing kids zombiefied by screens! Was it the way she took off her sunglasses when she said: 'It's just Nicolai and me.' Or was it quite simply

31

Nicolai himself, Nicolai's Henry-like face – apart from the ears he looked nothing like his mother – that beautiful, chubby little boy on her arm. Four months older than my boy, Helene's boy, was it the feeling of responsibility towards this stranger-child that made me blurt it out? 'I've just taken over the maternity leave – maybe we could meet up one day for a play date?'

I could have followed my instincts, said actually I wasn't that interested, that it was funny to have bumped into her and nice to have met her, but I felt no pressing need to get to know them, especially since Henry already had a big brother. Or I could have mentioned Helene, blamed her, said that she would have found it extremely difficult – there were countless ways I could have got out of it. But I chose none of them, I chose to act upon the feeling that I had to be loyal to a stranger, and had I had access to a little self-insight right then, I would have thought about what my old doctor used to say about how I needed to practise setting boundaries and stop trying to please everyone all the time, but self-insight evaporates in life's times of crisis, and I hadn't the faintest idea of what was sown in that moment.

THE KITCHEN CUPBOARDS are crammed with containers, packets and cans. On the bookshelves – which I have to take down – there are still books, while on the sofa towers of baby clothes and equipment I'm going to sell are accumulating. I just have to place the ads online before I pack everything away in separate boxes. Have I set aside enough time?

If there's one thing I'm hoping to find as I go through our things, it's the old Casio watch I've had since long before I met Helene, a common sight on lesbian wrists in the 2000s, and apparently also favoured among terrorist networks' bomb-builders, because it's both cheap and can be relied upon when you need to initiate a countdown. 09:18, says my wretched phone screen. Monday, 10th July.

It isn't only Mayliss who'll celebrate her birthday in the summer. When I was a kid, the countdown would have started long ago – to the family gathering with strawberries and cream, the birthday song and a neat row of knees lined up along the sofa. Don't speak too loudly. Don't be rude. Smiling, smiling, remembering that saying no will have consequences. Working hard to come up with something impressive and preferably a little precocious to say, perhaps dazzling our guests with my times tables or showing them the badges on my Scout's uniform so they can exclaim how extraordinarily clever I am. Me and my sister – look, see how bright they are. If Pappa is home from the North Sea, he sits in his recliner with his hands in his lap. Nobody seems to notice him picking at the skin around the fingernails of his thumbs when he's nervous, but I do. Mamma serves cream cake decorated with sliced kiwi fruit and even more strawberries, the guests are delighted even though it's the same cake she bakes every year, they simply cannot get over how talented she is.

How old will she be next week – sixty-two? Or was that last year? I haven't spoken to her since New Year's Eve, and she was the one who called me – I had finally picked up after ignoring her first four calls – but on her birthday there'll be no doubt as to where the responsibility lies. I'm dreading it. When I'm feeling on top of things, I can manage to both be in touch with her and to laugh afterwards at what was said and the emotions stirred up in me without too much effort, but in my current state it'll be danger-ous, because she can sense it, she'll hear it straight away, that I'm practically transparent, she'll know just how little it will take for her to find a crack through which she can sneak in. 'I've been to the shopping centre and bought some new bedding for the boys. Are you coming to stay this summer?' And Helene isn't here to help me drive her out, to help me meticulously close myself back up again, as if I'm a threadbare womb that needs stitching up after yet another life-threatening birth.

Our house was built in 1987, the year my mother became pregnant for the first time. It's easy to fall into the trap of thinking that all pregnant women are alike. All the detached properties I can see from the big living-room windows are identical, with the exception of those that have managed to add extensions to their fronts. Before we moved here, I was entirely unprepared for just how much I would obsess over how it feels to be surrounded by such… monotonous architecture. I hate it, I really do. I want to saw down all the thuja hedges, spray the blank façades turquoise and pink. That Helene and I are A4-lesbians with kids and a car and straight jobs is one thing. But what does it say about me, the fact that I've moved to this conformist suburban dump? Would we storm the barricades if it were required of us, or would we stay here in the comfort and safety of our Daz whiteness, light a fire in the log burner and open a bag of crisps?

When the Oslo Pride Parade took place in June, for the first time since the pandemic, we were away on holiday at a cabin.

A friend of Helene's, who lives on an upper floor of one of the apartment blocks in Enerhaugen, said: 'We watched from the balcony as the police got themselves set up – there were sharpshooters on the rooftops all across Grønland.'

It doesn't help that the neighbours, who are all outdoorsy but sweet types, go on about how happy they are here. Or that guests who come to visit call the area things like cosy and idyllic. And you're so close to nature, they say, to Marka and Ulsrudvann! You have everything right on your doorstep! I'm not sure I can so much as point in the general direction of Marka from here, and I certainly wouldn't know how to get home should I ever find myself lost there. The lake I've been to once – on one of the hottest days in June I dragged myself and the kids through the sunburnt and swollen crowds of parents and their young children, walking in a zigzag so as not to step in all the goose shit that lay scattered like small indignities across the dark-grey sand.

'Do you know what it's like for me when you take that attitude?' Helene says. 'You're the one who didn't want to stay in Torshov. You're the one who talked me into all this.'

*

As I was driving them to the airport yesterday, it suddenly began pouring with rain. Out beyond the city limits I still think the sky above Eastern Norway is almost eerily vast, like that above the Great Plains in North America. Dark clouds covered half the sky. I was nervous – Helene almost always does the driving, I no longer dare, I often imagine myself doing something that ends up with both boys becoming paralysed or brain-damaged. And for Helene it's easy – she learnt to drive in her father's rickety HiAce, she borrows other people's vans with no problem and has manoeuvred rental cars through the middle of New York City. But always having to be the driver irritates her. 'We have to be able to take it in turns,' she says, 'what if something happens to the kids when I'm not there? Do you want to be one of those doddery old biddies who can't reverse or parallel park, or are you going to book yourself a few refresher lessons?' I can't stand it when she speaks to me like this. I hate how we have to be equals in every conceivable situation. If she were a man, I often find myself thinking, I'd have been more easily let off the hook.

But this time, yesterday, I also felt a certain relief in driving. At having to concentrate on the road, at not being required to talk and therefore not having to risk letting the cat out of the bag. We listened to Captain Sabertooth songs; in the back seat the boys constantly chattered and sang. The rain flowed off the lorries that passed us, and outside the car's fogged-up side windows purple lupins lined the roadside verges. I didn't dare to drive a single kilometre over eighty. 'Are you finding it stressful?' Helene asked. And I could hear it. I could hear how she softened her voice, made it kind. 'Just try to relax as best you can, okay?' I didn't answer, just concentrated on my breathing, on keeping the thoughts of hydroplaning and huge elk bounding out in front of the car at bay. Suddenly, she put a hand on my thigh.

That touch: once it would have sent a tremor through my entire body. Then, for a long time, it fostered a warmth in me, reassured me that I was loved. More recently it's taken on a new function, has become an attempt at reconciliation, often after an argument, and sometimes it's enough, sometimes it has caused the hardness in me to soften.

But now: I felt nothing. She may as well have placed her hand in her own lap. Can you really not see it? I thought.

Just then the tiny ping of a text arriving cut through Pinky's song. I cast a quick glance at my mobile but didn't manage to see who the sender was before the notification disappeared. I knew, of course, that Mayliss and Nicolai had no travel plans – it was high season, she was probably standing in the hotel reception checking in some sweaty tourists right then – there was no chance of us bumping into them at the airport. I glanced at Helene, who sat scrolling on her own phone with her free hand. I tried not to let myself be swept away by my indignant reaction, but I just couldn't help it: 'There's no need to speak to me as if I've never driven a car before.'

As we stood in the departure hall and said our goodbyes – Henry hanging in a baby carrier at Helene's chest, while Olav clung to my leg and repeated in a wheedling, high-pitched voice that I mustn't go – I felt sad. Not because I thought this might be the last time Helene and I would say goodbye to each other like this, but because any sense of longing seemed entirely absent, the relief that I would soon be alone so great. And that would have been fine, entirely understandable, if in this relief there had also been joy and anticipation. But there wasn't. I was sweaty after hauling the suitcases onto the baggage belt, overcompensating for all the hassle and stress I would soon be spared. I agreed to give Olav a piggyback as I walked over to the special baggage drop with Henry's folded-up pushchair on a trolley; he kicked me in the hips with his light-up shoes and held on too tightly around my neck, but I didn't tell him off, as I might otherwise have done. Henry's nose was snotty, his hair wet from the rain after the walk from the car to the terminal. I kissed him on the forehead, then crouched down in front of Olav. He stared at the polished airport floor as if it were transparent and a frightening animated fairy story was playing out below it.

'Have a nice time with Grandma, okay?' I said. 'Mamma,' he mumbled, 'I want to stay with you.'

In order to appear calm, and perhaps because this was like countless farewell scenes I'd seen in movies, I took his little hands in mine. At his request, Helene had painted his nails a pale shade of pink earlier in the week, and now the polish had almost completely peeled away. Something had stirred in me the day I saw the nail polish, as if some creature deep inside me were flicking its tail, but I'd held my tongue.

'Mamma has work to do on the house,' I replied, 'so I'll come and join you in a little while.' 'Grandma and Grandpa are really looking forward to seeing you,' Helene said. Olav peered up at her. His eyes were brimming with tears, which was so typical of him. 'I know that,' he said, his voice thin. 'But I want Mamma to come, too.'

I wanted to shake his hands off me, to shake him, to shout: Come on now, fucking pull yourself together, you're embarrassing me! But I swallowed that down, too. And that's what makes the crucial difference.

Helene and I kissed. It was cold, sterile, like politely hugging an old great-uncle at a Christmas party. As her breasts grazed my arm I felt a pang of unease, like when that same great-uncle holds the hug for just a little too long. Jesus, I thought, things cannot go on like this.

'Bye then,' I began, 'bye Olav, bye Mamma Helene, bye Henry. Can you wave?'

Henry waved, then blew me a kiss. I blew one back, grateful that was all that was required of me. Then I walked away, but when I rounded a sports car that stood there on display, I stopped and watched them from behind it. Helene's expression was stern and focused as, along with the other overloaded parents with young children, she hauled her way down the family lane. She was wearing a new pale blue linen shirt she hadn't told me she had bought. Her long, damp hair hung loose down her back. When I see her from behind, I often think it can't possibly be her.

The crowd began to close in, but I glimpsed Olav helping to lift the hand luggage onto the belt at the security check. Henry was pointing at everything and kicking his legs, and Olav patted him on the thigh in a big-brotherly gesture. That gorgeous, sweet little boy. How I love him. And Henry too, of course. Of course.

And Helene. In a different way, but still.

My family.

But as they were waved over to walk through the metal detector, I thought it again. The thought. It isn't true. It's shameless and false and childish, and I didn't want to think it. But I did.

There they go with my child.

Just then a man bumped into me with such force I had to steady myself against the sports car, marking its paintwork with the prints of my clammy, traitorous hands. 'I am so sorry,' the man exclaimed, with such bewilderment it could hardly have been anything but an accident. I wanted to punch him. Instead, I turned and walked away. As I walked, I finally checked the message on my phone, but it was just some online shop's advertising I keep forgetting to unsubscribe from.

THE FIRST ENCOUNTERS are a seductive pitch, independent of all future costs. They have nothing to do with what will happen later. Still, these are the times people cling to, replaying them over and over and calling them the beginning. The intensity of the desire, that feeling of finding and being found: the stronger it was, the more dangerous it is, because then you simply can't stop hoping you'll rediscover it. It compels you to keep going, even as you stray deeper and deeper into the fog.

I recognized her from her profile picture straight away. She was sitting on the edge of the Sjømannsmonumentet, her legs spread wide, torso hanging forward a little and with her elbows resting on her thighs, like some relaxed and liberated ship figurehead. Yes, I thought. I want this. She was masculine, but with a certain finesse. Butch – not in that trashy, garish way, but like a cover girl on the kind of alternative lesbian magazine I hoped to discover every time I scoured the shelves of the Narvesen newsagents. Her chestnut hair was short over the ears, her fringe swept back (how did she get it to sit like that?); she was wearing turned-up jeans, a white T-shirt, and – and it was this garment that made me think there was no going back, now everyone would see me for what I really was – a short, open waistcoat. It suited her, actually. When she caught sight of me she smiled, a kind of warmth radiating from her, a self-confidence that wasn't coy, but generous – she was still able to look at people that way back then – and she held my gaze as if, at the bottom of the monument's pool of water, she had already glimpsed how the evening and the coming years would be tipped in our favour.

As an ironic comment on the extensive chatting we'd been doing online over the past few days, we introduced ourselves with a handshake. Silje Marie – you can use both or just Silje, it's all the same to me. Helene. Then we laughed a little, and I realized immediately: we might end up saying each other's names many times, in many different ways. I just had to play my cards right.

'So here you are,' she said at last.

'So what do you fancy doing?' I asked. 'Shall we walk?'

I knew very well that she had a summer job as a receptionist at a dental surgery and would soon be starting her final year studying dentistry. Over in Lyder Sagens Gate was where she worked on her thesis. 'Well, where do I start?' she said as we sat down with our beers outside Café Opera, 'I'm from a… pretty unique farm. My brother was always determined to do something in IT, so my parents pinned all their hopes on me: they wanted me to take over the farm or, failing that, to become a vet. But I didn't want to. I think I would have enjoyed working with animals, but not full time. And running the farm is out of the question. It's far too much work, far too lonely. It's… demanding. Pappa is working himself to the bone.'

I didn't follow up with a question about what made her family's farm so unique. Instead, I tried to be funny. 'So you're becoming a dentist instead. A stress-free life, completely devoid of responsibility. Isn't that one of the professions that carries the greatest risk of suicide?'

She smiled, said something about how she'd have to apply for a job feeding the penguins at the National Aquarium if her mind began to unravel, it wasn't very funny, but I laughed: I loved listening to her talk. I loved that she didn't look like a dentistry student, loved that in one of her profile pictures she was standing on a longboard, wearing a patterned shirt. Say more, I thought. Tell me. Then she ordered two more beers and a bowl of chilli nuts from which she greedily scooped great handfuls, which I was happy to see. All these skinny, hyper-intelligent girls with self-control not of this world – in their presence I could hardly think of anything other than how chubby and inferior I felt.

'So are you happy,' she asked, the corners of her mouth red with chilli powder, 'in your job?' She leant forward slightly, the waistcoat gaping so I could see she wasn't wearing anything under the T-shirt. 'How does it make you feel?'

The sensual voice was a joke, but its effect on my body was acute, as if she had just stuck a hypodermic needle into my thigh. I began to fiddle with my hair, to look at her from below my lashes. Now I'm blushing, I thought, she's really done it now.

'Fairly happy,' I replied, feeling that I couldn't have said anything more inane. 'I've always liked maths and thought I'd end up working with numbers. I would have liked to stay in Copenhagen, actually, but then I was offered a really good job in Oslo. I'm sure it'll be fine. The most important thing for me is that I don't end up back on Sotra.' 'So you're not planning on becoming a Cub Scout leader any time soon?' 'Did you google me?' 'You mean you didn't google me? You looked so cute in the photos in the local paper.'

Night fell. There's nothing finer than Bergen on a summer's night. The smell of the Bergen lilacs is enough to make even perfumiers swoon, and every building and crooked alley provides the perfect backdrop for a proposal. People sing in harmony outside Burger King. The windows of the houses scattered across the dark mountainsides shine like stellar constellations. On the park benches, alcoholics sleep as deeply as infants drunk on milk, and the fountains of Lille Lungegårdsvann flow as if all the world's despondency can be washed away by water.

She was three years older than me, a little taller and much fitter. Before she had changed subjects to get onto the course in dentistry, she had studied nutrition and backpacked around Asia. She had recently broken up with her partner, who was constantly surrounded by an entire flock of friends, albeit none close enough for her partner to call when Helene had said she wanted to move out. 'There's something disconcerting about people who don't have good friends,' she said, 'don't you think?' We spent a long time walking the streets, talking constantly, high on the chemistry between us that made the conversation flow so easily. But as we passed the familiar apartment building up in Fosswinckels Gate, I prattled on about the time my grandmother came to visit me in Copenhagen; she had wanted to wash her hair and didn't realize that the reason the shower was behaving so strangely was because Joachim had put an anal douche head on it the night before – one of my funniest stories. I glanced up at the pale yellow brick building. I used to live up there, on the second floor, with my best friend, I should have said. But I didn't. What did that mean? Probably no more than that I didn't want to interrupt the flow of the conversation. The first lie.

She walked with me to the bus stop next to Hotell Norge, where all the buses from the surrounding rural areas stop. My old bus stop, where in my youth I had stood countless times, waiting to be picked up and carried away from the city's extraordinarily boundless streets and over the Sotra Bridge, which stretched out like a tongue, and straight into the jaws of small-town life.

'I live not far from here,' she said, 'if you fancy a nightcap.' 'Nobody in Bergen lives far from here,' I replied, and when she didn't smile I nudged her, lightly, as if I were a young boy and puberty had me tongue-tied. 'Can we take a rain check?'

She looked hesitant. Embarrassed, or disbelieving? I should have slipped a hand up the back of her waistcoat, kissed her as compensation. Kissed her because I should, so I wouldn't leave her in any doubt, to avoid the discomfort of disappointing her. Who hasn't done that? I had done it many times. I was tipsy, I wanted to, it should have been easy. But it was late. People were shitfaced. I was no longer in Copenhagen. I saw nobody I knew for the moment, but it was surely only a matter of time.

I clasped my hands together and shook them in a begging gesture. 'Please, *please*,' I said, 'can we take a rain check?'

On the bus I took out my phone. I was more drunk than I had realized, had to focus in order to get the spelling right: *They say it's best to wait a while before texting someone you've just been on a date with, but clearly I can't control myself. Thanks for a fantastic evening.*

After sending the message, I put my phone on silent and resisted the urge to check it as the night bus sped through the tunnels. As we drove over the Sotra Bridge I cast a glance in the direction of Askøy, where the pearl necklace of the Askøy Bridge hung as if to adorn the very road to God's kingdom, arcing high above the fjord. The first girl I ever kissed was from Askøy. Nobody knew about it.

The youths at the back of the bus were shrieking so loudly the driver had to tell them to keep it down. A girl frantically pushed the stop button while yelling that her friend needed to puke. I tried to close my eyes and rest, but time after time I noticed my eyes were open again. Not until I had stepped off the bus and was making my way past my sister's house did I dare to take out my phone.

1 unread message.

Only the outside light was on; they had gone to bed. I let myself in, undressed, peed and brushed my teeth, then lay on my bed in my childhood bedroom where I was staying for the summer, my face lit by the phone's greenish-yellow glow, feeling something tugging at both my heart and between my legs as I read: *Speak for yourself. I'm the one who can't control myself.*

M Y YEARS in the accounting department have taught me that a lack of structure and concentration not only makes me frustrated and irritable, but can also whip up an entire melodramatic chorus of existential misgivings: Do I deserve to live, when I can't even get these invoices done before lunch?

I created myself a schedule even before they left. Planned every day in detail, but I already appear to have fallen behind. Wednesday after breakfast – rip up the floor; Friday evening – second coat of paint. It's a factual but also false list, which in no way describes what I'm actually going to work my way through this week. I add to it neither Mayliss nor any of the other things that haunt my thoughts. Were my newly married, heavily eyelinered self to encounter me today, she'd hardly recognize me. I've become an expert at omission. I've practised and practised, and I now know all there is to know about how to proceed without leaving behind any evidence.

The pictures need taking down from the walls. In addition to renovating the kitchen and the big bathroom, the Latvian decorators are going to remove the old Anaglypta, install new panelling and plasterboard, paint every single surface. There are pictures hanging everywhere, framed prints and photographs I stuck up with Blu Tack when we moved in, in a desperate bid to make the place feel cosy, like home. Pictures of the kids, my mother- and father-in-law, Helene's friends from Trondheim. Joachim and me at a

47

garden party. Janne with a teeny-tiny newborn Henry in her arms. A Christmas card featuring a photo of Lucie, Olav's best friend from his old kindergarten. But no photos of Mamma and Pappa. None of Helene and me.

We had countless photographs taken when we got married, but we've never framed any of them. Even though the wedding ended up excessively traditional, a framed photo of the brides just felt like the cherry on the heteronormative cake, an almost unpalatable boast. But yesterday evening, when I opened one of the many boxes of miscellaneous items and papers I'd hastily thrown together when we moved from the apartment in Torshov and found the bundle of leftover thank-you cards, printed with the only wedding photo to exist in physical rather than digital form, I grew sad. Why didn't we get this photo enlarged and put it on display while we still felt like these people? Might it have made a difference? We're standing in front of the bus shelter in a tangled embrace, so happy, Helene facing the camera and laughing, showing her gums, while my glistening eyes are full of stars because I'm looking at her. In that moment we're soaked through with joy at having found each other and chosen each other, in defiance of all the resistance we've encountered since I came out.

I remember Mamma asking: 'So you're going to get married in a suit?' 'In a suit?' I replied. 'Are you mad?' Both the threats and the boycotts had come to an end. They attended the wedding, all of them. My sister hugged all my friends who came over from Denmark. Pappa kissed us on the cheek – he'd reassured us beforehand that Mamma wouldn't make a scene, that deep down she was very happy for us. Mamma smiled and smiled. Nobody has a smile more radiant than hers. During the ceremony she sat in the front row and held my sister's hand and sniffled so loudly I could practically hear my friends thinking: Oh, look how moved Silje Marie's mother is – we knew it would all work out in the end.

The guests blew bubbles for us outside the courthouse, and then we took the 37 bus to the allotment belonging to Helene's sister-in-law's family, where a long table had been set and decorated between the berry bushes. I was a stunningly beautiful bride. We were two stunningly beautiful brides, in two even more beautiful dresses. Not a rainbow in sight. When we chose our dresses, the last thing we wanted to look like was lesbian brides. We never told anyone this – it was part of our own private lexicon – but we mocked the typical wedding photos of short-haired, overweight female couples from rural villages and American provinces, kissing in their bright white suits and matching ties. Yes, we mocked them – I remember we actually *laughed*. As if relieved that we weren't ugly, that we had much better taste, that we were able to raise ourselves sky-high above the stereotypes we secretly thought it was understandable people might feel provoked by, or despise.

Y ES – BECAUSE THE FACT that I always used to wear make-up? It wasn't just about trying to be attractive and happy. I wanted to be a hot lesbian, free of wallet chains and wide-legged, sagging jeans; no mohawk, no hiking rucksack or boxer shorts. Free of all the stereotypical signs which, back in the day, had made me shout after Torunn in Class C that she made us all sick to our stomachs.

Joachim has said: 'Being gay on Karmøy in the nineties wasn't just nauseating, it was dangerous.'

Janne has said: 'I just can't keep up any more – everyone at Maja's school is non-binary, we parents hardly know what pronouns to use when referring to our kids these days! In Mikkel's class there's even a group of boys who are planning to march in the Pride parade. Thirteen-year-old boys! Isn't that touching?'

Yes. It is touching. And it's touching to see uncles and grandparents in PROUD T-shirts, and it's touching to see the news story about the old lesbian couple with their walking frames and dementia who have been given a double room at the nursing home, and it's touching to hear the king speak about inclusivity, and it's touching that the only gay in the village can tell the reporter from the evening news that now Pride has come to his home village, he finally has the courage to show everyone who he really is, and it's touching that people say, 'Imagine having two mothers – it must be twice as nice as having just one!', and it's touching that the financial elite put their money where their mouths are and set up an alternative event when their children's Pride celebration is cancelled due to threats, and it's touching that Mamma's friends sent me tiny knitted garments for Olav just after he was born, even though I've hardly seen them since I left home, and it's touching to see girls holding hands, and it's touching to see boys kissing each other, and it's touching to see men with and without masks on sashaying their way through the parade wearing saris and with their chests smothered in glitter, and it's touching that parents say they support their kids no matter whether they identify as he or she or they.

People change. People have to be allowed to make mistakes.

But wasn't it some of precisely these parents who once stood and watched behind the chapel as Joachim's friend was so badly beaten he ended up with several cracked ribs? Wasn't it precisely these people who were once members of the group of ninth-grade girls who wrote a letter to our form teacher stating that we refused to shower with Torunn? And Mamma? She can go around calling herself Grandma, she can sit in the front row at my wedding baring all her pearly whites. But she was the one who chose to say: 'If that's the way you want to defile your life, then I'm afraid you can no longer live here at home.'

IT HAD TO BE HELENE. She came over as soon as I'd started my new job and moved into the small apartment in St Halvards Gate. Even though it was obviously going to happen, I was surprised when, the moment we'd closed the door behind us, she kissed me. She pushed me up against the wall, opened my mouth. But this time I didn't laugh, or just pretend I was turned on, too. How much of what a person does is because they've seen it done by others, and what comes from within? This came from within. I opened wide. Our front teeth clacked together. Her nibbling bites were hard, her mouth utterly soft. Taut and elastic – a contrast I couldn't resist. When she began to unbutton my shirt, it was like being injected full of contrast fluid and pushed into a booming MRI machine. Luminescence flooded my bloodstream. My heart lit up, as did my crotch. My fingers, the skin at my neck. Afterwards, when I went to the toilet, I could have sworn my piss floated neon yellow in the toilet bowl before I flushed it down. I was young. I had no idea what this would be the start of. The darkness that follows early attraction like a shadow – all the murk that commitment and stability drag after them – I knew nothing about. It's unthinkable that desire will fade, that all that free-flowing incandescence can turn viscous and pitch-dark.

She seemed so experienced. But afterwards, she was nervous. 'There's something I have to tell you,' she said, lying there with her head on my chest. The walls and the old wooden floor glowed golden in the autumnal light. Her fringe tickled my armpit, and I wished I had an ashtray, that my tenancy agreement permitted me to lie in bed and smoke – it would have looked so cool. I kissed the top of her head. She smelt of hair wax, something solid and clean. 'Tell away,' I said. 'Okay,' she replied. 'It's actually a bit embarrassing. But I'm just going to say it. My partner… his name was Jon. I've never been in a relationship with a woman before. I don't know why I haven't mentioned it until now. Does it matter?' She raised herself up onto her elbows. 'I don't want you to think I'm a tease. That I'm just testing this out.' I smiled – she was so serious. 'Really?' I said. 'Because if you are, your testing is very convincing.'

Did I mean it? Yes – it really didn't matter. On the contrary, I felt… honoured? Relieved that she hadn't slept or gone out with half the clientele of Fincken. But I was also surprised. Her big hands, the haircut, the naturalness in the way she slung her strong arm over my shoulders as we sat on the tram from Oslo Central Station – it surprised me that she could be turned on by men. Maybe I'm old-fashioned. But then again, I didn't grow up in the city.

'If it's any consolation,' I said, 'I haven't come out to my parents yet. Which is to say, my mother read my diary when I was seventeen and threw me out for a few weeks, and since then I've never mentioned it again. Does that matter?' She looked at me askance. 'You're kidding? What – did you grow up in a sect or something? Or is she a devout Christian?' I shrugged. It was a cocky gesture, one that couldn't be helped. 'You could certainly call it a sect,' I replied, 'but it's one that only consists of my parents, my sister and me.'

THE BOYS' TRIPP TRAPP high chairs are crusted with dried food, like the cradle cap on Olav's scalp. I make a half-hearted attempt to moisten the scabs and scrub them away, then carry the chairs up into the loft – I have to fill the loft with as much stuff as I can, to give the decorators space to work. Olav's chair is cobalt blue. Henry's is bottle green. I'm the one who painted them. What are the boys doing, right now? Probably something idyllic, something cut out of some brochure about how important cross-generational attachment and relationships are. Is Henry sitting on his grandfather's lap, gently swinging his short legs, while Grandpa wolfs down leftover pieces of rusk with kefir? Is his big brother standing on a chair beside his grandmother at the kitchen counter, helping to peel apples, to measure out flour, sugar and milk? Outside the windows the wind rushes above the fields and the enclosure containing the neighbour's harness-racing horses. In the farmyard stands the large, empty barn. Henry opens his mouth wide as his grandfather offers him a spoonful of kefir. Olav dips his finger into the baking bowl without being told off. And Helene? She's taking some rare time to herself in the living room, where she stretches out on the pale pink leather sofa and flicks through one of her mother's copies of *Home* magazine, or maybe she's gone down into the basement and crept up onto the water bed where we used to have sex during those first times I visited, giggling because we were afraid we'd either make a hole in it or the old plug might catch fire.

I love being in that house. I feel welcome there. They've always allowed me to feel that I'm family, that I am one of them. If only they knew.

My shoulders ache. The buzzing of the fridge, the lawnmowers, the distant drone of the E6: it really is quiet in here. I should probably make the most of it and put on a podcast or an audiobook. Go wild and connect the record player to the speaker, blow the dust off some vinyl. Pappa was so happy when I asked if I could take over his old collection – he lit up, as if he felt I suddenly saw him as the person he truly is. That was a long time ago. My former life is the life of a ghost. It feels as if the only times I'm happy are when I decide not to care about the approaching night's hellish screaming, crack open a beer and stay up late watching old episodes of *Absolutely Fabulous*. Or when I put on music. Playlists Joachim and I listened to on Fridays when we lived together in Copenhagen; eighties music videos on YouTube. This has to happen when Helene is either sleeping or out. Because every time Helene comes into the room, she turns off the music or lowers the volume so much it simply becomes noise. 'My head is totally fried,' she says. We no longer make playlists for each other. I used to know what kind of music she'd like, but now I know nothing.

'Everything will be better once the kids get a bit older,' Janne would have said, or in fact did say, this past winter, when she stopped by for lunch while I was home with Henry. 'Just give it time. Get out for some daylight whenever you can, drink wine out of a coffee cup while you make dinner. Nobody is of sound mind when getting so little sleep.'

I sleep better now. Helene says: 'You seem brighter than you did during the winter, at least.' 'Much brighter,' I reply, 'it's actually

55

gone pretty quickly – to think he'll be starting at kindergarten soon! I'm so looking forward to getting back to work!'

When I was little, I was bitten by a stranger's dog that stood tied up outside the local supermarket. Pappa had discovered the bite that evening, as he was getting me into my pyjamas. 'We don't need to tell Mamma about this,' he said. After I'd been to the botanical gardens with Mayliss and Nicolai, I mentioned only the botanical gardens when Helene asked how Henry and I had spent our day. Every time Helene wants to know if I defied the screams of protest she heard coming from the bathroom and brushed Henry's teeth properly, I say that I did.

AFTER THAT FIRST MEETING at Pride in the Park, the overriding feeling was one of wanting to throw up. Queasy and dazed, I sat on the number 12 tram in the bright, baking heat with Henry on my lap and thought: a half-sibling. Fuck. Holy fuck. How many of them are there? What does this mean? Why have I never truly *understood* this before? A real live little boy. And an unknown mother. To whom I had given my phone number. A real live little boy, an entirely concrete reminder that our family is not like other families, no matter how earnestly we might insist that it is, no matter how well I might manage to hide the thoughts I've struggled with ever since Henry was born.

'We're unfortunately out of sperm from the donor you used last time,' the doctor said as we sat there in the clinic at our so-called 'sibling discussion'. Helene and I glanced at one another, and despite the gust of disappointment – Olav was perfect, so of course we wanted to try the same *magic formula* one more time – we couldn't help but laugh, because how could we not laugh, it was absurd: we're terribly sorry, but the product you're after is sold out, we might get it back in stock but there's no guarantee, would you like to wait, or would you like to try using a different one?

Nobody at the clinic mentioned anything about the other half-sibling, nobody asked a single challenging question, and we smiled and nodded and trusted them – why wouldn't we trust these people who had been doing this for so many years? – and we'd never heard a single horror story, none of the other lesbian couples we knew who had children had ever uttered a word of doubt, and we already had Olav, and we loved Olav, our blonde-mopped 'Let It Go'-singing son, and now Olav would have a younger sibling, three would become four, and although Helene and I might be going through a bit of a rough patch, there was never any doubt that expanding our family was something we wanted to do. The fact that there was first one and then two outsiders, two real live men with unknown motives who had made this possible, it was abstract, it wasn't something we really needed to think about – the clinic would even select the donor for us. Everything would be done by the book, in accordance with the rules; there was nothing to stop and reflect on, everything we were doing was laid down in Norwegian law. We didn't feel we were being short-sighted and greedy, we didn't feel like lesbians who only see children as products and who inflict a handicap upon them, as the philosopher Nina Karin Monsen put it before she was awarded the Fritt Ord Prize in 2009 – because how could anyone in their right mind argue against this monumental and extraordinary and entirely fundamental human impulse: the desire to create and care for a tiny life.

But when I stepped off the tram and pushed Henry's pushchair towards the kindergarten gates, and Olav came running towards us – dusted brown with sand and with his T-shirt stained with blueberry juice, eyes glittering as he threw himself at his brother, utterly overjoyed to see him – all I could think was: have we done something seriously wrong? Are we deceiving them?

When she got home, Helene was tired. She'd had to work overtime again, an upper-jaw procedure that had turned out to be more complicated than expected. Of course I should have told her the moment she walked into our apartment in Torshov and kicked off her shoes – You won't believe what happened when Henry and I were at Pride in the Park today – I simply should have said I'd been blindsided into handing over my number, so Helene, slightly irritated but firmly, in the way I love that she can be, could say that naturally I was going to cancel: Just text her and say you're not interested – after all, you don't owe her anything.

But I didn't manage to say a single thing. I was clearly no longer capable of saying anything, not without planning it first, without weighing up the consequences. Why didn't I do it? Because the first thing she said was: 'This place is a complete pig sty'? Because it was one of those afternoons on which it was utterly impossible to speak – at least when it came to bringing up something so immense, something that risked sending a fissure down the middle of the life we were pretending to live? This fragile life of ours.

Olav threw a raging tantrum because the macaroni and carrots on his plate were touching, then refused to both go pee and to have his hair washed; Henry wouldn't sleep, despite being breastfed for hours. Exhausted, we fell into bed as the evening sun finally disappeared behind the neighbouring tower block.

I had the chance then. It would have been easy. I simply could have said: 'You know what? The craziest thing happened today!' She even tried to *establish a connection*, as Janne told me her couples counsellor put it. 'Is everything okay?' Helene asked as we lay there. I could sense her scrutinizing me. 'You're very quiet.' I hesitated. The face of the strange child had popped into my thoughts at regular intervals all afternoon, and I'd intended to bring it up once everything had settled down and the mood between us had improved, but now I felt unsure. What good would it do her to know? How stressed might she become? Would she take the news calmly, or get angry at me for not having called her, right there and then from Pride in the Park? I had promised never to keep anything important from her ever again – that was the very condition of us staying together. And what if it gave rise to a sense of unease in her, inflicted upon her even the tiniest morsel of doubt as to whether it was right that we had created these children in this way? It was no great drama, it was no crisis, but still, it was a possibility I wished to avoid at all costs. Because to see her begin to doubt, to get the feeling she was starting to change her mind – it would break my heart, make me feel unsafe and afraid.

Or would she simply shrug, shake her head and say: 'Don't give it another thought. We don't actually know whether they're related, it could well be just a coincidence that they look so alike. And even if they are related: what does it matter?'

But when I met her gaze, I was caught off-guard. Her expression was hard, and I knew immediately what that hardness meant. She spat it at me, the wretched sentence that made turning away in denial and dejection the only possible answer I could give: 'Are you thinking about *her*?'

In the night I got up, went into the bathroom, sat down on the toilet with my phone and navigated to the fertility clinic's website. The text there stated that each donor can provide children to a maximum of six families. But it didn't say that almost all the sperm is imported, that it's distributed all across the EU from Denmark, and that each country sets its own maximum number of families. I tapped my way to the sperm bank's website and opened the list of available donors – it wasn't long, it consisted of little more than twenty or so men. And yes, there he was. DANDY. *Eye colour:*

Brown. Hair: Brown. Occupation: Sciences student. Height: 185 cm. You could pay for more information – see childhood photos, hear his voice, read a letter about why he had chosen to become a donor. But I didn't want to. It wasn't him I was looking for. I tapped on the sperm bank's contact form. *I'm just wondering how many children each donor can father, globally?*

Then I somehow found myself reading a Swedish newspaper article. *Several of the expectant parents* Dagens Nyheter *spoke to were surprised – they were unaware that sperm from Livio Sperm Bank can also be sold abroad. 'Just imagine if my future child is told "you might have half-siblings in five other Swedish families", but then it turns out they have fifty half-siblings scattered across the world. I think that would come as a huge shock,' said one woman, who wished to remain anonymous.*

I did some more googling, then sat there and read an interview with a young Swedish woman who was critical of her own birth story. *The purpose of the donation industry is to satisfy its customers – that is, people longing for a child,* I read. *To make money, and to make a profit. But I think we have a right to know who our close relatives are. That we have a right to know if, after several years, our donor develops an illness, or if someone in the donor's family has a condition that might be relevant to us and our children. And if your only option is to use an anonymous donor or to not have children at all? Well, I don't think the desire to have a child should come before people's right to know their own genetic identity!*

Anonymous donor, I thought, almost relieved – at least that wasn't us! But then I came across a Norwegian article, about another donor-conceived woman of around my age. She was angrier. *It's already a huge emotional burden to be donor-conceived with many half-siblings in different families, all with differing family dynamics, and then you might suddenly learn you also have lots of half-siblings abroad,* she said. *This sends the message that these children are just a product, that they don't have*

the same rights as other children. Having so many half-siblings makes me feel
mass-produced. It feels a bit like being only half a person.

Product? Mass-produced? What happened to the research we'd had at the back of our minds when we were newly married and looking into things and booking our first consultation at the fertility clinic, about how the children of lesbians are slightly better off than the children of heterosexual couples? What about the recommendation from the doctor at the clinic, who a few years later believed it a good thing that there was no longer any semen available from the donor we'd had Olav with, so the child Helene hoped to have wouldn't discover their biological origins several years too early, should Olav wish to seek out his donor as soon as he turned fifteen? Half a person. Nausea oozed into my mouth. Like morning sickness, or like being small again, having been caught red-handed by Mamma after eating all the sweets my sister and I were supposed to share. Waiting for the punishment. The terrible period of waiting before the punishment is handed down.

When I finally stood up, I didn't go back in to Helene and Henry, but to Olav. I crept over to his child-sized bed and snuggled down next to him, in the same bed I'd sat on the edge of, that morning before they left, only now it has more stickers on it than it did when we lived in Torshov, and there's hardly space for me any more, his legs are longer and thinner, and the room in the apartment has been swapped for a room in this house, and now he's gone, he's on holiday with his other mother, still entirely unaware, still longing for me to come into his room at night and snuggle down beside him.

I N THE NEWS that is broadcast ahead of Pride, everyone seems to agree that people who vote against their housing cooperative putting up a flag, or who won't permit their children to participate in the kindergarten's rainbow parade, need to get with the programme. They're the ones who are passé. Everyone says: Research shows that the children of same-sex couples do at least as well as any other child. Very few know precisely what research they're referring to. The famous blonde lesbian couple in their cute dresses, who say that 'people forget that all that matters when you have children is that you show them love', fail to mention the Danish bank account into which they have transferred thousands of euros – and why should they? The law is finally being changed, so the people behind the organizations that offer conversion therapy now risk prison time. The out-of-work losers who send the famous blonde lesbian couple messages telling them that they're unnatural, that they're child abusers, are mentioned only as a reminder that the fight must continue for a little while longer. Some lesbians travel to Barcelona for a long weekend, to have an embryo created from donor sperm and their partner's egg implanted in their uterus. A few years later, the same procedure is repeated, but with the partner's uterus and the first's egg. Even in the smallest villages, the parades are growing longer and longer. Of course people can't help but smile to see them. Joining a Pride march is like being teleported to a carefree utopia.

In the midst of all this, hardly anyone asks: But are we entirely sure? Could it be that those who go after the primary school's Pride flag, night after night, year after year, have concerns that ought to be heard? Nobody in their right mind says: Diversity is great, but a good father might be the greatest gift you can give a child. Only fanatics say: Yes, we have a national limit, but why do the sperm banks refuse to provide information about how many more half-siblings the child might have in other countries? Absolutely nobody asks: What about all the unknowing biological grandparents who have no right to even the tiniest glimpse of how their family blood-line has uncoiled – does anyone think about them? Not a single surrogate baby-daddy makes himself comfortable on the sofa of *Good Morning Norway* and says: Of course, we used our privilege to create this little life. The parental quartet consisting of two same-sex couples, one male and one female, never asks the question: And what if we split up, can we actually stand by the choice we've made? No co-mother staggers onto the Pride festival stage and says: It doesn't feel as if the child is mine.

M Y BOSS HAS SENT ME AN EMAIL: *I hope you've enjoyed your maternity leave, and that you're having a great summer holiday. We're looking forward to having you back in August!* Who is it they think they're getting back after this year's absence? Perhaps having children will have made me into a more productive employee, if I can only get myself back into the office. But I'm more quick-tempered. I'm bitter, from getting so little sleep. I don't want to learn everyone's names, or charm the clients when they drop by for coffee. I no longer have the patience to advise those who are crass and disrespectful towards me; I no longer allow people to call me outside of working hours, even when I know they're in the midst of a crisis. When one of my clients had problems with the tax office last year, simply because he'd been careless, I sat and stared at the unbalanced accounts, thinking: Serves you right.

I've changed. I look different. I've stopped going to the hairdresser so regularly. Wrinkles spring forth between my eyebrows. I don't exercise. I live in a house in suburbia and no longer walk up flight after flight of stairs. My expensive, ethically produced work blazers no longer fit me, and after this blasted renovation project I probably won't have the money to shop anywhere other than H&M or Zara. Every day, I feel bigger. Every day, I stop at the mirrors in the house and pull up my shirt while hoping my stomach might look flatter. It's never flat. My words might claim otherwise, but I don't believe big bodies have the same value as slim ones. I'm ashamed to join the crowds of mothers with flabby bellies as I walk down the beach, hand in hand with my boys. I'm not proud of what my body achieved four years ago – it's immaterial, I want to be thin, but I just can't seem to make it happen. I'm the worst body type, neither skinny nor morbidly obese, everyone can tell just by looking at me that I'm weak-willed, a mother without discipline or ambition.

Mayliss doesn't care about that sort of thing. She pulls off her T-shirt in the sun, sits in the park wearing only her bra, does nothing to hide her belly.

The story's heroine must have a goal, some kind of drive, a desire to change something, to take fate into her own hands. I would never root for someone like me. My new doctor didn't want to prescribe me antidepressants when I went to see him last winter – he thought lack of sleep was my biggest problem. 'It'll soon improve,' he said, 'this is just part of life.' I nodded, smiled feebly, and said: 'Of course I know how incredibly privileged I am, being able to be on leave with Henry for so long, it isn't about that.' 'Try to enjoy yourself, too,' he said. 'They grow up so fast.'

Enjoy myself? Now, at thirty-five years old, the only thing I know anything about is being a mother. The only drive left in me is to keep the kids clean and happy, the house in some semblance of order. What I spend most of my time doing – and which others might therefore mistake for my main interest – is handling dirty and freshly laundered clothes. I wash sweaters, I wash shirts and jeans, I wash socks, I soak pastel-coloured woollen underwear, I boil cotton underpants, I hang up silk garments, sort T-shirts and bodysuits and tights by colour, put bras in washing bags for delicates, fold sweatpants and long johns. I carry piles of clothes up the stairs, I put the clothes in the wardrobes, I put the towels in the bathroom, I put the kitchen cloths in the cupboard beneath the hob. The cloths for the floor and for cleaning the bathroom have no set place, but Helene hasn't noticed that.

IN JANUARY, just after Henry's first birthday, I booked an appointment to ask if antidepressants might be an option, because since the move I'd felt so unfathomably sad. Of course I had to take Henry with me. It was a hellish morning – he'd slept badly, he had a cold and was whiny, with a runny nose and cheeks that looked as if they'd been scrubbed raw. He struggled, refused to sit on my lap, but when I set him down on the waiting-room floor he only wanted to be picked up again. The woman on the chair opposite me tried to entertain him. I could hear that she wasn't Norwegian – this was presumably why she was interacting with him – and when she tried to make him laugh by hiding behind and then peeking out from her magazine, I gave her a friendly smile. But when she began to speak to him and asked: 'What's the matter? Do you want milk? Would you like your mamma's milk?' I wanted to stand up and slap her across the face. No, I don't have any milk. And even if I had, I wouldn't have wanted him to have it.

PACKING UP THE BOOKS TAKES TIME. The first few metres of shelving I empty straight into one of the big blue IKEA bags but then regret it – I actually have the time to be selective, to get rid of the books I'm never going to read or regret buying. But Knausgård and Margit Sandemo's *Legend of the Ice People* series and the old Bokklubben hardbacks I'll keep, of course, along with all Helene's textbooks, *Health Legislation for Dentists*, *Topographical Anatomy*, *The Central Nervous System* – I remember I was so impressed, the first time I saw her extensive collection. I loved that she immersed herself in bite physiology and radiation damage; that she knew what was going on in my nervous system when she breathed against my neck and kissed the point where my ear meets my jaw.

I opened the last, two-day old text exchange with Mayliss:

In the middle of dinner, call you after?

Okay.

She hasn't texted to apologize for the things she said, but nor has she sent any angry tirades since, so surely that's a good sign? Perhaps she's slowly coming to the same conclusion herself – that it'll be best for everyone if we just draw a line under this. But no. It isn't that simple. 'I'm the kind of person who doesn't forget if someone is mean to me,' she once said with a laugh. 'So if anyone ever does anything against Nicolai, God help them!'

*

Helene messaged me at six this morning, while I was still asleep – a frustrated text about a bad night, arguing with her mother. I replied with hearts, sympathy, *hang in there, baby*. It's time to get in touch again. I have to make sure she doesn't grow suspicious; try to keep her irritation at a minimum. First I stand in front of the empty bookcases, but the light is poor in that part of the room, so I go over to the dining table where only one chair remains, stretch the hand in which I'm holding my phone high into the air, make an ironic thumbs up with the other hand, and laugh a little at myself, at the stupid photo. *Hey, check it out – progress! You guys all good?*

For a moment I consider sending the photo to Mayliss, too. To smooth things over – I could act as if nothing has happened.

WHILE I REARRANGE the storeroom to make space for all the things we're not putting into storage while the decorators are here, I set up my laptop and put on a Netflix show with Marie Kondo, the tidying queen who's made multimillions off getting people to rid their homes of personality, and who helps the selected mess-makers to part with things they don't need by thanking each object. I quickly grow tired of the formulaic show. I quickly grow tired of standing hunched over, going through things I'm unsure whether or not we want to keep. Because why am I doing this? What will come out of it? We'd thought this would be the best solution, that Helene and the kids should go away while I did the sorting – I'm the one who likes to keep things tidy, and it's impossible to get anything done with the boys romping around. But it was a mistake. She should be here, too – she's stricter than me, less sentimental. And it isn't right that I have to make every decision. It's as if, in being left alone with the responsibility for our things, I've also been left alone with the responsibility for the direction our life should take. I hold it all in my hands. Two adapters, the garish vase we were given as a wedding present, ski boots nobody uses, an old packet of Danish cigarettes, the winter footmuff for Henry's pushchair, which he may well have grown out of by the time it's cold again… keep or let go? It's a complex, far-reaching assignment, both practically and mentally. Maybe I ought to start sorting things in a different way, simply labelling the various boxes with either her name or mine, and then that would be that?

Because the situation can also be interpreted like this: I'm alone for a week, I sleep and eat alone and think thoughts I'm never able to think with the three of them present. It's as if I'm steeling myself, preparing for the time that will come if I can't force my heart to fill up again, to flood my entire being with a light that makes me shine so intensely she won't be able to take her eyes off me, and therefore have no chance of discovering all that's going on behind her back.

I'VE TAKEN CARE of Henry every single day this year, but during the nights he's belonged solely to Helene. Only in January was Helene first absent at bedtime – she was going out to meet friends for the first time since we'd moved. I had put Henry to bed only once before – it had been easy, but it certainly wasn't easy now. I sat as agreed at his bedside, but he didn't want me to sing to him or hold his hand, he threw himself around, flung his dummy onto the floor and carried on, howling with resentment because he was allowed neither milk nor to come out of the cot. For a good while, I was patient. Then I felt the rage starting to flare up, as if a dark rash were spreading from my chest and up towards my face. Sit there, comfort him, just sit there. I was exhausted, the house was a bomb site, Olav had already spent far too long watching children's TV – how long was I supposed to bear just sitting there?

Helene isn't here, I suddenly thought. It was like seeing the light. Then I broke rules. I walked out of the room. I let him scream. He howled, louder and harder, while I stood outside the bedroom door and waited. Go on, scream, I thought, you fucking brat. After a while, I went back in – he looked terrible, his mouth a distorted black hole, eyes and nose streaming. The screaming subsided. He reached out his arms towards me, but I took hold of him and pushed him down onto his back. He screamed again, tried to get up; I took hold of him and pushed him down onto his back; he screamed.

I left the room again, hands shaking – the door slammed shut behind me, I didn't mean it to – I waited, went back in, the screaming subsided, he reached out his arms towards me, the tears flowed, I pushed him down, he screamed, I pushed him down, I thrust him down, far too hard, and the back of his head grazed the bars of the cot, but he didn't slam into them – thank God – I left the room and stood outside the door again, where I shouted through gritted teeth into my palms, there was nobody to help me, and I couldn't simply cry out, because then Olav would hear me over the *Paw Patrol* marathon I'd plonked him down in front of while I was putting Henry to bed. I noticed I was on the verge of tears, and with this realization something within me clicked into place, and all at once I was able to feel sympathy for him, the poor little soul. I went back into the room, he screamed, he reached his arms out towards me, I picked him up, his hands had a primate's grip, he clung to me as he continued to scream, the scream had lodged in his throat, I stroked his back, his pyjamas were hot and clammy, 'I'm sorry,' I said, 'Mamma didn't mean it.'

As I rocked him to sleep, I thought of the book my previous doctor had recommended, which featured observations of small children who, after having fallen or experiencing a knock, staggered towards their mother for comfort while simultaneously holding one arm protectively in front of their face. When the caregiver is a source of fear, it causes an upset in the child's biology. One of the greatest risks to a child's development is growing up with episodic violence. With a caregiver who is caring some of the time, who doesn't always fly into a rage at something the child expects to be scolded for. It is the exceptions, those moments of kindness, that the child will cling to. Like a loyal and steadfast little tin soldier, the child will wait and wait in the hope of receiving its mother's delectable love once more.

I F ONLY JANNE had been home, I think, as I unscrew the blinds from above the windows over the kitchen counter, this week might also have been a gift. I could have invited her over, bought some olives and pulled out the garden chairs; we could have drunk wine together under the apple trees – her kids are so big now, she finished serving her time long ago. I could have said: 'I know I've behaved badly.' Perhaps I might have ventured to ask if she could help me out a little. With the painting, at least. To ask friends for annoying favours is a declaration of love. Or at least, it is for me. But Janne and Peter are in France, staying with some friends I don't know. I haven't seen her since we took the boys over to her place to celebrate Constitution Day on 17 May.

I'm sure things will work out between us. But I'm ashamed of how little effort I've made. That I didn't invite her to Henry's naming ceremony is one thing – it was a simple affair, we kept it small, so as to invite as few people as possible, to have to wait upon as few guests as possible – when my mother is present, I can hardly focus on anyone else. But that I didn't offer to go pick up Mikkel and drive him home, the night someone called to tell her he was pissed off his face at some party in Gamlebyen. Or that I didn't attend her master's degree celebration, the degree she had spent two years commuting to Bergen for... that was a mistake. She had only invited me a few days before – it'll be totally low-key, she said – and I misunderstood, or wanted to misunderstand. I thought it wasn't important, that it didn't really matter one way or the other if I gathered round the table in her old wooden house with her friends from Nittedal, who I don't know and in whose company I feel shy. In fact, I thought it would probably be best if I stayed away, because I'd only sabotage the mood, and I didn't want to have to make the long journey back to Oslo, and certainly not to stay overnight, to be forced into small talk with Peter the next morning and afterwards come home to Helene, who would be half-dead and angry after being both up in the night and getting up early. I sent Janne a breakfast basket with croissants and orange juice and flowers. And she texted to thank me, and told me they'd had a nice little party the previous evening. But I knew, of course – I should have been there.

What would Janne have said if everything were good between us, and she was here right now? Probably something along the lines of: 'Ugh, you've got yourself into a bit of a mess this time, haven't you!' But she might also have fished a cigarette from the pack I found in the storeroom, and said: 'You know what, Silje Marie? This idea that we're supposed to live lives free of pain – it drives me nuts. We're here to have many emotions and experiences, and if you can expand your repertoire, you can, at least in theory, develop a greater capacity for compassion. The idea that everything is supposed to be easy – you can just let that go. There's something reconciliatory and freeing in that. Private and personal happiness should actually be secondary, it's capitalistic, about nothing but the private sphere. My aim isn't to be strong and independent. My aim is to enter into a context, to be part of the community – with all the vulnerability that entails and everything else life brings.'

I HAVE TO TELL HELENE WHO MAYLISS IS. About where Henry and I were last week. About the things I've said, which I never should have shared with anyone. But I say nothing, because I know it will trigger a landslide. Open up the possibility of a reprise of the scenes that played out after my indiscretion, the schizophrenic swinging between sobbing and nasty comments and desperate kissing, but this time the bond between us will be irreparable, it will be broken for good, and Helene will never again think of me without noting how contempt seethes within her, she won't be able to see me in any other role than that of fraudster, and she'll tell everyone she's close to, and they'll take her side, and our boys – presumably she won't tell them, because whatever else she might be, she isn't like that, she won't want to be one of those people who inflict pangs of anxiety and stomach ulcers on their children, who use them as psychologists and go-betweens, and she'll probably be keen to ensure that we maintain a decent enough parental collaboration. But of course she'll subconsciously transfer her grief and hatred onto them, they'll grow up marred by the fact that mother hates mother, carry that pain, be worn threadbare between us, struggle with the dream of us getting back together and wanting to take both our sides, but of course, if they have to choose – if they really have to choose – they'll be loyal to the mother who was deceived, not to the one who, time and again, put her family's very existence on the line.

*

And that's why I can't use how alone I've felt since we moved here as an excuse, either. It's my own fault, I'm sullen and distant – I know that, I'm not stupid, although it doesn't make it any easier to bear. I can't tell her that I often pretend I want to kiss her, that I pretend I condemn keeping secrets, pretend I never have any doubt that she did the right thing by giving me another chance. I pretend, almost all the time, because if I'm honest with her now, she won't have the strength to handle it, and if I'm honest, she'll grow angry again, too, and I won't be able to stand it, because she has every right to be angry, I'm the one who did something that justified anger in this relationship, and who thereby made this relationship insufferable.

How long can I keep this up for, exactly? Until Olav has settled into his first year at school? Until Henry starts high school? Until the children have moved out? Or until the renovation is finished in September, so it's easy to just put the house up for sale before we've even moved back in, with all our junk and stacks of nappies? Or until the love comes back, with full force. Surely that could still happen? 'I've said it before, and now I'll say it again,' Janne said at some point during the winter, 'you need to go down to the family welfare centre. Peter and I got so much out of it. You just need to start making repairs, and if the two of you can manage that, then maybe there's hope.'

But often it doesn't feel as if I want hope. I don't want to make repairs. I just want to be left alone. Why are we never allowed a fucking break? From life. From motherhood. From the obligation to send texts and from the suspicion that clings to us no matter what we do, like chewing gum in a matted braid. Helene's gaze. Helene's new voice. It's like the old one, absolutely, but the difference is palpable if you listen for it, like when the

TV production company employed a new kid to dub the latest season of *Peppa Pig*.

When I think about what I should feel for Helene at these times, it's like staring at the pages of a puzzle book. I look and look, but Wally seems to have vanished into thin air. I've been searching for a long time; it's beginning to take its toll. Sooner or later, you start to lose hope of finding anything other than a mirage. And I can't bear to think about who comes to the fore on those occasions when Helene really sees and listens to me.

I WAS ONCE SOMEONE WHO CRAVED MY FRIENDS. And my friends craved me. Every Friday and Saturday night we would crowd before the mirror, the four of us girls who shared a bathroom in the folk high school's dormitory – the girls I worshipped, and with whom I moved into a shared apartment in Bergen the following autumn. The girls I thought would be my friends for ever, but whose surnames I now can hardly remember. I remember only Janne. She hadn't been living with us all that long when she buzzed me in one evening when I'd forgotten my keys; I was soaked through, it's a myth that everyone from Western Norway dons their rain gear and carries an umbrella at all times. 'Sit down and relax,' she said, and made me a cup of tea, because that's what young women in flat-shares drink when inviting one another into a kind of polite confidence; she gazed at me in such a mild, motherly and mature way that I didn't dare say a word. How old was I – twenty? Twenty, with no idea what I wanted to be, or how I was going to manage all the freedom that had suddenly been dumped in my lap. All I knew was that I didn't want to stay on at the bakery when this year came to an end. That I'd soon have to trawl the streets for girls to make out with. That I would never live on Sotra again.

'So you all went to the same folk high school? I actually thought you were older than the others,' Janne said. But she was the one who was older, by almost seven years; she had long since completed her training as a physiotherapist – she now treated hip patients using the Mensendieck method in a sports hall out in Åsane – and had taken over Birgitta's room because Birgitta had fallen in love with an off-road motorcycle rider from Alta, and because Janne needed a temporary place to stay after breaking up with her high-school sweetheart just months before they were supposed to be married in a humanist ceremony on a mountain farm. 'Best thing I've ever done,' she said. 'Life is so good now!' All the other doors in the flat-share were closed that evening. The rain streamed through Fosswinckels Gate's darkness as my jeans dried on my thighs. 'Would you like a bun?' I asked. 'I have cinnamon or custard.' I always brought treats home from work for my flatmates. Still, when Janne said yes, I felt like a child being praised for having learnt something new. She wasn't attractive, I thought at first, all her features seemed sort of big on her, her head, her lips, her eyes – she was large and rough. But the more she told me about herself, the more charming she became. She could speak French. She had two younger sisters. She, too, had been a Cub Scout, but only for a year. She'd seen Michael Jackson live in concert, and could just about still listen to his music. She was absolutely certain she wanted children. I felt immature for understanding neither why it was a point that she could still just about listen to Michael Jackson's music, nor the seriousness of the question of children. I was surprised and happy every time I said something that made her laugh, or took the conversation in a new direction. Because it felt so good to sit there, I found myself wanting to get up several times, to say I had to open the bakery early the next morning, in order to extricate myself from the situation before I said something stupid, before I revealed what a stupid, boring doormat I really was. But Janne said: 'I'm not sure how long I'll be staying here for. I'm going to view a new place next week. But if you ever fancy a chat, all you have to do is knock on my door.'

I couldn't quite believe she wanted to be my friend – I was sure she must see me as a kind of charity case. Even though I was the one she called after she slept with Peter for the first time. Even though I was the one she invited to a New Year's Eve party out at a cabin with no electricity. Even though she added me to the group chat she had with her friends, where they mainly just shared funny cat videos and photos of men with exceptional style. I wanted to dress like those men, although I didn't say that, of course. The fact that I so often began to stutter, that I would apologize mid-sentence because I didn't feel smart enough and was having a mind blank, and then would also proceed to comment on it – it irritated her. 'Can't you just try to chill out a bit?' she said. But she stayed all the same – even after the time we went to IKEA, and I only half-jokingly referred to her as my support worker.

And later, in Copenhagen: by day, I was an economics student, but by night, I stepped into a den of lesbian iniquity. I couldn't believe it. All around me, the city was teeming with amazing women, and I was consumed by them, the way you're consumed by new friends when you're young and have the time and desire to cultivate those relationships and what those relationships make you feel you really are. I spooned with them, and danced to Britney and Ace of Base at afterparties with them, and watched Julie compete in roller-derby tournaments out in the Danish countryside, and was the only one with a driver's licence and therefore the person who drove Mette and her girlfriend to Hamburg so we could all attend an event known as L Beach, where huge German lesbians in swim shorts swaggered around topless in an indoor water park and eyed each other up before hurrying away, squealing, every time they caught sight of Leisha Hailey, who was there to perform with her band.

Mette put her arm around me and said: 'My dear Silje Marie, will you ever forgive me for bringing you here?' I would have forgiven her anything. All these queer, Danish friendships – it was as if they formed a wall of the most beautiful, glittering crystal around me, and far beyond the wall lay my childhood and all I'd been before, everything I had struggled with, but which I had never really been able to look at or managed to put into words.

Several of my Copenhagen friends were invited to my wedding, and they came, and they hugged me, and Julie wore Converse without a hint of shame, and Mette stood alone and smoked a cigarette when the guests thronged together to take a group photo, and they said Helene and I looked beautiful, and that even though they didn't know Helene, they could tell we were going to be great together. And, like me, they probably thought our friendship would endure, that we'd call each other often and visit one another and go on holidays together, even though I'd moved back to Norway.

The wall shattered, of course.

Of everyone from Copenhagen, Joachim is the only one left.

He was the hottest guy at Copenhagen Business School, like a young Bruce Springsteen, with narrow eyes and dark, dishevelled hair. The first time I saw him, he was wearing a white vest and a black denim jacket, and he stood out among all the straight, sleek economics students. You, I thought, are someone I want to be seen with. I never would have guessed he was Norwegian. 'So where in Norway are you from?' I asked as we made our way to the lecture hall, 'Sørlandet?' He grinned, tossed his head. 'Wow – you're worse with dialects than I am,' he said. 'I'm from Karmøy, mostly famous for unsolved murders, heavy chapel culture and Flipper the dolphin.' 'Flipper?' I repeated. 'I've met Flipper! It was one of the greatest moments of my childhood, petting that dolphin – I was high on it for an entire summer. I remember I wrote in my diary: *it was so lovely and smooth…*' 'Eeeew!' Joachim cried, waving his beautiful, slender hands around. 'Stop!'

Maybe I started hanging out with Mayliss because I'm lonely. But the fact that I'm lonely doesn't mean I no longer see people. I have friendships of convenience, people I meet up with because they also have children, or because both Helene and I get along with them. Of course I'm grateful for that. But they're not Joachim, who bought me champagne on his credit card and took me to his father's fiftieth birthday party in Tuscany and made green break-fast smoothies for me when we lived together, and who woke me, crying, in the middle of the night, because he'd fallen in love with yet another married man. They're not Janne, who invited me to celebrate Christmas with her family when Mamma froze me out, who drove down from Nittedal with freshly baked sourdough bread and a hand-knitted baby blanket the day after I came home from the hospital with Olav. Even though I once didn't even remember to let her know I couldn't make it to Mikkel's naming ceremony.

That I was so close to them… during those first years Helene had found it appealing. She went to great lengths to try to charm them, came up with ideas for what we might give them as Christmas gifts, suggested that we spend time together in the holidays. 'Joachim is so funny,' she declared affectionately, 'you never know what he's going to come out with next! And Janne – she's just so incredibly smart.' But after a while, as life grew ever more constricted, when the blows fell and she realized that I revealed and confided things to them that I never told her… she didn't say anything, has never said anything, but she no longer looks forward to seeing them. She speaks politely with them, comes over to Janne's place if the entire family is invited, will have a drink with Joachim before she makes her excuses and says she needs to get going, but I note her coolness, see her wariness. And, naturally enough, it rubs off – maybe that's also one of the reasons I've gradually cut contact with them: I don't want Helene to be unnecessarily reminded of my betrayal. I don't want her to feel that she isn't my top priority. Because she is. In spite of everything: she is.

'To be with someone – that is, to enter into a committed, long-term relationship,' Janne said, long before our friendship began to falter, 'is to give your life away. Nobody realizes this, of course. Because everything seems so incredible and vital and safe. Super safe! But you give your life away. You share your most intimate thoughts and darkest fantasies, your bank account, family and friends. You buy a house together, you have children together, and you have no idea that life has been turned to delicate glass until one of you is standing there clutching it, ready to hurl it at the wall.'

I F I HAVE TIME, I think, as I pick Blu Tack and double-sided tape off the walls and cast a glance at all the boxes of the children's stuff, on one of these upcoming days I'll sort their toys by type and material. Toy vegetables and the mini porcelain tea set, Lego, Playmobil, colourful bits and bobs, all the plastic animals from Schleich… In the newly renovated house awaits a fresh sense of order: the boys will know where to find what they want to play with, and afterwards they will – following encouraging but firm instructions from their mothers – put the toys away again. Dream on, Janne would have said. She and Peter live in a state of chaos much wilder than ours, an utter pig sty, I think I hear my sister say, but I've always loved being there, the mess is pleasing because it reflects Janne as both a person and a mother, down-to-earth and self-assured. She doesn't feel that she's drowning in all this crap, that it erases her and is a manifestation of the fact that she's making no effort in her life.

Something is sticking out from under the sofa: it's the bit of wood Olav likes to pretend is a fence when he brings the plastic animals to life.

I have countless indications of the fact I'm making no effort, neither in my own life nor in that of my kids. The only thing radiating from me is resignation. Something dead. Like the fact that I don't have a hobby the kids can be inspired by. Like the fact that Olav has hardly ever been to the cinema, even though he's almost four and a half, or that I haven't taken Henry to the library more often, or that I so rarely make plans for the weekend. But sometimes we go to the children's farm at Ekeberg on my initiative. I can fake initiative. When were we last there – just before Easter? It was after I got to know Mayliss, at any rate, because I was nervous about us potentially bumping into her and Nicolai. Because if we did, what would I say?

The two calves were the first animals we saw. The fence around the farm isn't electrified, and as we approached, the calves stuck their heads through the gaps in order to reach the new shoots of the almost fluorescent-green grass. Cautiously but astonished, Olav patted one of the calves on the neck, while Henry pulled up clumps of grass which he then threw at the other calf, squealing enthusiastically as he did so. Helene and I stood close to one another as we watched them. 'Can you take a picture?' I asked. She shook her head. 'I left my phone in the car.'

What a shame, I thought – it was the perfect image, the two kids in woollen sweaters together with two beautiful calves, in beautiful weather one beautiful spring day, and weren't we also a beautiful family, didn't I have a beautiful wife? I glanced at Helene – she was wearing her old, aviator-style glasses, and in the pale spring sunlight her skin appeared even more sallow than usual, but of course that wasn't everything, couldn't I simply swipe that away, as if I were changing the filter on my phone's camera, and find the original image beneath? The way her cheeks had once burned when she caught my eye, or after I had made her come. Her eyes when she gazed at me, or after I had made her come.

I should touch her, I thought, a loving gesture – how long was it since I'd last done that of my own volition, outdoors? I stuck a hand under her thick ponytail and laid my fingers against her neck, at her hairline, and rubbed a couple of times at the points where I knew she held tension. Would she stiffen, ask what I was doing? Instead, she closed her eyes. She sighed, 'Oh,' she said, 'that feels so good.' It was a lot. It was too much, far too intimate. How she yearns, I thought, how she truly longs for this. All at once sorrow surged up in me, it felt as if my lungs were being filled with wet clay, as if they grew twice as heavy in my chest. Olav began to laugh – 'It's licking my hand,' he shouted, 'look!' 'Yes, look,' I replied. I withdrew my arm, suggested he might try to let the calf suck his fingers. 'It doesn't have teeth,' I said, 'so there's no need to be scared.'

I crouched down behind the boys, only now noticing how many other families had arrived, keen to have the same authentic experience as us. A little girl came toddling over with a fistful of grass; I made space for her so she could come all the way up to the fence, and that was when he came running, the boy who spat, hitting one of the calves right between the eyes. The boy laughed, a frenzied and stone-cold laugh, before he sped on, straight past his parents, who didn't do so much as raise an eyebrow to reprimand him. 'What the hell?' Helene exclaimed, 'what a total brat.' 'What's that, Mamma?' Olav asked. I stared at the calf as it unknowingly tugged grass from the little girl's hand with a trust that was almost unbearable.

I N ANOTHER CITY, another moment of impact on the timeline to which only Helene and I have access: we're waiting for the bus. The mountains that surround Bergen cast shadows on the streets; it's too late in September for the patches of morning sunlight to provide much in the way of warmth. Helene is wearing a baseball cap and a black leather jacket, she kisses me again and again, even though my breath must smell terrible. I stick my hands under her leather jacket, under her shirt, up her smooth, strong back. 'Jesus, your hands are so cold,' she says, but she doesn't push me away. 'Do you always forget your gloves on purpose?' I'm here on a weekend visit from Oslo, and I haven't told my parents I'm in town. We have no idea that we'll move into my apartment together before a year has passed. We've hardly slept. We both find ourselves in the psychotic state in which we think we'll die simply at the thought of being separated for eight hours. The light-rail network is still under construction. The bus is a few minutes late. More and more people crowd the stop, but only one person is looking at us. The curls of her perm are perfect, her coat neatly buttoned up. First, she turns to look a few times, demonstratively. Then she begins to stare – furiously. Helene is standing with her back to her; I don't mention it, because it's ridiculous. I want to go over to the old woman and say: you're ridiculous. But when she spits, straight onto the pavement, I'm the one who pretends not to notice what's going on.

I WISH I HADN'T TOLD MAYLISS ABOUT THE SPITTING WOMAN. But I did – I got carried away after she told me about how she would never walk hand in hand with her ex in Grønland. 'And at work,' she said, 'the odd male guest has realized what I am and let me know in no uncertain terms what he'd like to teach me up in his room.' 'And what do you do when they say that?' I asked. She only grinned, shrugged. 'Gah – I joke around with them, have a laugh. I mean, it's funny.'

I know nobody else who takes this kind of thing so lightly.

Before the terrorist attack, and perhaps after it, too, I've often thought that it's almost become a kind of sport, to be indignant, to be as frightened as possible. Everywhere I go, I encounter people who tell me about the handful of uncomfortable experiences they've had, like minor sensations, episodes you can collect and laugh at while taking the piss out of homophobic idiots. I have a suspicion that these episodes make us feel that we're special – that there's so much more to our lives than the usual stalwart everyday Norwegian existence. The suffocating, normal everyday Norwegian existence. The pressing weight of anonymity. But then again, what do I know? I'm not trans. I'm not the feminine guy who thoughtlessly kisses his boyfriend in the taxi queue. I don't receive online threats. I haven't heard the shots of an MP 40 in Oslo city centre.

When Joachim was almost dragged into a service-station toilet by two men, the case was dropped, even though the whole thing was caught on the station's security cameras. He says: 'It still gives me the heebie-jeebies, whenever I smell Thousand Island dressing.' He shook as we sat together in the police station and filled out the report. But Joachim makes no apology. Out of everyone I know, I think I'm the only one who apologizes. But if anyone ever spits at my boys, I will kill them.

OUT OF THE OLD COFFEE TIN I kept when we cleared out my grandmother's house – I had to let my sister take the framed Theodor Kittelsen prints – rolls Olav's little shell collection. Mussels. Conches. Sea-snail shells. He loves to mess around with these kinds of things. To gather treasures, meticulously sorting and arranging them with his tiny hands. The tiny hands that grab hold of my face. He wants to kiss me on the mouth with his small, dry lips. 'I have two mammas,' he says. I ask him if he thinks that's silly. He cocks his head to one side: 'I don't know?' He doesn't understand why I'm asking.

One afternoon, when I sat brushing Olav's hair and trying to get him to tell me whether it was him or the two big boys in his class who kept pulling out his elastic, he pretended not to hear me. 'Why is the sky above us?' he began. 'Why is the sky higher than the houses?' Maybe his curiosity was genuine, but he knows me – he knows how I turn soft and gooey when he gets all philosophical, thinks boundless thoughts. I don't want to live in a world full of children who only ever put on an act in order to please, but I'm in the process of shaping such a child myself. We spoke about his birthday for a bit. 'Did you know it's the third of November today?' I asked. 'That means it's exactly two months until you turn four, and right after that Henry will turn one.' 'Will I get cake?' Olav asked in reply. 'You will,' I said. 'Can Isak and Bo come over and visit me?' he said. 'Maybe,' I replied, 'but only if they stop being mean to you.' 'Oh,' he said. 'Okay.'

Then he suddenly got up. Henry was sitting on the play mat – Olav went straight over to his little brother, knelt down and bent halfway over him. Henry laughed. Olav blew on his neck, Henry laughed again; Olav tickled him, and Henry grew breathless with laughter. 'Be careful,' I cried, 'remember he can't say no!' Olav stopped tickling his brother. He put his arms around Henry and rolled over, so Henry was lying on top of him. Henry giggled. Then he set his head against his big brother's chest and closed his eyes in one single huge and breathtaking declaration of love.

My boys. The bond between them. Who's to say that such moments don't make up for everything?

Mayliss is the only person I've told. It wasn't hard. I just came out with it. That I hadn't actually wanted to go to any sibling discussion; I didn't want another one. I didn't understand it, how I was supposed to love another child. But I couldn't deny Helene the experience of being pregnant – in fact, I'd promised her: 'If I can be the one to get pregnant this time, it'll be your turn next.' And Olav – was he supposed to spend his life alone with us, shouldn't he have a sibling with whom to play pirates and argue and kick a football around and go trick-or-treating and build sandcastles in the endlessly long summers of our future? The best thing a child can have, I once read somewhere, is a good father. But I think the most beautiful thing you can have is probably a brother.

'If I hadn't been completely sure, I never would have had a kid,' Mayliss said. She spat a pouch of snus tobacco into the bushes beside the bus stop we were standing at. 'But I'm the kind of person who follows my gut.'

JUST A FEW DAYS after the terrorist attack came the text from the unknown number. Would we like to meet up? *Hugs from Mayliss and Nicolai :).* But I had already decided: I didn't reply. Then I heard no more. We went to Spain, in August we ended up in a bidding war for the house, and then came autumn with the move that consumed us, the hatred for the house that united us. We forgot the horrors and testimonies from that night in June. The sea of withered flowers in Rosenkrantz' Gate was gathered up and cleared away. Queen Elizabeth's coffin was carried through the city of London. Iranian women took to the streets, their heads uncovered. Mice swarmed and scurried in the loft, while Olav stopped using nappies at night and started eating tomatoes. Amid the smell of blocked drains, Henry learnt to pull himself to standing. We became a pair of mother hens. Mother hens on the sledging hill. Mother hens at the swimming pool. Misty-eyed mother hens with cameras at the kindergarten, watching the Saint Lucy's Day parade. Helene's parents came over for Christmas, and my mother-in-law said: 'I'm sure the house will be lovely, but you've grown so thin, Mamma Silje.' Pappa transferred me some money so I could buy some presents for the kids. Mamma sent such huge gifts in the post I was sure she must have bought them on credit. My sister messaged: *It would be nice if you could spare a thought for Mamma, too, and visit her soon.* And I thought: I'm right to just forget about all that, just forget it ever happened.

*

But then she was there again, sitting on the floor of Grønland Church. It was February, frost and white light everywhere, a dead light that stung your face and burned in the gaps between your jacket cuffs and gloves. Inside the big church it was chilly. The deacon who led the baby music sessions was yet to arrive. But Mayliss, she was sitting there among the other exhausted parents, wearing tight jeans, a strip of purple in her bleached-blonde fringe. Nicolai had grown a lot, and so had Henry – he'd just learnt to walk. 'Well, hello there!' she exclaimed. 'It's you, isn't it?' I wanted to turn around, to just leave, pretend I'd forgotten we had an appointment at the children's clinic. Instead, I said: 'Is this spot free?' She moved closer to one of the others in the circle, a dad with long, skinny legs. 'Here,' she said. 'Sit yourselves down.'

She was so friendly. It was suspect. I glanced around the circle at the other parents – had they noticed? No, nobody said anything, presumably they had enough to worry about with their own kids, who were crawling around and stuffing egg shakers into their mouths, and had it not been for the fact that we were at Pride in the Park when we first bumped into each other, I probably wouldn't have noticed it, either. She leant towards me and whispered in my ear, as if we were old friends. It was as if her hot breath reached some point deep inside me, a sensitive place that had never before been touched. The smell of her – cheap hairspray, melted cheese. 'Nicolai is actually getting a bit big for this,' she said, 'but they let us come anyway.' 'Same here,' I replied, slowly drawing away from her, 'this little guy doesn't start kindergarten until August.' I realized I was staring at Nicolai. He was standing next to Mayliss, his thumb in his mouth. His eyes. They were Henry's eyes, in the middle of a strange child's face.

What had I imagined would happen? That I'd hold my breath and count to ten, and they'd just disappear? But here he stood. A thickset little boy with a fire engine printed on his sweater, born just a few months before Henry was pulled out of Helene. A little boy who was growing up in the same city, and who was in all likelihood descended from the same man, a man who, one day, for reasons unknown, had registered his interest in becoming a sperm donor, and who, after being put through multifarious personality tests and health checks, had given the sperm bank a few childhood photos from his mother's photo album and composed a handwritten letter about his motives for undertaking this deed, and signed to confirm that he consented to all his future descendants both learning his identity and being able to contact him.

If Nicolai and Henry, as teenagers or young adults, were to log on to the national health service website in order to find out who they were descended from, they would find exactly the same story, an identical explanation, the same names would appear on the branches of the family tree which until that moment had remained in shadow, and maybe it wouldn't mean all that much to either of them – perhaps Helene and I would have succeeded in all we hoped to achieve, in helping the children understand that biological relatives are not the same as family. That it was the four of us – Olav, Henry, Helene and me – who constituted Henry's family, even if Olav and I were nowhere to be found on any of the tree's branches.

But perhaps it wouldn't work out like that. Maybe they would come to write each other off, my children, one day turn to each other and say: Look at us – we're not real brothers. Maybe they'll abandon Helene and me, slam doors and scream, *You're not my mother*, an eventuality we will of course both need to tolerate and be prepared for. Maybe they'll say it to hurt us, or because they're going through a difficult phase, or maybe they'll really mean it, maybe it will be something they've always felt because they noticed that we, no matter how hard we might try to hide it, treated them slightly differently – for example by always saying good morning first to the child to whom we had given birth – and maybe also because they simply felt it at the very core of their identities. Maybe they'll try to hide it, too, loyal and loving as they are to both of us, but if they ever hurt themselves, or are away at summer camp, or experience something amazing or frightening, it's the longing for Mamma that will begin to hum, to quiver within them, and at those times the word Mamma will be linked to one body, one voice, one face. To the nature we like to pretend we have tamed and conquered.

In front of us, the deacon sat straddling a little drum. Her curly hair stuck out comically in all directions, and over her polo-necked sweater she was wearing a kind of tunic made of grey linen. 'We'll start by singing a round of the children's names,' she shouted, and I pulled Henry down onto my lap. I had long since stopped demonstratively expressing how embarrassing it was to give oneself over to these kinds of activities, and now it was a relief to concentrate on keeping time with the deacon's drumbeat and sing *And Ada is here and Synne is here, and how lovely that Emilio-Milan is here*, to rock Henry to the same rhythm, to take my eyes off Nicolai and what I had discovered, the thing suspended in the air between him and Henry, a thin, glimmering thread. What was it? After we had sung Henry's name, when I was sure Mayliss and the other parents had their attention turned on the next child in the circle to be introduced, I lifted my hand and tried to waft it away. But my hand went straight through it. And at that very moment, Nicolai turned and looked at me, and it gave me chills, as if I had just made eye contact with a relative I had always believed to be dead, and I thought: Who are you?

When Helene and I ate dinner that day, and I yet again neglected to say anything about the meeting or what Mayliss and I had agreed, I realized she was back. That it wasn't me sitting there at the table, but my clone, of whom I had been completely unaware until she began to flirt with Fitness Guri, but who apparently had been living inside me my whole life, just waiting for an opportune moment to take my place. She was like me in every way except one: she had no scruples about lying. She withheld crucial information without the slightest hesitation.

The following week they stood waiting in the snow outside Victoriahuset. Since New Year I'd been trying to create a routine for Henry and me, so I wouldn't 'completely lose it', as the worn-out Swedish mum of twins I sometimes bumped into used to say. On Mondays I went to the open kindergarten, Tuesdays to the central library, Wednesdays to the botanical gardens, where I could walk and walk and listen to podcasts while Henry slept in his pram. On this particular Wednesday I had Henry in the baby carrier, so I'd have the excuse of needing to go home and put him down for a nap after an hour. It was a long time since I'd carried him, and he was radiantly happy, pointing at dogs and cars and kicking his legs as if he were a tiny infant again.

There she was. In a puffer jacket and blue scarf. Ugg boots and a Kari Traa-branded beanie. Research into fatphobia shows that our immune system can interpret obesity in certain people we meet as an infectious disease, but it wasn't her excess weight that made me want to turn around. That woman and I have nothing in common, I thought, what the hell am I doing here? But for her it was presumably different. The person she saw approaching, was – in spite of the expensive fair-trade woven baby sling – confirmation that she belonged to a community, that there was another mother, many other mothers to whom she would always be linked, whether they liked it or not. It was simply the consequence of the choice they had made.

'He's so cute,' she said. 'Then again, I would think that, wouldn't I, ha ha! What's his name again – Henrik, was it?' 'Henry,' I said. I lifted him down into the snow, but he didn't seem to notice Nicolai, who was crouched down and playing with a little toy tractor. Nicolai's jumpsuit was blue. His hat was too small, it didn't cover his ears properly. 'My wife always liked the name,' I said. 'And you and your wife don't have any other kids?' 'Oh yes,' I replied, 'we have a boy who's just turned four – his name is Olav.' 'There's another one? And does he look just like these two?' 'No, Olav and Henry don't share the same donor.' 'No? Isn't that a bit weird?' 'No, why should it be?' 'I mean, didn't you want them to have the same father?' Father? I'd never heard anyone like me refer to their child's donor this way. What an absurd conversation this was. 'To put it bluntly, since you asked: they were all out of sperm from the first guy. So that's why we had to use a new donor with Henry.'

Henry reached out his arms towards me; I picked him up just as Nicolai was about to round the corner of the greenhouse. 'Nicolai,' Mayliss shouted, 'come to Mamma!' She went to get him, then came back to us. 'We have to introduce them to each other properly,' she said. 'Nicolai, this is Henry – he might be your half-brother!'

Half-brother? Could she really just come out with it, just like that? The boys eyed each other for a few seconds. They both had all their front teeth, dark lashes. Nicolai held his little tractor in his hand; Henry reached out to grab it. The likeness between them was like a composite sketch. I didn't want to find out who the suspect behind the composite was.

'I know they're only little, but I don't think we should use the word half-brother,' I said. 'I don't want to confuse them.' 'But is it really such a big deal,' she replied, 'if that's what they are?' 'Henry's family is the family he's growing up in,' I said, and immediately felt ashamed at how pre-programmed I sounded. 'When he turns fifteen, he can decide for himself if he'd like to initiate anyone else into that circle.' 'Okay,' she replied, a little sharply, clearly puzzled. 'You just seemed quite keen on the idea yourself, that's all.' 'Don't worry about it,' I interrupted. 'Are we the first you've met?' she asked. 'Do you know of any others?' 'Others? God no, luckily enough,' I said. 'Well, I think it's pretty cool,' she said. 'You know, to be a few of us in the same boat.' Jesus, I thought. What an idiot this woman is.

We went into the Victoriahuset greenhouse. Mayliss had never been there before, she said, the poor country bumpkin. The close, damp air made Henry squint, as if he thought he was about to be sprayed with water. After Christmas I'd often sat in here while he slept outside in his pram, warming myself up and trying to coax the carp in the more-than-a-hundred-year-old pond over to me. I would occasionally glance up at the chart that hung on the wall, which featured an antique photograph of a child who had been set on one of the gigantic waterlily leaves in order to demonstrate how much weight they could bear.

In their thick jumpsuits, the boys toddled along between the damp, tropical plants. Lotus flowers. Lianas. Coffea. Algae grew on the stones. Mayliss talked about herself, laughing often – maybe she was a former bullying victim who, as an adult, was taking a sort of revenge for a decade of muteness and fantasies of turning invisible during school lunchbreaks by talking the ear off everyone she came across, in the belief that it was impossible to see through her, to see the kind of loser she had been all her life. I was polite. I nodded and smiled and asked follow-up questions. How long had she been working at the hotel? Did she regret moving to Oslo to be closer to her mother? Oh, that's right, your mother can look after your child while you're at work, that's so great for you. And for him, too – of course.

Nicolai had stopped toddling around. Now he squeezed his way between the plants, making for the pond. 'There fish!' he cried, and I saw the carp's smooth back – it broke the water's surface just beside his hand. Two words. Henry wasn't even close to uttering anything like that; at a stretch, he could just about manage Mamma and no. But there was an ocean of time between them, an eternity for such young children, it was utterly meaningless to make comparisons. Again, I thought: What am I really doing here? What had I expected – that seeing Nicolai up close would give me some answers? A kind of peace of mind? The sense that it was irrelevant, the fact that he existed, and that there were probably many others like him out there?

And what about Henry? Was it right to drag *him* into all of this? Even though he didn't understand what was going on, even though he wouldn't be able to tattle on me? Or, to put it another way: would I have done this, come here, if the child I'd met at Pride in the Park had looked not like Henry, but like Olav? Would that not have triggered the opposite reaction in me? Wouldn't I have withdrawn, done everything in my power to keep Olav to myself, far from strange mothers and children I knew nothing about? I clearly wasn't all that concerned about Henry's well-being. I was unable to imagine Henry's inner life. That was obviously what this was all about. With Olav, there was either no problem or a huge problem – I could see every future worst-case scenario in vivid Technicolor before me. But not with Henry. It wasn't just about the fact that he was still so young, that I still knew so little about his weaknesses and vulnerabilities, about who he would be in the world – no, I clearly just wasn't connected to him. He was a small child I was linked to, but not by any true motherly bond. I had dragged him here with me today, but I obviously didn't care about the consequences this might have for him. And it was awful – utterly horrendous, in fact – that I could have such meagre feelings towards and take so little responsibility for a child who, according to legislation and the life I lived, was mine.

OUR NEIGHBOUR, Bjørg, who in all probability isn't away on holiday because she doesn't have anyone to go with but can use the fact that she has a dog as a convenient excuse, stops just outside our garden while I'm out on the patio in the rain, stamping flat a ruined box. Her tiny, half-blind dog cocks its leg right next to our steps. She doesn't tug on the lead, just lets the dog pee. 'So I see the two of you have made a start, then?' she shouts, nodding at the waste-disposal sack beside the apple tree. 'Yep!' I reply. 'Or I've made a start, at least – the others have gone on holiday.' 'Well, be careful what you leave outside,' she goes on. 'I saw someone snooping around here a few days ago. It's peak season for break-ins at the moment.' 'Oh gosh, really?' I reply. 'Well, thanks for letting me know, I'll keep an eye out, enjoy your walk!' A perfect show of small talk. It's something I've always been good at. When I was little, it saved me often: if you can play to the gallery, you can get away with almost anything.

I'll do anything, whatever it takes, to please. I put on an act. I adapt. I lie. I'm a fawning, laughing fox. I've known this ever since I read an article about a set of experiments performed by a Russian researcher in the 1950s. He wanted to find out more about how, at some point in history, dogs were tamed. He studied not wolves, but foxes. From a fur farm housing thousands of animals, he selected those that exhibited the least fear of humans, and in just a few generations of selective breeding, the foxes changed. Not only did many of them seek out human contact, but many were born with entirely new colour patterns to their coats, curly tailed and lop eared, and some began to wag their tails, bark, and communicate by making a sound similar to human laughter.

Exactly, I thought. I feel you, foxes.

I decided not to mention this experiment when I was introduced to my father-in-law's mink farm.

I think I have the makings of a good hostage. One weekend, I went over to Joachim's place. He was seeing a huge Danish bear at the time, who'd just been to Germany for work, in order to attend a safety course. While the bear served us crazy varieties of Swiss cheese and poured wine into our glasses – and I noticed Joachim constantly trying to catch my eye to get me to confirm that I, too, thought this bear was *just amazing* and *marriage material* – he shared his top tips from the course: never book a room above a hotel's reception area, because that's where suicide bombings happen. Always run in a zigzag if you're fleeing an active shooter. Starting to panic? Breathe in, hold your breath for four seconds, then breathe out – if you're fearing for your life, you can manipulate your body into believing you're relaxed, and thereby regain some self-control. If you're taken hostage, you need a strategy to change the hostage taker's view of you from day one – you want to rise through the ranks, from enemy to human to friend. Or perhaps even more – you want him to want to become your rescuer.

I THOUGHT SHE WAS STUPID, not all that much upstairs, per-haps. I thought to myself, I'm going to conclude this now, finish it politely, end of. She walked with me to the Metro station. An icy draught streamed through the underpass in which we had stopped. Henry was utterly still in his carrier. Was he feeling the chill? Were his feet cold? Did I even care that he might be freezing?

'This was so nice,' Mayliss said. I nodded. 'It really was,' I replied, casting a glance at the departures listed on the screen – I couldn't make the excuse that I had to run, it was seven minutes until the next train on line three. 'I'm free Monday and Tuesday – shall we get together again?' There – there it was. My heart sank. I hate having to reject people, I need extreme reasons for doing so, only then do I do it, in cold blood. But I tried. 'It's been really nice to see you,' I said, 'but I'm not sure. I think it might make things complicated for my wife.' There – easy, not exactly a lie, just something I couldn't substantiate knowing for sure. But she didn't get it. 'What's so complicated?' I looked at her. Um, that they might be half-siblings? I wanted to say. That I'm tampering with my family? She leant down over Nicolai's pushchair and smiled. 'Phew, I think someone needs a new nappy!' She turned back to me. 'Well, you seem like you need it. You seem a bit lonely, to be honest.' Lonely? I laughed, and heard how fake it sounded – it's always so embarrassing to be caught being fake. 'Maybe you think I'm being a bit forward,' Mayliss said, 'but I like to say it as it is.

That's just how I am. And there's no need to feel ashamed – you're not the only one. I'm lonely, too.' 'You need to watch out that he doesn't get an ear infection,' I said, 'that hat's a bit too small.' She bent down again, straightened Nicolai's hat. 'And you think it's fun to play with other children, don't you, Nicolai?'

I looked her up and down. She was so unlike my friends, so… insipid? But also unafraid. Since she just came out with these things. The fact that she was so direct – wasn't that precisely what I went around missing, here among all these cautious, self-aware city dwellers: straight-talking people? I stroked Henry's back through the carrier. He yawned. It was awful, me laying it on thick like this. *Of course* I cared about him. *Of course* I felt a motherly bond. But he was still so little. Endless spring months of parental leave stretched out before us. He got bored when we just stayed home, I saw that. And of course he didn't understand who Nicolai was – and it wasn't even certain that Nicolai was what I thought he might be. And it would be so good not to have to go to the open kindergarten for once, so good not to have to traipse down to the children's clinic and its cesspool of germs along with kids whose names I never learnt. And getting down on my hands and knees in the children's area at the library every Tuesday to pick up the books Henry ripped from the shelves, or sauntering around the botanical gardens alone on Wednesdays, weren't exactly the most stimulating activities life had to offer – not for me, or for him. And if there was one thing Helene was keen to ensure, it was that Henry should be stimulated. And if there was one thing Helene often expressed concern about, it was the fact that I spent too much time alone. Yes, of course we ought to meet up with them again, I told myself. After all, she's a single mother! And one who's not all that well off! She's probably so glad to have met some people like us! And Nicolai, who otherwise only ever went to his grandmother's house… socializing with another child would surely do him good. And that child needn't be anything more to him than a somewhat peripheral friend of the same age.

A SO-CALLED NEW FRIEND. A so-called new home. This house. We should have just redecorated before we moved in, in fact we never should have bought the place – had we read the survey a little more closely, we would have realized that there were challenges far too great for us to take on, that it was madness to pay the asking price. The sewage pipes, the chimney, the patches of damp on the beams up in the loft. The mice! *Mice have been observed in the loft*, it said in the report. 'We're talking about one, maybe two mice a year at most,' the estate agent had said. Why didn't we send the prospectus to my father? But we had put in an offer, knowing full well that we hated the house's current style, that we would redecorate, using only the most beautiful, most sustainable materials. We'll just have to wait a little while, we said, until Henry gets a bit bigger, until he's sleeping a bit better. Next summer, we said to each other, once we've lived there for a bit and got to know the place, that'll be best. Best! Packing up the apartment in Italiagården had almost broken me, but we didn't realize that renovating the house would demand another packing-up, a kind of move within a move; that the house would have to be emptied, you can't just shove everything into a corner. Nor did we know that I would come to be so lost, so confused, this summer. Wandering in the forest, which even in midsummer is dark, my anxiety like an irascible, internal infection.

*

Because nobody is watching me, I stretch out on the sofa as I download the app for the company that offers storage services. I have to pay per object I want them to take, and then they'll come and collect everything – all I have to do is check off the relevant items in the app. Two sofas. One dining table. One desk. One large rug. How many armchairs? All the beds? Collection date: 15 July. Saturday. No surcharge. Making the booking is boring, it irritates me. Why couldn't Helene do it? I'm finally alone – the sole thing I've wanted – and now I have to spend my time on this house, on cleaning up all our shit. If I only knew I wanted to stay here, at least. Knew that I will come to feel at home.

So many people are moving into the area, I encounter them at the kindergarten and the health centre, they're so content, they clearly don't feel the way we do, the way I do. I never should have left the city, never should have joined the army of make-up-free mothers in all-weather jackets. Joachim would have said: 'You look like you've joined a lesbian hiking club.' And even though Helene sings the praises of the ski trails in Marka, I know that she, too, feels trapped among the high-rise buildings and trees. We're from the country, I from the coast and the rain and the West Norwegian heaths, the stone walls that line the overgrown pastures, the hikes taken along the rocky shoreline, the sound of the sea and the breakers and the helicopters that come flying in with the oil workers – when I was little, I always hoped Pappa was in one of them, that he had come home early. And Helene, she can fix damaged mouths, send safe-guarding reports about injuries to palates and necks, help firemen who are terrified of the dentist, go on courses, receive bonuses – but this isn't really where she's meant to be. She actually belongs to an agricultural landscape, among the smell of fertilizer and burning rubbish, with meat and cabbage soup and karsk and lefser and Toro

Mexican Stew packet mix in the kitchen, everything that's the same as it has always been. I know she suffers from homesickness. She used to say: 'You could easily get a job with the local municipality. Or maybe we could live in Trondheim?' But since my indiscretion, she's never again asked if I might consider moving there.

The first time Helene took me home with her to Trøndelag, I had been dreading it. It wasn't much help that she said the secretly filmed footage that appeared on the news every year or so wasn't representative of the industry – that there were black sheep, individuals who operated their farms irresponsibly, but that her father was of a different school. 'I'm not saying it's all sunshine and roses,' she said, 'but it's so much better than people think.'

Her father picked us up from the airport; looking back, I can see that he was nervous, because he spoke quickly, incessantly. 'You have good timing,' he said, 'you've arrived right in the middle of birthing season, the tiny peeps and squeaks can be heard all over the place!' 'How exciting,' I said. 'It must be a wonderful thing to see.'

As we turned into the farmyard between the house and the barn buildings, my first thought was that it looked like an ordinary farm, but then I noticed the fences – weren't they unusually high? 'Escape-proofed,' Helene's father said. 'Smart,' I played along. Because what was I supposed to say? I felt I had to watch my mouth so as not to come out with predictable criticisms about the livelihood of the parents of the woman I'd fallen in love with, and who I wanted to be with, with an intensity greater than that of any of the other girls she'd brought home. And not only that – I wanted her parents to feel the same, to take her aside after dinner and say to her, their voices low and with a gleam in their eye: 'Oh, she's a real keeper, this one.' I wanted them to love me. And I wanted to love them. They made it easy. They were such nice people, both of them: he soft-spoken but cheerful, a heavy smoker; she with a kind of platinum-blonde Eli Hagen hairdo, a hand-crocheted top, and the positive but never overly elated demeanour of someone who's spent their entire life getting their hands dirty.

'So what do you think about the fur industry?' Helene's mother asked as we sat around the kitchen table eating a welcome lunch of fried eggs and meat patties. 'Are you one of these people who goes on protest marches?' 'Oh, no, no,' I replied, shaking my head, smiling. 'I certainly don't go on marches, but I have to say I'm not exactly the kind of person who would wear a fur coat, either.' 'If people only knew,' Helene's mother said. 'If people only knew how we actually run this place. But they don't know. And nor do they want to. People think we're animal abusers, that we've put loads of wild animals in cages so we can torture them for fun; enjoy a cup of coffee while we watch them chew their own legs off.' 'No, God no,' I replied, 'of course I don't think that.' 'Okay, not that,' she said, with a wink at me. 'Good to know.' 'You'll have to give her a guided tour, Pappa,' Helene said.

Helene didn't join us when I accompanied her father across the yard. It felt like a declaration of love, she wanted and trusted him and me to build a relationship on our own. I thought I should ask plenty of questions, take an interest, but I couldn't think of anything to say – not until he had unlocked the door and led me through to a changing room, where he handed me a white full-body suit he asked me to put on. 'They're vulnerable to infection from outside,' he said, and all at once he looked so sad I felt I ought to cup his big, stubbled cheek with my hand. He sniffed. 'Last year I had to slaughter almost the entire stock after a night-time visit from some so-called animal welfare activists.'

We walked through the cool barn, the small cages packed close together, each of them divided into an inner and an outer section, like apartments with glassed-in balconies of netting. The limber brown mink soon began to slip forth as we approached. Several stood on their back legs and peered at us – they seemed bright and alert, almost happy. 'This is the 160th generation, so they're not actually wild – all of them come and smell my fingers,' Helene's father continued. 'Would you like to hold one?' Smiling, I shook my head and thought: He must have cleared away all the dead and injured ones before we got here.

IN THE LAUNDRY ROOM are boxes we've never managed to unpack. I should probably just put them straight into storage to save time. But the point of me having this entire week is to sort out all the things we otherwise never get around to – to go through the drawers, make a trip to the dump. (Especially that!) To throw things away. I open a box labelled BABY STUFF and rummage through it, there's little of value inside. Old muslins. Cream for sore nipples. But there's the electric breast pump! I can sell that online. If I price it right, I'll probably be contacted fairly quickly by some terrified new mother with painful, tumour-like milk cysts in her hard breasts. Breastfeeding is so brutal – women will pay anything for a sliver of hope that they'll one day feel good in their body again. Helene inherited the pump from me. After Henry's birth, she had struggled to get the hang of breastfeeding. I tried to guide her, sat close to her as she put Henry to her breast. 'There – he's opening his mouth, get him latched now!' I directed, and for the most part she tried to follow my instructions, and I could therefore bask in a feeling of solidarity and superiority. But then – often completely without warning – she might suddenly freeze up, adopt a cold, sharp tone, and I'd have to pull away, because I knew that at that moment she was most likely filled with thoughts of what I'd done, what I'd done with Fitness Guri, which was in sheer violation of her trust but which we still hadn't had a chance to talk about, and then I had absolutely no right – or desire, for that matter – to sit close to her and be her breastfeeding guide, or even to be in the same room as her.

But I had to be in the same room. It was my role. And I had to prove that it wasn't something I questioned. The snow drifted down over Torshov, we heard the tractors and snowploughs working tirelessly through the night, as if there had been an avalanche. The Christmas star still hung in the window. Only one of the bulbs in the bedroom lamps worked. Olav, who had just turned three, reacted to the baby by suddenly becoming obsessed with wearing his summer trainers to kindergarten – every morning he threw himself to the floor and screamed. His hungry little brother screamed even louder. He writhed, flailed his tiny arms, got himself into such a state that Helene exclaimed in desperation that it was just never going to work, but eventually she grew adept at it after all, and without us ever consciously agreeing on it, it became my job to take him when he was done feeding and put him over my shoulder and wind him. Did Helene do the same when Olav was little? I couldn't remember, I remembered only that she was always there, within reach of the baby, she adored Olav, sang and prattled away to him and changed all his nappies before she reluctantly had to go back to work. 'He's so gorgeous,' she might spontaneously exclaim, 'and he just smells so damn *good*.'

When Helene was pregnant, all those terrible long months, I tried to reassure myself with the thought of how wonderful it would be to experience the scent of a newborn again. I reminisced about how I'd sat wide awake in the dark on the maternity ward and breathed Olav in; he had smelt sweet, like those perfumed erasers collected by little girls, only even better. It was utterly incomprehensible, I thought, high on my hormones and the intense certitude that I had given birth and therefore performed a miracle, that a scent could be so intoxicating.

But Henry didn't smell all that good. Everybody else seemed to think so – my mother-in-law, Helene's friends, even Olav – just not me. As I walked around with the tiny bundle hanging over my shoulder, stroking his back in an upwards motion to bring up the air he had swallowed, I searched his neck for something that reminded me of the smell I had longed for, but found nothing. He smelt only faintly of milk, sick, shit and fabric softener, and that isn't so strange, you might say, I didn't have the hormones to help me out this time around, but still I couldn't quite stop asking myself if this meant something. What did it mean? Henry's smell elicited no emotion in me – had I been blindfolded and led all the way over to his bed, I'd have stood no chance of sensing that what lay there in heavy, blissful sleep, right in front of my face, was my own son.

I don't like to think back on that time. My silent atonement, my penance. I'm ashamed that my actions cast such long shadows into the nursery. The story of that time is twofold. It was the delicate first weeks of Henry's life – a marvel. And it was also the first months of our razed life, after I had stuck two fingers up to everything known as loyalty, and stuck my fingers deep into someone else. Of course it was challenging. Like being locked up inside a self-contradiction. Wanting to cry or shout or sneak away and hide, but not being allowed to, because you always have to act gently and lovingly out of concern for the vulnerable little child that lies there naked on the changing table under the harsh bathroom lights – or, if I spool way back, out of concern for the mother who refuses to allow any emotions that make her uncomfortable to be expressed. Anyone would understand that life's streets weren't exactly paved with gold back then.

Nor do I like to think back on how things were in our bedroom. The intimate smell of lochia, the dark milk stains on the fitted sheet, all those damp, bare breasts we let our new son sleep on – even Helene's sister-in-law unbuttoned her blouse – it was so feminine, all of it. Suffocatingly womanly. But, one might protest, this is how it's always been, throughout the ages – the mothers and girls take care of the infants, while the men hardly ever see them. But I can't shake the feeling that the fact we never asked ourselves if this was okay – or rather, the fact that we never asked one another whether our choice could be defended – will at some point come back to bite us.

I AM THE OTHER MOTHER. The other mother reads Amnesty International's newsletters. The other mother listens to podcasts in which gay asylum seekers describe how they have almost been lynched, or asked to inform on their friends. The other mother knows what's going on in the world, but she can't really *grasp* it, just as she can't really grasp that there were once gas chambers and slave ships. Only when Russia invades Ukraine does she realize. It's a kind of tedious, protracted realization: day in and day out, she follows NRK's news updates, even when it's time for cake or the wine raffle at work. At weekends, when her wife, still suffering the after-effects of her C-section, is out at some playground or other with their eldest son, and the baby to whom her wife has just given birth lies dozing on her chest, she simply lets the live news broadcasts play. The baby sleeps as apartment buildings are razed to the ground. He sleeps as people throng onto train-station platforms. He sleeps, despite the fact that, just within the chest on which he rests, beats an anxious heart. For the other mother, it feels as if the connection between the horrors of the past and present is growing ever clearer with each day the war advances. She thinks: They can do whatever they like, and nobody is going to step in. International condemnation achieves nothing. They can start to intern children, and nobody will step in. They can ban the language. They can ban certain sexualities. They can start to execute people like us and be met with condemnation and sanctions, but nobody is going to step in.

THE CHEST OF DRAWERS in the hallway is stuffed with old batteries, hair elastics, receipts, half-empty packets of throat lozenges, keys, a boarding pass from March, from Easter. We spent that holiday with Helene's parents, too. Mamma sent me no texts, no accusations, no money for Easter eggs for the boys. I wasn't used to it, the silence, but after a few days I began to relax.

I remember the flight well. I wonder if I'm ever going to stop worrying about causing offence. We left on a Friday afternoon, in the middle of the Easter rush. Henry was unsettled, perhaps coming down with something again; I was the one carrying him but he constantly reached for Helene, who was irritated and hot; Olav had chocolate around his mouth and all over his fingers, and we had too much hand luggage. 'No, Henry,' I said, 'no, you're going to sit with Mamma Silje.' Henry was strong – he kicked me with his little feet, hit out. 'No hitting!' I shouted. 'No hitting,' Helene said. She sighed, had given up. 'I can take him,' she said, 'you board first.' It was a relief to exchange him for Olav. Olav is big and sensible, Olav knows what's expected of him. Aboard the packed plane the infant seat belt lay ready on my seat; Henry and I had 21B, Olav 21A, while Helene had 7D – we had checked in too late to get seats all together. As a member of the cabin crew passed by closing the overhead bins, I stopped her. 'This belt is for my son,' I said, 'but he's changed seat, he's sitting in 7D with… another member of our group.'

'WHAT DO YOU THINK,' Helene said, 'about having a baby?' It was the year after we'd got married, we'd never spoken about it before, the thought had hardly occurred to me. But clearly little more was needed, because from that moment on I had it on the brain – I want a kid, I thought, I want to be pregnant. Pappa had recently called and said that this was it, he finally felt able to leave Mamma – this time it was serious and he was moving to Haugesund – and maybe that was why, because it became so clear to me that everything lay wide open, my old family had dissolved and now it was my turn to create a life, to have a child, a happy child.

A few weeks later I visited my doctor, a commanding but patient woman in her fifties who, since I'd moved to Oslo, had been helping me through the difficulties with Mamma and my sister, including when Mamma learnt of my relationship with Helene – and took a smear test. Once I had dressed, I asked her if she had a little extra time: 'There's just one more thing I wanted to discuss…' She sat up straight in her chair and looked at me, friendly and professional, unaware of what I was about to ask of her. I hesitated – it was an intimate situation, after all – but then I decided to just go for it and said that my wife and I had started talking about having children, and how should we go about it, could she refer us on the national health service, or should we go private? The friendliness vanished from her eyes, but what replaced it wasn't something stern or condescending, it was more a kind of despair, or shame perhaps. She fumbled with her paperwork, found a Post-it note and scribbled something on it. 'Here's the name of one of my colleagues,' she said, as she handed me the yellow scrap. She smiled, sorrowfully, as if I were a little girl who had just told her she had an ugly nose. 'Unfortunately, for reasons of conscience, I don't do referrals for assisted reproduction.'

A T FIRST, I felt like superwoman all the same. We sat shyly side by side in the waiting room, and I sneaked glances at the other couples there, heterosexual couples, and secretly exulted – there was obviously something wrong with them, lifeless sperm, ancient eggs, but here came the pair of us, two young, healthy women. My cockiness quickly dissipated when, after our fourth attempt, the pregnancy test remained just as negative. But I wasn't prepared to give up – I must have a child, I thought – my thinking stretched to no more complex reasoning than this. The process was complicated in many ways; the rules for receiving fertility treatment meant we had to submit criminal record certificates, be tested for HIV. We grew irritated, felt we were being discriminated against, wondered why all the other people making babies didn't have to go through the same procedures.

And now? Now I wish the doctor in her green scrubs, who once a month emerged from the insemination room's back door with the little tube of warmed semen in her hand, had at some point given Helene a brief nod and leant over me as I lay there half-naked with my legs spread, jabbed her index finger against my chest, and asked: Have the pair of you really thought through the consequences of what you're about to do? Are you really sure enough of yourselves that you know you can make a stand for this form of family, even if the kid ends up being bullied for it or starts asking critical questions? If I were to tell you that I've inseminated three or four other women with semen from this very same donor this year alone, what would you say then? And you, Silje Marie – or do you just go by Silje? – the fact that you're so desperate to birth a child: don't you think it's partly about you seeking a kind of recognition you've never before received in your life? Have you actually thought about how the trauma of your own upbringing might be activated and play out anew when you yourself become a mother?

WITH OLAV IT WAS EASY; he was the first and only, and we were two mothers who were utterly consumed by him. We went to baby swimming together, to baby music; we sat on the floor and watched him as he lay on the mat and practised pushing himself up or rolling over or shaking a rattle, as ridiculously in love as only first-time parents can be. Had anyone asked me if I felt there was any difference between us, I would have shaken my head a little dismissively and said that of course Olav prefers the body that gives him milk, but otherwise we're exactly the same, we both love him the same, we do the same things with him, and I never feel that he and Helene are not related.

I wouldn't have mentioned how at first I would almost feel a malicious glee whenever the screaming began while Helene and I were out for a walk with Olav in his pram, and everyone could see that I was the one who sat down on the bench and began to unbutton my shirt. It would have been inappropriate to tell people how I felt during those first weeks, that every time I walked into the bedroom and saw Helene sitting there naked from the waist up, with Olav sleeping between her breasts in only his nappy, I wanted to snatch Olav from her and tell her to cover herself up.

It was so delicious, that he only looked like me.

A T THE CHILDREN'S CLINIC, at my mother and baby group, the other women and I gathered around an old television set. On the screen played the classic films about bonding that all Norwegian mothers are shown, with the infant who does everything to attract its mother's attention, while the mother stares at the child with a blank expression. First the child tries to be charming. Then it grows frustrated and angry, and then sad, really sad – it cries inconsolably – but in the end, when any reaction from the mother still remains unforthcoming, it gives up, looks away and becomes apathetic.

'What did you just see?' the public health nurse asked in a gentle voice. 'How do you interpret this?' I glanced at the others, waiting for one of them – perhaps the try-hard social climber from Southern Norway who had decked out her five-week-old colicky daughter in a tight white headband with a rosette – to reply. Olav hung heavily over my shoulder. He was knocked out by milk; I had sick down the neck of my shirt, but it didn't matter. He was my child, I'd known it since he lay bloody on my chest after the birth and I recognized the tiny jerks his body made – the movements were exactly the same as those I had felt inside me. I thought being a parent was the easiest thing I'd ever done. I snorted at the women who asked themselves if they were a bad mother, when that obviously wasn't the case. I will never, I thought, have problems providing adequate care to my own son.

S OMEWHERE UPSTAIRS MY PHONE DINGS. I have to search for a while before I find it, I've put it under one of the sofa cushions in the upstairs lounge, where I usually hide it out of sight from the boys so I won't be tempted to pick it up more often than is necessary. The text is from Helene, and suddenly I'm afraid, as if I've just realized that I'm making my way onto the motorway in the lane flanked by a STOP! TURN! sign, because what if Mayliss has completely lost it, what if she meant the things she said literally, the last time we were in touch? *If Helene only knew.* What if she's gone online and entered our address in the online directory and clicked on *People and businesses at this address* and saved Helene's number and composed a message with one of the photos taken at her place last Tuesday and tapped send, and what if Helene is now texting me: *Why have I been sent a photo of a woman with Henry and a boy who looks just like him sitting on her lap?*

But this is just an ordinary text, a smiling selfie, she's out and about, I can see the misty Trondheim Fjord far behind her. Presumably she's at the top of the mountain she likes to drag me up whenever we go there together. *With no kids!!!* she writes. She's red in the face, her plump, round cheeks. She hates that several of her patients have asked if there's another one on the way. When she undresses in the evenings, I avert my eyes. The scar on her stomach. It doesn't make me feel warm and tender towards her. *Wish I was there*, I write. *Be sure to make the most of it.*

*

The top floor of the house looks straight out over a small forest. It was one of the reasons we chose this place. Still, I've only taken Olav into the trees a couple of times, and when I did, it felt as if I was doing something illegal, as if I was wandering around in someone else's garden in the dead of night. And Marka? Forest scarred with gravel paths, no lookout points, no soul. Our family friends say: 'Don't be so high and mighty, Marka is a fantastic place!' But in this so-called 'Oslo nature', I know I'll never really feel at home.

Indeed, the autumn before Henry was born, when we still lived in Torshov, I lay awake and thought: We've forgotten that we live in nature. Train lines that are snowed under during the night; deadly, spear-like icicles hanging from the gutters in the rear courtyards of apartment buildings; torrential rain that floods the streets; an autumn day with angry gusts of wind that tear at tree branches, road signs and suede hipster caps – all this triggers the same reaction every single time. When nature reveals itself to people, to the people of Oslo, they feel neither shock nor unease about climate change, but are instead almost indignant.

On this particular night, the temperature had hit a new heat record. The bedroom windows facing the street were open. I woke suddenly, an intense pressure in my chest. The act itself was yet to happen, but I knew things with Fitness Guri had already gone too far. Now the birds joined the chaotic chorus of my thoughts. They perched on the rooftops and in the public trees that lined the road's central reservation and twittered, singing as if possessed. As if blind to urban expansion and the destruction of nature and insect decline, not to mention how the season was off kilter. Like a victim who doesn't realize she's a victim. The child who continues to laugh and play silly games upon the lap of its abuser.

From the vase of carnations on the bedside table came the smell of rot. Between Helene and me slept Olav, he lay at an angle so that his naked feet pushed into my hip; the curls at his neck were sweaty. Helene's back was large and unmoving, her belly hidden in the darkness beneath the duvet. I reached an arm across Olav, under the covers, and put a hand to Helene's stomach. The foetus wasn't asleep, either. I felt a little foot, or maybe it was a hand, an elbow or a knee. I gave a gentle nudge, a greeting to which I hoped to receive a reply, but he moved away, withdrew deeper into his mother's abdomen. There were only three months left until his due date. There was nothing I could do.

WE WERE A GROUP OF WOMEN who had started weight training in the office basement gym every Tuesday after work. I've never liked those sorts of terms: girls' nights, weekends away with the gal pals, women friends – they make me embarrassed, perhaps because they remind me of how it is back home, the insane gender segregation, even among people my own age. My sister's friends are like that, the women have a club, the men watch sports, no married woman changes her car tyres. Olav was two years old. Gleefully malicious clichés spewed like vomit from the mouths of everyone who learnt Helene was pregnant – Oh, just you wait till number two arrives, then you'll really have your hands full! Get your exercise in now, while you can!

I didn't have much experience training with weights, but I liked it, rotating the dumbbells above my head, the way I had to tighten my core when doing deadlifts – it wasn't long before I could lift my own body weight. This, I thought, is my thing. No starting blocks, no exercise bike, no round after round on the football pitch. Just me and something heavy I have to move.

Sometime in the spring, attendance thinned out, and my remaining colleagues agreed we should invite some friends to train with us – no boys, though, thank you very much! Who should I ask? They have kids. They've moved. Janne, who had long been going on about how important it is for mature women to do some strength training, replied only *hahahaha* when I texted her the invite along with a photo from a bikini fitness competition. And Helene lay at home, throwing up. I had no allies when one day, Fitness Guri was suddenly standing there beside me at the squat rack.

She had blonde hair cut like a man's, was much younger than me, a friend of one of my younger colleagues – at first I'd thought they were a couple. The endorphins made me high, extroverted. How about we start rounding this off with a beer, I suggested, and they agreed, almost all the women – they could at least manage just the one beer or glass of red wine. The evening sun was warm. The beer tasted fantastic. It was utterly classic, the fact that Fitness Guri and I ended up being the last two sitting there, even as the sun went down and we had to ask the waiter if we could borrow some blankets. I should have noticed the tiny adjustments I made, the way I ran a hand through my hair, the way I insisted she might as well stay a little longer, now we were there, the way I tactically offered up several amusing anecdotes from my life because I felt such intense satisfaction at making her laugh, the way I didn't mention Olav until Helene texted to ask where I'd got to and I realized it was time to leave. 'You've got kids?' she exclaimed, 'I never would have guessed!' Only young people can say things like that. I'm not even interested in young people, they're so unfinished, self-centred, have far too childlike, pinchable cheeks. Another son on the way. A pregnant wife. I didn't tell her about them. Why should I?

Of course I noticed that she was interested. That even though my wedding ring glimmered on my finger, she was disappointed when in the middle of one of our training sessions a colleague asked how it was going with Helene and the pregnancy. During the summer holiday she sent me long texts, asked me to promise to let her know if I needed anyone to go for an evening swim with. If only I could, I texted back. And I was entirely sincere, I did wish I could be where she was, instead of battling with Olav, trying to get him to sit still so I could brush the tangles from his long hair, while Helene went around moaning about pelvic girdle pain and worrying about how we were going to manage with yet another kid when we were already arguing constantly.

But what I didn't realize was that Fitness Guri wanted to have sex with me. Not even when, sometime in the autumn, she invited me back to her place so I could borrow a book she could have simply brought along the next Tuesday. Nobody was home in the apartment she had bought with a friend. Her room was cute, pink, with an old concert poster of Ani DiFranco above the bed. 'I'd completely forgotten about Ani DiFranco,' I said, without mentioning: I never understood why all the lesbians listened to her. Her mouth – suddenly it was just there, right in front of my face. I was confused, but I couldn't simply push her away. Okay, I thought, are these the signals I've been sending? I mustn't hurt her, I thought, I can't make her feel foolish, or let her think that I've tricked or used her. So I returned the kiss. All I had to do, after all, was part my lips. She touched me, over my sports bra. 'You're so gorgeous,' she said. 'I want you.' Okay, I thought again, we're getting a little explicit now! But it was too late. I had kissed her, and so I reasoned I may as well go all the way. I touched her, over her sports bra. I didn't consider Helene, not in any other way than this means nothing, and therefore it's fine.

She scissored me, was too heavy-handed, too fast. I pretended to come. When she pressed my head to her crotch, I closed my eyes. Afterwards, I locked myself in the bathroom and sat on the floor with my hands over my face, crying because she wasn't Helene.

THE FOLLOWING TUESDAY was easier, perhaps because of all the tension I'd been carrying since last time, the feeling of guilt I'd stuffed deep down inside me as I built Playmobil with Olav, or massaged Helene's feet and calves as we watched the first season of *Succession*. The anxiety built up, was stored in my chest and the folds of my vulva. I glanced at Helene when I felt sure she wouldn't meet my gaze. Can you really not see it? I thought. Can you not see who's sitting here beside you? Only Fitness Guri could free me from that identity. Entirely without protest I allowed myself to be led over to the bed – this time I was the one to kiss her first – and after I had come, I began almost immediately to think: The fact that this is happening, that I'm seeking this out and my body is going along with it, is probably a sign from above that I can't continue to live as I do.

A WOMAN ACCOMPANIES her pregnant wife to the clinic, where she reverently listens to her unborn son's audacious heartbeat and feels relief at the midwife's declaration that the fundal height measurement is following the curve, even though the bump is small. After the check-up, both women must return to work – they part with a kiss at the entrance to the Metro station. 'See you in a few hours,' the woman says, 'it was so lovely to be with you today.' There are dark clouds above the buildings. The cramped square smells of hash, hotdogs and piss. With a deep and stimulating feeling of tenderness, the woman watches her wife walk cautiously down the steep steps, remembering how she had constant lower back pain during the final months of her pregnancy. Wow, she muses, to think that there will soon be a little brother.

But the moment her wife is gone from view, she takes out her phone and swipes her way to a woman's name. As if by magic. As if Dorothy is standing over by the pedestrian crossing and clicking her red heels together as a signal, causing a crowd of people to storm forth and tug and pull at the surroundings – they're actually just stage backdrops on wheels. The pigeons take flight. The well-dressed trio at the Jehovah's Witnesses stand are sucked up into the sky. Click, click, click.

Outside the apartment building with a view of the park, the falling rain is protracted and intense. The woman's bra smacks against the floor. They haven't even paused to turn on the light. Her breasts are pale and small, they look so innocent under the hand that kneads them – how could anyone suspect someone who possesses such a body? How can what the woman is doing be wrong? She listens only to her heart and clit, she wants only to live truthfully, it is brave and entirely right, and soon – tonight, perhaps, after her two-year-old son has been put to bed – she will liberate both herself and her pregnant wife from living a lie. She feels a sense of dread. She is prepared for it to be awful. But one day, she thinks, as she feels the tip of a tongue graze one of her buttocks, her wife will thank her.

THERE WERE NO THANKS. The day Helene called me at work but remained utterly silent on the other end of the line, I was terrified. 'What is it,' I asked, 'tell me what's wrong,' but she didn't answer. 'Is it the baby?' I continued, 'is he moving enough?' I was standing in the lunch room, I was alone, apart from the new temp, who was sitting over on the sofa and staring at his phone – God knows what his name was, and I couldn't care less. I heard how I continued to make my voice strong and practical. 'If the baby isn't kicking,' I said, 'you should take a taxi to the hospital right away, he's probably just sleeping, I can meet you there, it's going to be fine!' 'No,' Helene replied suddenly, 'you don't need to do that.' Her voice was meek, but she spoke so calmly, and just as abruptly I felt myself turn completely numb. It isn't the baby, I thought. It's much, much worse. I grew hot in the cheeks. Nausea flooded me at once, as if I had been squeezed in some sort of vice. I stood there in the lunch room, and I didn't worry that Olav's kindergarten had called about an accident, or that someone in the family had died or received a serious diagnosis. She's found out, I thought. Now she knows everything.

When, a few days earlier, I had met Janne for coffee, a dried stain from Fitness Guri's crotch on the thigh of my jeans, I said I was on the verge of a breakdown because I felt like a terrible person – that I couldn't believe I could behave so inconsiderately, so selfishly. 'I feel guilty,' I said. Which was a lie, of course. Any traitor knows that conscience is subordinate to the right to covet and be coveted. 'Well, you should,' Janne replied. 'You can't carry on like this.' I refrained from hugging her outside the coffee shop, because I'd forgotten to wash my mouth before leaving Fitness Guri's apartment. I saw my own reflection in the café's windows and thought: If Helene finds out, this incredible, precious thing will be taken from me. Helene, I thought, is first and foremost someone I need to get out of the way so I can get laid more often.

B ECAUSE WE ARE pack animals and driven by attachment, we are biologically programmed to make our relationship the most important thing in our life. Which is why we also react so intensely to being abandoned: stress hormones immediately flood the brain, the circulation system changes, the body prepares for fight or flight. The break-up is experienced as a question of life and death: it's as if you're being hunted out on the plains, and even though the sun is shining and it is utterly still, not so much as a breath of wind, the body senses that over in that copse of trees lurk predators, and across what at first glance appears to be a peaceful meadow there are trenches, where soldiers are now silently preparing to take aim and shoot.

S HE HAD BORROWED MY LAPTOP and seen a message. I had forgotten to log out of Facebook, or perhaps her suspicions had prompted her to log in. Exchanging passwords is at the very core of a modern marriage. I immediately deleted all the messages that might be deemed racy. How many relationships go to the dogs after a digital blunder? A few words to the wrong person – that's all it takes. She looked as if she had just fled down a street strewn with the bodies of executed prisoners. She was in shock, hardly recognizable as the person who that same morning had done her make-up, put up her hair, complained that her fingers were now swollen too, soon she'd no longer be able to work. At first I watched her as if through a glass pane in a zoo, a wild animal on the verge of madness, as it slowly dawned on me that the reason she was behaving this way was because I was standing on the other side.

'Our relationship is one thing, but what about Olav?' she shouted. 'He's only two! And the baby? I'm pregnant, for fuck's sake! How the hell could you do this?'

All at once a dark reality revealed itself before my very eyes: death and decay wherever I turned. The shame. Suddenly it was entirely incomprehensible that just a few hours earlier, I had been a person capable of feeling other emotions. The shame was everywhere, on the furniture, in the streets, over my eyelids and lips, like radioactivity, it radiated and radiated, right through my skin, straight through me. The inside of my chest and stomach ached and burned, as if my entrails had been sprayed with gasoline and set alight. It doesn't take much to move from shame to pure terror.

'It only happened once,' I said. 'We were off our heads. I really thought it didn't mean anything, that's why I just let it happen.' 'Who made the first move?' 'I don't remember.' 'Oh, come on, of course you do.' 'No, I mean it, we were so drunk, it was after the summer party, you know we all got shitfaced that night.' 'Where did it happen?' 'Why do you want to know that?' 'Where was it?' 'It was at her place, we'd gone back there for an afterparty. I was practically passed out, all the others had left. I didn't realize what was happening until it was too late.' 'Didn't realize what was happening – are you in love with her?' 'In love?' 'Don't play dumb.' 'No, I'm not in love with her.' 'Then how come you're blushing?' 'I'm not blushing.' 'You're blushing, and you always do that when you're lying. Are you in love with her, or is it just the thought of fingering her that gets your blood pumping that bit harder?' 'Ugh, no, you need to stop this.' '*I* need to stop?'

She looked at me. Her face, it was no longer marred by shock, but evil. An evil, sinister face. It felt as if she was filled with a dark force, as if she might turn me to stone or cause my clothes to catch fire at any moment. I had to get away. Run, crawl into the ivy and disappear until after sundown. 'Is she in love with you? Does she know that I'm pregnant? I mean, what have you actually told her? That she can look forward to January, because then she can come along to Ullevål Hospital and meet your newborn child?' 'No, stop it! Of course I haven't said anything like that!' I shook my head. I was trembling, as if somebody had ordered me to hold out my arm to receive a lashing. I mustn't lose my composure. I needed to get my story straight. Create a specific narrative, weave together truth and lies into a perfect, tight braid. Hold that braid together for the rest of our lives.

For the next few days, Helene took Olav with her to Sunniva's place and rarely answered the phone. I texted that without her and our little family, I would probably die. *I really didn't realize what I was doing. YOU HAVEN'T SAID ANYTHING TO OLAV, HAVE YOU?* She always left me on tenterhooks, waited a long time before she replied, and I had no right to complain. *What do you think?* she finally replied. *Of course not. I've just told him you're away on a work trip.*

Like a grieving dog, I slept curled up in Olav's bed, unable to eat. I deleted and blocked Fitness Guri's number, removed her from Facebook. At lunch I couldn't bear to go to the cafeteria out of fear that her friend might confront me, and what if she'd already gossiped to the entire weight-training group? At night I spoke to Joachim for hours, he told me to get signed off work and come to Copenhagen; I told him I couldn't. 'I have to be here, I have to wait for her.' Janne invited me to Nittedal, said I could stay there with her, or that she could come stay with me in Oslo. 'You shouldn't be alone right now,' she said. I accepted, then declined. 'It's okay,' I said, 'I'm managing.'

On one of those mornings, Mamma called. It was entirely unexpected, and I felt afraid – surely Helene hadn't bitched about me to my sister, surely she didn't hate me that much? Did she? I let the telephone ring, scared to touch it, terrified that I might answer the call by accident, let the cat out of the bag, give her something she could use against me, and that's when I realized: without Helene, I don't stand a chance.

*

But in the midst of all this, I loved the change in my appearance brought about by the crisis, almost overnight. Without its padding of water and fat, my face became sort of angular and refined; my gaze lost its veil of indifference. The face in the mirror – it was attractive and intriguing. I would have chatted me up in a bar. My senses grew sharper: out in the city I noticed new street art, hair elastics and dummies and other tiny lost objects. I felt the cold more easily, even indoors; my jeans hung from my frame, it was glorious to feel that I had no excess weight.

After almost five days, I'd had enough. I texted Helene to say that even if she didn't want to come home, I was at least going to collect Olav from kindergarten that afternoon. She could come over whenever she was ready to talk, but she should know that I had told Fitness Guri in no uncertain terms that I had made a serious mistake.

The way in which Fitness Guri reacted, it haunted me. She behaved as if I'd been her girlfriend, as if by kissing her I had made a solemn vow. She told me to go to hell, didn't want to hear my explanations and excuses. 'Spare me,' she said, but then she began to cry, like a manipulative little girl who's certain she'll get her own way, as she berated herself for believing me, for believing everything I had told her.

I said I couldn't remember what I'd told her.

I felt sick at the thought she'd seen me naked.

Upsetting people has always made me feel distraught, but with her it was different: her tears had no effect. I hardened. Lost any capacity I might have had for nuance or empathy. I thought: Don't you dare come here and disrupt my life again. You should have known better.

*

The only other tears that can summon this hardness in me are my mother's.

But I knew her number off by heart. I couldn't just stop thinking about her – it had become a habit, after all. And I looked for her everywhere. All the time, even long after Helene had come back. Because every time I thought I saw her, it felt like having a harpoon thrust through my navel; I shook. And even though it was stressful, even though it felt life-threatening, as if I was about to take a running jump at a high-voltage fence, I couldn't help feeling slightly jubilant about it: it was an indisputable reminder that there was no longer any doubt that I was human. Someone who felt fear. Someone with fragile longings. With desires so strong that, for a brief time, I had completely forgotten I was a mother.

THEY WERE THERE WHEN I GOT HOME. I slunk in from the past, like some caught-out Casanova with a downcast gaze. Olav hardly noticed me, he was sitting with his headphones on, watching children's TV on Helene's laptop. Helene did most of the talking. She rubbed her belly – I wanted to grab hold of her wrists and tell her to stop.

'What would you have me do now, exactly?' she asked. 'What do you want?' 'I'm an idiot,' I said, 'I want to be with you, to be a family. That's the only thing I want. I just can't comprehend how I could have behaved like this, but I understand that it's utterly, utterly unforgivable.' These were the kinds of sentiments that flowed between us, back and forth, for what must have been hours. She flitted from one state of mind to the next – it was like watching a light being turned on and off in a haunted house, she might be affectionate, or give a ragged laugh: 'I don't even remember what she's called, fucking Fitness Guri whatshername!' But then, as she realized what she was laughing at, the room would seem to dim, her eyes darkened, and everything in me turned completely black.

'Is it really true, that it only happened once?' I nodded. I looked her in the eye. I was calm, made my voice deep and warm, as if I was speaking to an exhausted child. 'I've told you everything,' I said. She wilted, deflated. Then she darkened again. 'If you lie to me one more time,' she said, 'then it's over. One more time, and you'll have nothing to do with this baby.'

Her tone of voice, knowing that I couldn't demand she immediately drive the hate from her words and thoughts: it was an experience of powerlessness and punishment I hadn't foreseen. She couldn't deny me access to the baby, not while everything we had popped the champagne corks for in 2009 remained enshrined in law. But the fact that she would do it. In anger or otherwise. Take my child from me – the baby who, to all intents and purposes, was my child. And that she would say it to me, too. I put my arms around her and thought: We'll never be able to forgive each other now.

I T'S AN AFTERNOON IN NOVEMBER. Outside, the temperature is minus eight, and there is a flamboyant pink sky above the area's bleakly identical roofs. The family – two mothers, two small children – are in the kitchen. All the lights are lit. Unopened moving boxes still line the walls. A log burns behind the sooty glass of the wood burner. The youngest child's other mother has the youngest child in her lap. She is feeding it a home-made burger and fries. The child has long been suffering from a cold, and therefore has a poor appetite, but now it puts the meat in its mouth. 'Look,' the other mother says, 'he likes this!' She has cut the patty into small pieces. The child opens its mouth and stuffs one between its five or six teeth. The other mother registers that the chunk of hamburger might be a little on the big side, but she's the one who's on maternity leave, she feeds her youngest child at least four times a day, so she chatters away with her oldest child, who is standing at the end of the table and loudly playing some imaginary game or other, and with her wife, who is emptying the dishwasher – she assumes she doesn't need to check how the child is getting on. Suddenly, the child begins to flail its limbs. It tenses, tries to cough and gag, but the floor before the child remains bare – the retching sound doesn't cease, only continues, without progress or relief. The other mother feels the terror physically, almost as if her abdomen is being torn open; she sticks two fingers straight into the child's mouth. The child's biological mother gives a start and rushes into action, grabs the child, puts it over her knee and thumps its back. The child immediately vomits up the meat patty and begins to cry. The child's biological mother clasps the child to her chest as she snarls: 'It's always me who has to take responsibility for watching him – all you ever do is sit there!' The other mother grows completely stiff, as she always does when scolded. She crouches down, picks up the pieces of meat patty from the floor. She cannot bear to look the child's biological mother in the eye. Nor can she bear to so much as glance at her eldest child, who jabbers on incessantly, presumably in order to compensate for the uncomfortable shift in mood. The other mother is deeply hurt by the biological mother's accusation – she watches this child day and night. She sleeps next to it, so it won't roll out of the double bed, picks up the older child's beads and Lego bricks from the floor, throws herself in front of sharp table corners whenever the child loses its balance. But at the same time, she is also sceptical, unsure. What is it she feels – is it shame?

It will soon be the child's first birthday. The other mother will love him. There is nothing to suggest that she doesn't. Ask anyone – he lights up every time he sees her. She makes him shriek and cackle when she swings him over her head, blows raspberries on his stomach, or allows him to blow raspberries on hers. If his throat becomes blocked by mucus at night, she lifts him so he can cough it up, even before she is fully awake. When he gets nappy rash between his cherubically chubby buttocks, she applies to his skin an expensive cream which she purchases at the pharmacy, without demanding that her wife cover half the cost. Every single day, she looks at her wife and exclaims: 'He's just so cute!' And when he lays his head against her chest after she has brought him in from his outdoor nap in his pushchair, she feels the same warm, wonderful feeling as when the horse she rode as a young girl might suddenly and unexpectedly stretch its neck towards her and allow its heavy head to rest against her shoulder, a feeling of being indispensable, of being chosen, bestowed with something sacred.

But she knows it isn't enough.

As if breaking apart a giant jigsaw puzzle, I strip the house of belongings and junk. Several times a day I have to answer the door to people who come to collect the things I'm giving away or selling cheaply online. A thin American sleeping bag. A footstool from IKEA. An unsorted box of miscellaneous Tupperware. Two brass wall lamps we had hanging over our bed in Torshov, but which have ended up languishing in a box.

The breast pump sold for 450 kroner. It was a new dad who collected it, he gave me a start, suddenly standing there in our garden yesterday evening. Who's that, I thought, hasn't he heard that this is where the lesbians live? We don't have our first names on the mailbox. We don't hang flags during Pride. We stopped that after we moved, not because of the terrorist attack. But I haven't forgotten what Joachim said: 'It really is heartbreaking to think that if somebody's out to get the gays, they can just look for the flag. That rainbow is like a signal. Wherever they see the flag, they know they can find us.'

I take a structured approach to my tasks. I've found my flow. The rain falls in tedious squalls, the garden sparkles in green, the flowers fall to pieces as if the rainwater is toxic. I've FaceTimed the boys twice, my mother-in-law's plush violet curtains and framed cartoons of fat naked women flickering in the background. 'Bessie only wants to go on a walk with me,' Olav shouted this morning. He hardly had time to speak to me; told me only that Bessie is the neighbour's dog. When Henry took over the phone he just smiled and blew me kisses again, playing to the camera – he loves watching himself on screen, still has very little language. 'And how about you?' I said to Helene. 'Are you there?' 'I'm here,' she replied, but I couldn't see her, and Olav shouted in the background: 'Mamma, Mammaaaaa!' It wasn't me he was calling for. 'I'll call you later,' I heard her say, 'when things here are a bit calmer.'

She didn't call, just sent a couple of photos instead, and isn't that actually fine, I thought, that for once I'm not up to date on absolutely everything going on in Helene and the kids' lives? I'll soon be back in the same old rut.

This is the first time we're not spending the entire summer holiday together. Joachim once told me about a gay couple he knew, who had brought home twins from a surrogate mother in Canada, and who from day one had divided up their time: each father spent a week with full responsibility for both children, while the other could continue to live his exclusive lifestyle featuring dinners with friends, trips to the opera and workdays that were as long as his job required. 'I don't understand why more people don't do it that way,' Joachim said. 'It seems like a nightmare to have to do absolutely everything together all the time. Why don't the two of you take the opportunity to define how you want your lives to be? Think outside the box – is there anything wrong with that?' 'I hear what you're saying,' I replied. 'But all I can say is, there's certainly no doubt that you're a man.'

I haven't heard so much as a peep from Mayliss. Is she trying to psych me out? Is she done? Is she not going to say anything else, accuse me of anything more? Her Instagram account is unusually quiet. Her feed consists almost exclusively of photos of Nicolai. Protecting her family's privacy, and the fact that children are entitled to a digital private life, are clearly not things she worries about. One of the photos was taken during the heatwave in May: Nicolai wearing only his nappy, with his round, bare belly, sitting on the floor in front of their fish tank and eating an ice lolly. I've done that, too – sat there, beside the fish tank. I could have been the one who took the picture. What is she doing, at this very moment? Does she have friends visiting from Elverum? Has she told them about me, about Henry? Surely she must have done? I have a hunch about it, just as I have a hunch that it's now only a matter of days until she texts me, or calls and says: I just wanted to warn you that I'm going to write about this experience in an op-ed. But 'op-ed' is presumably a term she doesn't know.

I T WOULD HAVE BEEN so easy to simply withdraw. Back out. I think about how I'm going to defend myself, how I can explain myself to Helene. Listen – here's the backdrop: we've moved, the trust between us is worn thin, we never sleep for more than two or three hours at a stretch. We've been through a traumatic time as a couple, we've never fully processed it. We're together because we can't bear anything else. We're together because what's best for the children is more important than how often we sleep together or talk things through. We're worried about Olav's tormentors at the new kindergarten. We have meetings with the architect and the Latvian construction manager; the architect wears docksiders in the snow and says things like: 'This house is going to be sensational!' We pick mice out of the traps in the loft and fail to agree on whether we're going to build a daybed along the west or the east wall. We have more than enough to deal with. So I say nothing about who I'm in the process of getting to know. Or, I say: 'I'm going to meet a woman from baby music tomorrow.' 'Oh, that's nice,' Helene replies absentmindedly. 'She has a boy who's a bit older than Henry. He won't start at kindergarten until August, either. Her mother looks after him while she's at work, so Mayliss claims the childcare cash benefit on top of her salary – a pretty cunning way to play the system, don't you think?' And of course I can hear it myself. Just how shittily I'm behaving. How do I think I'm going to get away with this? Is it self-sabotage? Am I actually just longing for her to ask a suspicious question, to say, Hang on a minute, rewind – who did you say that boy is?'

But Helene doesn't take an interest, doesn't ask, she isn't interested in my drab maternity-leave life, isn't interested in my colourless inner life – all she cares about this winter and spring is the kids. Especially Henry. He clings to her, hardly looks at me when Helene gets home from work. Begins to scream if I try to lift him away from her exposed breast, which she constantly allows him to attack, as if they're both animals. She says: 'Oh sweetie, Mamma's here.' Without asking how Olav's appointment at the hairdresser went. Without noticing that I'm still upset because she slammed the front door without saying goodbye that morning. So I continue to lie. Because the lie is loyal. The lie doesn't turn its back on me simply because I don't behave like a good little girl.

The weekend after we'd been to the botanical gardens, a text dinged in. *What about Leo's Playland, have you been there? Great for kids. It's just around the corner from you :) :)* I hadn't been there. Olav, of course, had noticed the building with the huge, glaring lion on its sign when we drove past, and asked me what it was. And I had deduced, when I got chatting with some of the other parents at the kindergarten, that it was where they tended to hang out on teacher-training days, the gang, the kindergarten parents' A-team, and I had thought that maybe somebody might invite Olav and me, but the training days came and went without any invitation, and I said to Helene: 'Well, we're lucky Olav will live in blissful ignorance of Leo's Playland for a little while longer.'

A bitter wind was blowing that morning, when I left home at around nine. Henry squinted against the drifting snow that swept down into the pushchair, but he seemed happy enough; I let him keep his dummy in, even though he was only supposed to have it at night. I walked quickly down the ploughed footpath, noticing that it wasn't just my pace that was causing my heart to pound, that made me slightly agitated, but also the thought that by choosing the route towards Leo's Playland I was doing something illicit, something forbidden – that now I was doing something that, no matter how banal it might be, would have consequences. I didn't know what, only that I would be yanked from the grey, stripped of the apathy in which both Helene and I had enveloped ourselves that winter, as if it were a coat of a fabric that, while it might certainly keep us warm, was also sprayed with disease-inducing chemicals.

I appeared to be the first person to arrive at the soft play. In the empty changing room just inside the entrance I stamped the snow from my boots, undressed Henry so he was wearing only his bodysuit and tights, and hung up our coats, before sitting down under the row of hooks to wait. The place smelt of popcorn. Henry pulled himself to standing using my knees for support – he had managed to stand unaided just before his first birthday, but he was still cautious, he never hurried off without being sure that the surface beneath his feet was safe. Just like his brother when he was small, I thought, and immediately felt a pang of longing for my big boy, a yearning for the time when it was just us – Helene, Olav and me – and we couldn't take our eyes off Olav, because he was our only child and everything he did was a miracle, our miracle, which we could enjoy undisturbed, as if we were sharing an enormous bottle of champagne in a secret garden. 'That?' Henry said. I peered down at him, and he held up a bit of blue plastic – it looked like the end piece from one of those candy dummies that were sold at the circus and in amusement parks when I was young. 'Yucky!' I exclaimed, and batted it out of his hand. He stared at me, bewildered, and I tried to smile, to radiate a kind of soft and warm authority, as I thought: Oh, sweetheart. It isn't your fault you're here.

She was more than a quarter of an hour late. 'We took the Metro in the wrong direction!' she laughed as she came barging through the doors. 'Have you been waiting long?' 'A fair while,' I said. Nicolai was wearing the same tight cotton hat as last time; he was red in the cheeks and glassy-eyed – was he ill? 'Hello, Nicolai,' I said. He turned away, hid his face in his mother's jacket. 'Oh, stop it, Nico,' Mayliss said. 'It's only Silje Marie!' She smiled as she took off her coat, smiled and smiled – What is it with her, I thought, is she one of those people who thinks she always has to act cheerful because she's fat? But I didn't actually think that. Because I could tell. I can tell the difference between a false and a genuine smile. 'Have you been here before?' she asked. I shook my head. 'Although I'm sure it's high time,' I replied, 'since I'm aiming for the full suburban experience out here.' Nothing in her face suggested she had picked up on my indolent quip. Instead, she hoisted her nappy bag over her shoulder and said: 'Okay, I'll go sort out our tickets.'

The soft play's long slides and cage-like climbing frames towered before us like a mountain range as in our stockinged feet we stopped at the ticket desk, and I thought she had meant she was going to pay for both of us. 'Two adults,' Mayliss said. The teenage girl behind the counter glanced at the boys. 'And how old are the kids?' 'They're under a year old.' 'Both of them?' 'Both of them.' The girl looked confused. I'm sure I did, too. I felt an automatic desire to chime in, to correct this incorrect information – and if I was going to do it, I needed to now. 'I'm afraid I have to ask for their date of birth,' the girl said. 'When were they born?' Mayliss smiled. And I – I simply stood there, passive and speechless. Because the tiny lie she had told escalated. 'I was actually hoping you wouldn't ask – it's a pretty complicated question, you see. Their due date was the seventeenth of February 2022. But they were premature. The youngest one here only weighed 1,200 grams. So they're not regarded as one-year-olds until their due date. Which is the seventeenth of February.' The girl looked just as confused. I squirmed. Was she really going to accept this? 'So… that applies to both of them?' At that moment I felt Mayliss's hand, its pressure against my back. 'Surely you've heard of children who have two mothers, haven't you?' 'Of course,' the girl replied sourly. She pushed the card reader towards us. 'Two adults will be seventy-eight kroner.' 'I'll get it,' I said.

I was hot in the cheeks as we walked deeper into the deserted soft play. What if the girl changed her mind, or her strict, older colleague popped up to inform us that no eleven-month-old is as quick on its feet as Nicolai, and asked us to therefore please repeat his date of birth? 'I can't believe you did that!' I whispered. Mayliss waved a hand, sort of nonchalantly, but also proud. As if, even before she had decided to lie so the kids would get in for free, she had known it would make an impression on me. 'Oh, they're raking it in,' she said. 'You aren't even allowed to bring your own food.'

She set down her nappy bag next to a low gate with a sign that proclaimed MINI LAND, and which led to an area clearly intended for the soft play's youngest guests. 'Come on, you two,' she said, bending down and walking through the gate, and Henry let go of my hand, he hurried after them, moving faster than he had ever moved before, towards all those fantastic, padded surfaces.

TAKING GLASS AFTER GLASS down from the shelf above the kitchen sink. Wrapping them in newspaper, before setting them gently atop each other in the box. It isn't long since I last did precisely this – I was on leave back then, too, so I was the one who packed up almost the entire apartment in Torshov. We've been together for such a long time. The house is teeming with objects of sentimental value. This blue ceramic cup, for example – Helene bought it in an arts and crafts shop when we were on holiday in Lisbon. She bought two – it was before we'd moved in together, before I could believe that she would want to buy two, and that's precisely why it became so important – all the confirmation I hungered for was right there, in two hand-turned cups finished with a royal-blue glaze.

To lose face. There isn't much that's worse. Without Helene's magnanimity there would hardly be anything left of mine. Scraps. Spoilt meat. Nobody wants anything to do with it. To conspire against life itself – to lie and sleep with someone else when you have a child on the way – who can sympathize with a person who does something like that? There are no extenuating circumstances, she can't even call herself an involuntary parent, someone who in the heat of a careless moment squirted a little semen into the mouth of a womb. No – this is a situation she herself has knowingly and willingly chosen.

This lesbian woman has been through a laborious process. She has thought and undertaken assessments and settled her accounts, signed paperwork to confirm that she is party to the attempt, even if she and her wife no longer talk about anything but the children and housework, even if she only truly laughs when she speaks with friends or joins her group exercise session in the basement with the women from her office's accounting department, even though her wife often looks at her in a way that makes her think: Do you hate me?

They try to make a child. That part is easy, because they don't even need to be in the same room while they do it. All she has to do is sign the papers. And transfer half the cost of the attempt to her wife. She makes transfer after transfer without thinking. Soon, she stops attending the monthly ultrasound of her partner's ovaries, and soon she might also fail to show up for the insemination itself, because of course it doesn't mean anything, to sit there and hold your partner's hand while a doctor yet again sticks a needle-like insemination instrument up between her spread legs. What means something, they say to each other, is to be there if the test actually shows +, if the + actually makes it and becomes a living child.

To Fitness Guri, I said: 'When she came out of the bathroom on the morning the test was positive, I somehow just couldn't feel happy about it.' I stroked her lovely blonde hair, cut in its men's style. In that moment, I wholeheartedly believed in the version of myself I was presenting; I've always had a strong sense of empathy, I'm always moved by final words, emotive speeches, it's just the way I am. Helene never needed to say: What the hell am I going to tell Mamma and Pappa? I saw it in her eyes, a black, explosive sentence, and I didn't repair it, I couldn't subject myself to that humiliation.

After she had moved back home again, I started to think about what I would say if Fitness Guri suddenly sought her out at the dental clinic: Do you know what she told me, about the day the pair of you found out you were pregnant? Or, and this was even worse: Has she told you we only slept together just the once?

But Fitness Guri never appeared. At night, Helene lay with her back to me. The birth approached. I screwed together the pieces of the flat-pack crib, purchased a pack of tiny nappies, baked and froze cinnamon buns, read book after book to Olav. I kissed the back of Helene's hand, said I would give her time whenever she brusquely shook me off. I praised her outfits in the mornings, flattered and fawned and told her she looked pretty. I sounded the way I did when I was little, when I spoke to Mamma. I bought Helene a pair of new trainers, even though the weather forecast predicted snow. I bought tickets to a performance at the Opera House and got her brother to come over and babysit. My cheeks burned. My shame glowed in the darkness. She said: 'Do you know what the worst thing about you fucking someone else is? That I didn't do it first. Jesus – do you think I haven't been tempted?'

I knew she had moved back in with me so quickly because it was such a short time until her due date. There are limits to how many upheavals a person can tolerate at once. But one day, she put her head in my lap, entirely of her own accord. Slowly, I was able to haul my face back to me again, to cobble it together, a pastiche of the person I once was. The person who, when I try to imagine her, I can no longer see.

ALL THE HUGE, shapeless IKEA bags full of books are in the way, I have to carry them upstairs, get them up into the loft. The Tripp Trapp high chairs, the refuse sacks of clothes, the piles of curtains and cushions: all of it has to go up. I open the ceiling hatch and climb the ladder; the heat hits me, like banked-up anger. I investigate the corners. The traps are still empty – as I had known they would be, the autumn is when they'll start to come in again. We heard the scratching in the walls the very first evening after we'd moved in. Then I found the tiny black droppings. Helene got the heebie-jeebies – she was terrified it might be rats. 'Relax,' I said, 'it's totally normal for a house to have a couple of mice.' I purchased traps, used peanut butter as bait. I hid the traps all over the loft, under the sloping ceiling, the beams, behind the chimney. I hid how stressed out it made me. Helene came home from work and asked: 'Was there anything in the traps today?' and I shook my head or said: 'No, not today, but on Monday there was one.' 'What should we do,' she went on, 'should we contact the insurance company?' 'No,' I replied, 'I'm taking care of it – they'll soon be gone, I'm sure of it.' I did it for her. And I hoped she was thinking: What would I do without you?

To love is also to suppress one's own fear. To know the other's traumas and strive to ensure they're not reactivated in her. To know everything about one another. And stay together all the same.

'We should get ourselves a cat,' Helene said, as I set the plastic bag in which I'd wrapped the day's catch out on the step. It was a Saturday morning, snow in the air, an ice-cold draught blowing into the house, and I heard in her voice that she suddenly realized what she'd just said, that my face had taken on *that* expression. 'Oh, can we get a cat?' Olav exclaimed, and Helene made a movement as a sign that I should look at her, and I did, I allowed her to look into my eyes, she was the only one allowed to look into me that way, and she knew that, and she didn't abuse it, she corrected herself, and the draught disappeared and the snowflakes melted on the hallway floor as she said: 'Oh no, Olav, I'm sorry, I forgot – we can't, because Mamma Silje is terribly allergic.'

T HERE'S THE TRAIN, I see it winding its way behind the trees as I close the hatch to the loft. It takes no more than eighteen minutes to reach the city centre by rail from here, but this isn't the city, it's neither city nor countryside – this is no-man's land, a social-democratic ecotone. I should have listened to Joachim. He hasn't been here yet. After we won the auction, he made no attempt to hide his scepticism. 'Kringkollen? Christ. You may as well have moved back to Sotra. Just what do you think's going to happen to your fashion sense, for example?'

He was in Oslo on a course; we went for coffee in Sandaker. Henry slept outside in his pram, parked next to another pram, a white one from an expensive brand, the owner sitting alone at a window table drinking tea, wearing a powder-pink cardigan. Her face was smooth, freshly made up, utterly devoid of credibility. Out on the street I saw several of the city originals, all with their characteristic shortcomings: the two friends pushing their dogs around in tilted prams; the limping alcoholic with piss stains on his trousers; the blonde in a wheelchair with her horrifying face, who looks as if she's spent her entire inherited family fortune on getting unscrupulous plastic surgeons to transform her into a cross between a porn star and Munch's *Scream*.

Again I said that Joachim would have to come visit us often, that he was more than welcome to use our guest room as a home office. 'When I'm done with my maternity leave, we can even work together,' I said. 'We can go swimming in Nøklevann, or you can help me in the garden, seeing as I know shit about plants.' 'Don't get your hopes up,' he said. 'We don't need to get carried away with these fantasies, everybody knows that the people who move out here sink to the bottom of the waters of oblivion.' He said it in a jokey way, but of course there was a seriousness in it, too – this was also about to happen to us. I had resisted for a long time, done my utmost to show that marriage and children comprised only a small part of me, and not least that I would never define my life as being more valuable or meaningful than his, and I meant this, truly I did, but soon it would no longer hold water, because my kids and the responsibilities I had towards them, and the conditions in which I wanted them to grow up, restricted me. In his eyes it must have been like watching some creature of the night gradually fade with the dawn – I no longer brought him witty anecdotes or despairing infidelity updates, which at least had an interesting energy. I had become colourless, uninteresting. All the disrupted sleep made me forget significant details; I always had to go home early on the few times we went out for a drink, and I didn't make it to the theatre production to which he gave me tickets for my thirty-fifth birthday, because both Olav and Helene had a stomach bug.

Now, on the rare occasions we speak, he appears to have given up enquiring how it's going between Helene and me, presumably because he can't understand why we would choose to stay together, to surrender to all the pain, all the doubt. The fact that I'm building a life over a chasm of distrust. That I didn't break up this life when I had the chance, that I didn't use to my advantage the damage inflicted upon us by all the business with Fitness Guri. This is probably where the alienation lies, most of all – he probably remembers that when we were in our twenties I always felt my intuition as a hot and surging inner stream, and that I allowed it to lead me, no matter how painful the cost. Now, he must look on, aghast, as all I do is work hard to divert it. He would have tried to hide a snort had I said: But greatest of all is the family. He would have called it resignation, a capitulation to antiquated and straitjacket-like norms, and I would therefore also have thought: He no longer knows me. Moreover, he doesn't even know when my kids' birthdays are.

THERE'S A BRIEF PAUSE in the rain, and it's so humid I can leave the terrace door open. After lunch I sit on the steps that lead down into the garden, light an old, dry cigarette from the packet I found in the storeroom, and send Joachim a text. *Darling, I'm home alone. Wish I was with you!* Bumblebees whirr above the clover in the damp grass; the tallest apple tree is teeming with tiny green fruits. I want to go visit Joachim in his life, not have him come here, into mine. That became clear the last time he came over, back when we still lived in our apartment. Helene and Henry were away, and I'd therefore invited Joachim over for a three-course Hellstrøm-style dinner. I plonked Olav in front of the TV with his Saturday sweets and spent hours prepping, cutting vegetables, making sauces and frying up excruciatingly thinly sliced mushrooms. The meal was magnificent – we sat at my grandmother's old teak dining table and drank and gossiped and laughed and listened to Bronski Beat, but just as we were finishing off the chocolate fondant, I heard the screaming from Olav's room.

Night terrors. I'd ended up sitting with my hysterical child for almost an hour, feeling guilty that not only had I left Joachim on his own, but that he was also forced to listen to the awful sounds of a child in the grip of the night terror's raging trance. The guilt quickly dissipated, however – as if someone had just given me a clip round the ear – when, exhausted and groggy, I came back out to him and apologized, but realized that not only was he having a fine old time, sprawled there on the sofa drinking crémant and chatting with somebody on Grindr, but he had left everything on the table exactly as it was: the plates, the bowls, the stains. He hadn't so much as considered doing the washing-up. I had used every last pan in the kitchen, and he hadn't washed a single one of them.

The three dots appear on my phone's screen almost instantly. *DARLING!* he writes, before sending a photo of the pair of us at a bar in Berlin from back when he lived there with Tobias. I've seen it many times before – it's a fantastic photograph, we're so happy and fresh-faced – but I also feel a sharp pang of sadness. Doesn't he have anything more recent to send me?

When we spoke before the summer holiday, he had complained about work, about the pressure he was under and his boss and his never-ending tasks; said he was struggling to sleep, to find the motivation to get up in the morning. 'If your job is killing you,' I said, 'don't you think you ought to seriously consider maybe doing something else?' 'But that's exactly what I'm saying,' he replied, 'the problem is I have no idea what else I would do.' 'Well,' I said, 'there must be something that makes you happy. The meaning of life is to try to enjoy it, isn't it?' He laughed. Just as I was thinking how much I love him when he laughs like that, he said: 'Yeah, and aren't you just the perfect role model?'

Come to Copenhagen, he writes now. *Catch the ferry to Denmark! It would be wonderful.* For a moment I can see it all with crystal clarity: I step aboard to the recording of the lively brass band that streams from the poor-quality speakers; take a dip in the grotty Jacuzzi on deck along with some already-drunk teenagers and dads with children in swimming nappies as the ship sets out from Vippetangen. Then I buy some Lego and a few bland but practical items of clothing in the duty-free shop and drink a large, watered-down beverage while a dreary live act plays Smokie songs on keyboard in front of a few single, tottering women on the purple light-up dance floor.

And what would greet me upon arrival? Joachim's Danish gay life, his party life, his jet-setter life. A Saint Lucy's Day party at a huge penthouse. Dick pics sent from users 800 metres away, 450 metres away, 20 metres away. Holidays with single friends on the Riviera. Credit cards and Fast Track and luxurious, always spotlessly clean clothes. His life is as far from mine as you can possibly get, and still we somehow maintain a kind of friendship, like a long-held habit it's both too late and too pointless to kick. There are so many others who I've lost touch with, withdrawn from; meet-ups I've cancelled, tentative coffee invites I've never followed up – I simply haven't managed it, because it's demanded my all: keeping the family together, keeping my little life going.

But after what happened with Fitness Guri I can no longer call Joachim in a crisis. I can't show my face in Copenhagen, feeling as wretched as I do now.

M OST OF THE SPERM offered at the Norwegian fertility clinics is imported from Denmark. The European Sperm Bank even has its offices in Nørrebro, just a short bicycle ride from Joachim's apartment in Rådmandsgade. I think the donor is Danish, both the donors we used probably were. But I can't imagine them, their faces and bodies, I'm not interested, feel no curiosity or anxiety – not for them. Only for the hordes of children they have spawned. The morbidly huge bands of children. And their parents.

'Have you ever considered it?' I once asked Joachim. 'Donating your sperm?' He shrugged, gave a brief laugh. 'Well, no request was forthcoming from the two of you, so…' I paused, taken aback. Did he mean it? Was he a little disappointed – perhaps even wounded – at the fact we hadn't asked him? Helene and I had toyed with the idea early on, but soon dismissed it: it would have been too complicated. These families with several parents, three, four, five. I envy that they know who the father is, have a handle on the biology – it's one less thing for the child to rage against, at least. But the happy photos that accompany the articles, 'Hilma Has Three Daddies'; the houses in which the child has one door to the mothers and another to the two fathers. I refuse to believe them when they go on about how enriched their lives are, how frictionless the partnership is, how they feel nothing but joy at having rediscovered that human beings are, in fact, pack animals. I refuse to believe that not a single one of them wrestles with jealousy. That everyone feels they have an equal right to the child.

Joachim's jealousy, on the other hand, was an illusion. Or at least, that's what he wanted me to think. 'No, no,' he exclaimed, 'I'm just kidding. You lesbians can take care of all that reproduction stuff and leave us out of it.'

Oh, how I miss him. I miss laughing, I miss going on road trips and long weekends to New York without being haunted by thoughts of burning forests and animal species facing extinction. I miss sitting on the balcony and hearing Jussi Björling's 'O helga natt' playing at full blast in the middle of the summer. *Will you be in Norway at all this summer?* I write, lighting another cigarette as if to ensure I'll be in the right frame of mind when he answers, but I end up sitting there and smoking the entire cigarette alone. It seems the window has closed – he's whirled off into his non-stop wild and wonderful gay life again. The phone's screen dims and remains dark, nothing but a mirror image of the house and my pale, pathetic face reflected in the greasy plastic that protects the screen.

Before we became parents, before I knew that I was pregnant, we were at a dinner party in Trondheim. Since Helene was back home, her friends from high school had arranged a get-together. Nobody else had brought their partner, but because we're two women, we have to hang out with each other's friends. Of course we can all be girlfriends together, the lot of us! I politely declined the wine. We said we were trying to get pregnant; that I'd recently been inseminated for the fifth time. 'How exciting!' they exclaimed, 'just think – you might be pregnant right now!'

Around the table, Helene's friends talked about how natural it is for two women to have children together; how family is what you make it; how today's heterosexual hell is passé. As if they thought I agreed with everything they said. Me – who finds egg donation a complex issue. Me – who isn't sure whether it's right that women are able to have children on their own, for the child to be in one person's power, without other witnesses. Me – who strongly believes in the ban on surrogacy. Try as I might, I simply can't grasp the arguments espoused by certain trans men, who believe there's nothing paradoxical about the fact that, one day, they will be able to be pregnant men. I don't want to stand in solidarity with everyone and everything – I want the right to have children myself. Am I simply selfish? They can call me selfish. But I know there are limits to society's goodwill. I don't think we should rock the boat too much.

I noticed Helene looking at me from the other end of the table. I sliced into the pink meat on my plate, said nothing.

'I read that lesbian couples can go to Barcelona and have an embryo using an egg from one partner implanted in the other,' Sunniva said. 'Like, you can carry each other's baby. Isn't that just the loveliest thing?' Helene looked at me again. 'Yes,' she said, 'I think so. But I'm not sure Silje Marie does.' All eyes turned on me. All those female gazes, the gazes of Helene's girlfriends. Didn't I love Helene enough to want to carry her egg inside me – was that what they were thinking? I tried to appear relaxed. 'It just makes things more complicated,' I said. 'Isn't it best that we just do it in as old-school a way as possible? That we don't mess around with nature any more than we have to? And anyway,' I added, 'it isn't exactly cheap.' Some of the women smiled and nodded, but nobody offered any follow-up comments, so I continued to speak. 'You're all so lucky, with your men at home – unlimited access to free sperm! If it doesn't work this time we'll have to start IVF, and then there'll be no expensive holiday abroad for us this year, nope!' Over at the other end of the table, Helene looked embarrassed. I understood – I sounded like an idiot. Sunniva smiled, then lifted her glass as if making a toast. 'Well then it's lucky you're married to a dentist!'

Afterwards, as we walked hand in hand towards the bus stop, Helene said: 'You really don't want to, do you?' 'What?' 'Carry my child.' She dropped my hand from hers. 'Do you think the kid would be ugly? Is that it?' I had no idea where this was coming from – I'd never heard her mention this Barcelona idea before. 'What if it doesn't work this time either?' she said. 'How long are we going to keep trying? Is it really so vitally important that you get to be pregnant, so you can pass on your mother's genes?'

When Helene speaks to me as if we're enemies, it becomes incomprehensible to me that she's the same person I said yes to. It's as if she's entered into a pact with Ursula, the Disney sea witch, as if Ursula has invaded her body, although it isn't obvious – in fact it's almost impossible to see, because she looks like herself and she speaks with her own voice, but she has Ursula's soul, Ursula's evil intentions. It's the sea witch's face I'll see, should I dare to glance at her reflection as she's putting on her make-up after we've had an argument.

'Have I upset you?' she said. 'I'm sorry. That was an awful thing to say.' She tried to take my hand again. It was too soon. I pushed her away, put my hands in my jacket pockets. I felt certain of one thing only: there was no way I could have children with someone who thought she could just say whatever she wanted.

How does a life change? First gradually, and then all at once. Mayliss turned everything on its head. My endless, lonely weeks of maternity leave were suddenly filled with something. I said: 'Maybe we could go for a walk together, the next time you have a day off?'

Throughout the rest of February and into March, we met up once a week. I made sure we always agreed on meeting places in parts of the city that were off Helene's route: nowhere near Helene's work, or where she caught public transport, or locations where we might bump into her colleagues and friends who were also on maternity leave. Mayliss didn't ask how Helene felt about me bringing her son along to our clandestine assignations. Presumably she didn't even realize I was keeping them a secret. She worked on reception at a hotel, taking most of her shifts in the evenings or at weekends, and she said she could get us a good deal, should Helene and I fancy booking a room at the hotel for a staycation. She listened to Iron Maiden and Staysman. She was one of those people with a certain attentiveness – she reminded me of the way children react spontaneously to their surroundings, hardly ever thinking of what's gone before or is to come. She didn't speak of the donor again. She never mentioned articles about children who feel mass-produced. She never even asked how Olav was getting on.

'Ah, so you're an accountant,' she said. 'Isn't that, like, really dull? I completely failed maths – I could have done with you to check my sums, ha ha! Although I'm actually pretty good at budgeting.'

Before she moved to the city, she rented a small apartment in Elverum – she'd had no chance of being able to buy there. She was a lesbian single mother from the country, but she hadn't anticipated all the prejudice she would come to encounter. She chatted with the young Muslim who worked behind the till at the local supermarket. She asked the overdressed hipster at the next café table where she'd got her shoes. She declined the advances of the drug-addicted *Big Issue* sellers on the street without rolling her eyes afterwards or making a point out of how she really, *really* did feel for them, but she simply couldn't help everyone. She gave Henry a packet of Smarties without asking if it was okay for him to have chocolate, since he was still so small. She spoke of her mother warmly, despite the fact that her mother had abandoned Mayliss and her little brother when Mayliss was just twelve years old. She said: 'Having Nicolai is the best thing that's ever happened to me.'

Nicolai was born in September. He was conceived in Copenhagen; Henry was conceived in Oslo. I don't know if they're half-siblings. But I can see it. And now that I've seen it, it's impossible to get it out of my head. Like when you discover an optical illusion in a painting, where what you think is the work's sole motif actually comprises the components of another. It's no surprise that the girl behind the counter at the soft play was fooled – we look like a family. Or at least, we look more like a family than Helene and Henry and Olav and I do. When I walk beside Mayliss along the bank of the Alna River, I'm filled with a curious mix of shame and self-satisfaction. I fret because she looks so drab, waddling along in her old Ugg boots. I fret because I care what people might think if they see who I'm associating with. But next to her, I feel thinner. I feel prettier and smarter. Most of all, I feel free.

Because it isn't entirely true, that it's impossible to unsee the likenesses. Soon, I forget them. The differences take over. Nicolai isn't Henry – in fact, he's quite the opposite. Henry is allowed to watch a tiny bit of children's television; Nicolai gets to watch hours of YouTube. Henry wakes at five in the morning; Nicolai has to be woken at seven-thirty. Nicolai climbs all over everything, Nicolai runs off, Nicolai refuses to eat slices of apple or seeded bread. His clothes are ugly and boyish; his nose is always snotty. When Mayliss changes his nappy in front of me, I see that his bottom is bright red, but she applies no cream to ease his nappy rash. Nicolai is a kid Henry waves to when we leave, a kid I'm only semi-interested in when we're all together. What Henry is interested in is going to pick up Olav from kindergarten. And what I'm interested in is talking. What I'm interested in is unburdening myself to someone who won't gossip or judge me or call me out on my shit.

Only once does she bring it up, the way in which we've had children. 'Do you think there's a difference,' she says one day, when we're sitting on a bench in the playground in Sofienberg, 'in having given birth to one kid and not the other?' 'Of course,' I say. 'There's no escaping biology. And the kids view us differently, too. But the love we feel for them is the same. Exactly the same.' 'Really?' she says. 'I mean, that's fantastic! But I don't think it would be the same for me. If I had girlfriend, I'd never dare let her carry the kid.' I glance at Henry, who is standing under the frame of the slide, seeming a little lost. He peers about him, he's looking for me. 'Can I be completely honest for a minute?' I start. 'I think this whole co-mother thing is fucking hard work.'

*

When did I last meet someone who says exactly what they want to? She reminds me of the people back home. The defiant inhabitants of Sotra, who always tell me how much they hate Oslo, even though they know I live there, and who, when they go shopping at the local Spar, don't even notice that right above the racks of semi-skimmed milk there's also a small selection of organic alternatives; who are against exporting electricity to Europe; and who think people ought to know better than to bundle onto some old rust bucket of a boat and set out from the North African coast – if it all goes wrong, they have only themselves to blame.

But at the same time, Mayliss is also so… pragmatic? She seems always to look on the bright side – I'm not used to people thinking positively like that. When I talk about how awful and worrying it is to think about our children growing up in an ever-hotter world, she says: 'Yeah, but you also don't have to stress too much about it. We might not want to think about it because it all feels too scary, but to the kids it will just be normal.'

I forgot myself after one of our meet-ups, as I served Helene tea and cheese toasties for supper. I had fried the sandwiches in a pan as we listened to a radio programme about how being surrounded by inflation and climate anxiety and threats of war is affecting people's mental health. 'But just because times are hard,' I said, 'doesn't mean people can't be happy.' Helene looked at me, frowned, then laughed and said: 'Well thanks, Miss hard-right-leaning Progress Party voter, for that insight.'

THE BRIEF TEXT EXCHANGE with Joachim makes me want to drink. I may not have anyone to drink with, but that doesn't mean I can't buy myself a bottle of wine. Or gin, perhaps? I have to allow myself a break now and then. I'm sweaty and tired. I'm looking forward to getting out of here – to feeling the breeze that blows across Trøndelag's fields on my skin. To taking walks in the forest. To sitting in the kitchen and being served coffee in the striped mug my mother-in-law always picks out for me.

If I'm even able to go there, that is.

On my way to the wine shop I pass the kindergarten, where before the weekend we had gathered in the playground for the summer party. The kids ran around, overexcited and worked up; muffins and fruit squash were served, and the staff lined up wearing wreaths of flowers on their heads and sang 'Idas sommervise'. The swings, the sandpit, the little wooden playhouse Olav sometimes stands in and waves to me from when I arrive to pick him up... all of it abandoned for the summer. The gate to the playground is locked; all the buckets and spades have been cleared away. Only a single small, pink mitten hangs from a branch up in the tree the kids like to climb.

I feel it in my throat. Sometimes, it's just too overwhelming. It descends on me, every now and then, like when Olav had just started at the kindergarten and I arrived to pick him up and saw him sitting ready on the kerb with his balaclava and bag, waiting, his expression serious. And it hit me, with a force that terrified me: he loves me. Because I am his mother.

To bring something into the world. To inflict upon a child all that love, vulnerability and dependence. The responsibility one has for stewarding it all… It's simply too much.

I remember one time I was here, back in the winter. In the snow outside the kindergarten gate stood a poor mother, overloaded with a bundled-up baby in a sling at her chest and a little boy of around eighteen months at the end of one arm. The boy was screaming at the top of his lungs and clinging to his mother, shouting: 'No, no, no!'

No member of staff went out to meet her. I passed her without thinking too much of it, mostly just feeling relieved that I'd managed to drop off Olav without any drama, and that Henry was still quiet in his pram. Over at the pedestrian crossing, as the light turned green, I noticed the same mother as she came up beside me. I looked at her and the baby and gave them a sympathetic smile. 'Well done,' I said, but she didn't reply. She only stared straight ahead, tears pouring down her cheeks, and I felt like a fool, as if I was acting as some spin doctor for this society that wants to send all its languageless, eleven-month-old citizens off to institutions, a society in which women's freedom and good sense are synonymous with handing your children over to other women.

I'm sorry, I wanted to say, you poor thing, that must have been really tough for you and your son, but she had already hurried over the crossing, while I was left standing there on the pavement. Now the light had turned red again. I looked down at Henry in his pram. It would soon be Christmas, he would turn one in January, he wouldn't start kindergarten until August. I was the one taking the government's cash benefit and staying home – I was the one who insisted we do it that way with both our kids, lost pension points or no lost pension points.

This wasn't a happy time. But it wasn't about my happiness. I was depressed and lonely; every evening I dreaded the next day I'd have to spend alone with Henry while Helene was at work. 'Why are you doing this to yourself?' Joachim asked. 'Is this some kind of attempt to make up for being unfaithful?' asked Janne. 'Are you trying to fix things by being an overenthusiastic mother?'

But I knew it was the right thing to do – people can call it privileged and hysterical and way too self-sacrificing if it makes them feel better, but I know that as a society we're on the wrong track, I know far too many people disregard the duty of care they have towards the children they bring into this world; they send them off to kindergarten as soon as they're able to, give them a screen instead of speaking to them. People who consistently stick an iPad in front of their kids at mealtimes ought to be called out on it, reprimanded for neglect. Mayliss is one of those people. But sitting in a café with her and Nicolai, I said nothing when she gave Henry her phone because he was whining.

O N THE BENCH outside the wine shop sits a man with a boy with learning disabilities on his lap. I hope the man is the boy's father. That he's a good father. When I was little, Mamma worked at a centre for adults with learning disabilities; sometimes she would take me along while she provided one-to-one care to the centre's users, accompanying them to a doctor's appointment, or to the Sartor shopping centre to play the slot machines. The centre's users would sit in the back seat with me, in my sister's spot. The men in particular terrified me. Their big, hairy arms, the smell of aftershave, their deep voices, the outfits from Dressman, which looked like Pappa's clothes. The fact that they were so manly but could also stare at me protractedly, with the intensity of a small child. Or that they might suddenly begin to rock back and forth, or dribble onto the scarf around their neck without noticing, or lean over the middle seat, stroke my cheek and say: 'Oh, you're such a nice girl.'

'There's nothing to be afraid of,' Mamma said. 'Most of them have had a hard life. If anyone should be afraid, it's them.'

During those first years we lived together in Oslo, Helene worked in the state dental service. But after she had been forced – for the second time – to make a safeguarding report regarding a child who had reluctantly opened wide only to reveal a large bruise on their palate, I found her sitting in the kitchen in the middle of the night with a cup of tea on the table before her. She shook her head and said: 'Will you think I'm weak and a coward if I move into private practice?' 'No,' I replied. 'I actually think it's pretty incredible you've stuck it out this long.'

Ever since Olav was a tiny baby, I've repeated myself endlessly as I've changed his nappies and washed him and helped him to put on his little underpants. 'It's your body. Nobody is allowed to touch it if you don't want them to.' The time it was revealed that a child in Janne's neighbourhood had been subjected to years of abuse, Janne had said: 'I can hardly believe it. She's such a funny and outgoing girl. And that's almost the most disturbing thing about it. You can't see it on her.'

MOST PEOPLE can't see it on me, that I am what I am. I look like an ordinary mother – with short hair, true, but in ordinary trainers, ordinary linen shorts, a blue striped T-shirt. With a wedding ring. When the rainbow flags are raised and hung from balconies at the housing cooperatives out here in June, most people don't know that I'm one of the people they're flying the flag for. I stay under the radar. I shop at the local discount supermarket and do the kindergarten pick-up and attend parents' meetings and do the vacuuming and rinse and dry the plastic waste before throwing it into the purple bag for recycling. I enter invoices in accounting systems and send invites to meetings on Teams. I live an ordinary life. But it isn't an ordinary life.

Outside the school, the ground has been painted in rainbow colours. This is the school's response to the vandalism. It happens over and over, and it's been happening for years. The headmaster must have an entire store cupboard full of flags in her office, from which she replaces the destroyed and stolen ones. Nobody knows who's behind it. It's probably just some young kids acting without thinking, who must be forgiven, for they know not what they do.

On the morning the shooting happened, when Helene had woken me, I almost felt a kind of… relief? My paranoia – it wasn't unfounded. I'd been waiting for something to happen, for years I had gone around thinking: That we can live so freely and celebrate in this way? It's just too good to be true.

And yet it isn't the extremists in yellow T-shirts that occupy my thoughts. It's the neighbourhood wives. The dads in the playgrounds. The supermarket employees. The bus drivers. The woman who sees me almost naked at Wax ON! Wax OFF! Never knowing what they might think or say, if I were to reveal who I am. I'm not afraid they might be unkind or become violent – hardly ever, it isn't like that. But simply noticing their disgust. That I make good, honest people uncomfortable. To watch the shifting expression on the face of the friendly carpenter who's come to give us a quote as it dawns on him: we have one double bed. And we have two children.

I T WAS MY TURN to have a lie-in that Saturday, when Helene came in and sat on the edge of the bed. She placed a hand on my back. 'There was a shooting at the London nightclub last night – several people were killed!' 'What did you say?' I mumbled. I turned over; she sat there with disbelief in her dark eyes. 'It must have been a terrorist attack,' she continued, 'there's no other explanation, it's just awful, I've been awake since five, I wanted to let you sleep but then I just couldn't wait any longer.' 'No, of course you had to wake me,' I replied, 'of course!'

Afterwards, I reacted like everyone else in our circle: over the next few hours my phone was never out of my sight; I scrolled through media updates as I messaged everyone I could think of who might have been out that night.

The reeling thoughts and anxieties triggered by my first encounter with Mayliss and Nicolai at Pride in the Park just a few days earlier suddenly felt insignificant.

The fact that we had both been grumpy the previous evening because Helene wasn't in the mood for sex was at once reduced to a joke.

We took turns taking care of the children. I put on a cartoon for Olav, *Winnie the Pooh*; I carefully fed Henry baby porridge with mashed banana, smiling and babbling and wiping up water from his tipped-over beaker as I exchanged the occasional glance with Helene. We had to remain calm in front of them, we couldn't cry – to be responsible for a child is to renounce one's right to react freely. Behind the open fridge door, Helene embraced me. Tenderly, for a long time. As if we were saying farewell before I embarked on a long journey to somewhere dangerous. 'What are we going to do about the parade?' I asked. 'I can't believe you even have to ask,' Helene replied. 'There's no way in hell we're taking the boys there.'

Pappa called me unprompted, from a sun lounger in Phuket. 'I agree with Helene,' he said, 'it sounds wise to stay home.' Later that day, after it was reported that the parade had been cancelled, I texted Mamma: *Just wanted to let you know we're safe.* She replied: *Safe from what?*

I S IT TOO EARLY to pour myself a gin and tonic? No. I pour one. It gives me a feeling of decadence, if nothing else. What should I do now? Start on the floors upstairs, so I can feel I'm really making progress? Or clear out the bathroom? I choose the bathroom. It's a fucking ridiculous job. We're two women: we own thousands of products – the cabinets are stuffed to bursting. Contact-lens fluid. Hair elastics. Moisturizing creams, dried-out tubes of mascara, sanitary towels. Half a bottle of head-lice treatment. The most romantic chemical in the house.

A month after Helene came back, when we could still go entire afternoons and evenings without looking at each other or speaking, other than to exchange simple practical messages (with the exception of when she would return to being furious and desperate for reassurance in her new role as the Humiliated Party, point the finger at me and ask: 'Did it really only happen once?' or, 'Do you swear you're no longer in touch with her?'), and I, with an unbearably well-deserved pain in my chest, had thoughts like, If this doesn't get better soon, then we're finished, Olav's kindergarten called and said he had head lice. 'He kept complaining that his head itched today,' his teacher said, 'so I had a little look. There are loads of eggs behind his ears.'

When I arrived to pick him up I saw that the staff had put Olav's hair in a bun; his teacher hadn't asked me to collect him early, but it felt like the only decent thing to do, and I wouldn't have managed to achieve much at the office anyway. We cycled over to the pharmacy, where the pharmacist said that everyone in the family ought to be treated. 'You have to treat everybody at the same time,' she said, 'otherwise there's no point.'

Helene was red-faced when she arrived home from work – she hurried into the apartment exuding an energy I'd thought I might never see in her again, and it was wonderful. 'Oh my God,' she exclaimed, 'I've been itching and scratching all afternoon! I really hope I haven't given them to any of my patients!'

She wanted me to check her hair using the nit comb; said she wanted to be sure she wasn't doing the treatment unnecessarily, because she'd read online this was something you shouldn't do, 'especially when pregnant'. 'I asked for a treatment that's safe to use during pregnancy,' I replied. 'The pharmacist asked how far along I was.' She looked at me, and it was a warm look, it really was warm. 'Oh, thanks, that's nice.'

I had already prepared a de-lousing station under the spotlights in the bathroom, lined up the bottles of treatment, set a chair in front of the sink. 'Bend over and look down,' I said. I pulled the elastic out of her ponytail, made a centre parting in her hair with my fingers. The skin at her nape was as pallid as the scalp I glimpsed beneath all the dark hairs. 'Can you see anything?' she cried, down into the sink. 'Can you see anything? It's so disgusting, I can't stand it!' 'Not yet,' I replied, 'I'll have a look with the comb now.' Were we alone? It felt as if we were alone, even if Olav, his hair glossy and slicked back with lice treatment, sat there on the tiles over by the bathtub, turning the pages of one of the *World's Most Beautiful Fairy Tales* books Mamma had sent, along with a passive-aggressive letter, in the post. But yes. It was just the two of us there. I felt how my heart beat harder. Not because I was afraid of finding lice. The sight of that bent, white neck. The access. To be permitted to share something so repulsive, something so intimate. Who else would I have done this with?

Suddenly, as if after panicked searching I had finally found her in a crowd, I bent forward and put my arms around her from behind. I pressed my cheek to hers, hard, insisting – I didn't give a shit if a louse crawled from her head onto mine. I closed my eyes and inhaled the scent of her – in recent weeks I had only smelt it while sorting the dirty laundry, that beloved scent, never again did I want to live without it, never – her mouth opened, her lower lip was dry, she didn't sarcastically ask if I had embraced Fitness Guri the same way, and nor did she tell me to let go and get a move on with the fine-combing.

WE PUT AN OFFER on the house in August last year, less than a year after I'd broken things off with Fitness Guri by saying I had acted like a reckless, sex-crazed idiot. Those were the words I used, it was easiest that way. Henry was eight months old and had an ear infection and screamed all through the viewing. Olav thought the German Shepherd tied up in the garden came with the house, and shouted that I was mean when he realized he'd misunderstood. Watching him feel ashamed makes my stomach churn; I get so angry when he reminds me of myself. I don't think anyone else has noticed this.

Helene and I weren't doing well. The baby weight wasn't coming off – she insisted on going straight from maternity leave to jogging from Torshov to the city centre, even though she was still sore and grew irritated if I asked her to take it easy. 'It's a long time since your body was able to run a marathon,' I said. She gave me a stern look. 'You think I don't know that?'

When, each day right after lunch, I stopped by the clinic with Henry so she could breastfeed him, she always spoke to me in a way that made me feel like an au pair. We never mentioned what I had done to her. We didn't kiss, we hardly looked at each other, and yet we got ourselves pre-approved for a mortgage and put an offer on a house next to a Metro station we hadn't even heard of before this. A new start. Was that what this was supposed to represent? After the viewing we told each other that children shouldn't be stuck in an apartment-building courtyard, that we wanted our kids to get to know the forest and people who are more interested in Gore-Tex than cashmere. I failed to mention all the other things that made me so eager, like the fact that Fitness Guri had also been to our place in Torshov, and that above the door to the apartment hung a flashing neon sign that said LIAR, 24/7. But had I let something slip, I would have tried to limit the damage by emphasizing that the only room anything had happened in was the living room.

Moving. I'd had no idea how all-encompassing it would turn out to be, no idea about all the new preoccupations to which it would give rise. But even before we moved in, I realized we had made a serious mistake. It wasn't just the mice, or the smell of drains in the bathroom. All autumn I thought of nothing but materials: floors, wall colours, how the textured wallpaper could be plastered over and made smooth. I thought only of surfaces, became obsessed by what we could do with them. Helene wasn't much better. The upcoming changes to the house became the only thing we could talk about at any length. Our shared indignation at all that was wrong with the house gave us the sense that our commitment to it meant we were still committed to our marriage, that it was about making the necessary arrangements for us to have a good life. But happiness can't survive on surfaces, on their complementary forms and colours.

At his new kindergarten, Olav became almost mute. 'He's a cautious boy,' the kindergarten manager said when he contacted us out of the blue, by calling Helene. I thought: Why didn't he call me? 'How cautious?' Helene replied. 'Should we be concerned?' If anyone ought to be concerned, I thought, it's me.

*

We just managed to make it into the house before the first frost. What had we moved for, after all, if not for the garden? From work, Helene sent a list of bulbs for me to go and buy. After Henry's morning nap I shoved a dummy in his mouth, hauled him into the car and drove to the garden centre. That evening, I stood for a long time looking out through the terrace door, watching as Helene crouched down before the flowerbed, side by side with Olav in the autumn darkness. Helene dug while Olav placed the bulbs in the holes, hesitantly, with the utmost care, as if he too was anxious about what might grow from this soil.

A FTER A FEW MONTHS, two older boys at the kindergarten began to bother Olav. They might refuse to speak to him, or take his mittens, and when he happily arrived for the carnival in February in his full Spiderman costume, they told him his outfit was stupid. The worst thing wasn't actually the exclusion itself, but rather that Olav continued to look up to his tormentors, to long for them – it's common, I read, for a victim to idolize their bully. And it's generally for good reason – bullies are often charming, popular, someone who makes the teacher laugh, and when a child becomes a bully it's rarely due to the fact that they're unfeeling or compensating for a poor home life – quite the opposite. He's an ordinary child, who one day just happens to realize he has power over another child, and when he realizes that his victim defers to him, he gets a kick out of it, and the experience of having this power is so intoxicating that it requires exceptional self-control not to want to invoke it again.

The episodes with the two tormentors weighed heavily on me, of course. What if this continues, I thought, what if he loses trust in people, what if they destroy his social confidence and he ends up alone at break times in primary school, becomes timid and weak and lonely and bad at football, loses out on the chance to have his first kiss, barricades himself in his room and refuses to speak to anyone other than the American and Finnish kids he games online with? But at the same time, I noticed that I didn't actually believe my catastrophic thoughts – it felt more as if I was going through an obligatory list of motherly worries that could have been cut from some tabloid website.

Helene, on the other hand – she lay awake staring at the ceiling, she woke me and said: 'I just can't stop thinking about it.' She sent texts and requested a meeting with the kindergarten manager. She passed Henry to me and pulled Olav onto her lap and with great earnestness told him to never keep anything from us. 'It isn't your fault,' she said, 'and you don't have to speak to them any more if you don't want to.'

I noticed how I compensated, in those moments when I saw she was on the verge of tears after Olav had told us about yet another episode. 'Relax,' I said. 'This is very normal. It'll all work out.' 'Work out!' she repeated angrily. 'Olav shouldn't have to put up with this!'

She has no history of bullying to speak of, no traumas to trigger. So how could she feel it more physically, be so much more worried than me? – I couldn't quite make it add up.

I T WAS A LATE AFTERNOON IN MARCH. Olav was at a friend's
house, one of the little girls from kindergarten. We'd been to the
supermarket to do a big shop, we just needed to get Henry into the
car and go pick up Olav and drive home. But it wasn't happening.
Henry didn't want to go in. He tensed his body in his car seat,
rigid and howling, terrifyingly strong – it was impossible to fasten
the tight straps. I lifted him out of the seat again. He was sweaty,
but he stopped screaming. 'Take off his suit,' Helene said, 'he's
too hot.' I set him down on the ground, between my legs, to slip
off his rainsuit, but he refused to cooperate. Suddenly he shrieked
and threw himself backwards – the back of his head hit the car
park's icy asphalt with a thud. He screamed again. An entirely
different scream this time. His pain was like a pressure wave in my
own body. I picked him up. 'Oh, sweetheart,' I cried, 'oh honey.'
Helene leapt towards me, tore him from my arms, pressed him to
her. She was angry. 'Why didn't you hold him?' she shouted. 'You
have to hold him – we've talked about how bad-tempered he gets
when he doesn't want to do something!'

Later, when I'd called the out-of-hours clinic and been told
that due to the risk of concussion we had to wake him every hour
throughout the night, I said: 'It feels as if you're saying I don't care
about him as much as you do. That I don't look after him as well.'
'Why on earth would I think that?' she replied.

T HE RECOUNTING OF THE INCIDENT, the subsequent argument, my terrible thoughts – I should have kept it all to myself. But Mayliss was the only one who asked why I had to cancel our play date the next day, because she was the only person I ever met up with. Mayliss told me to spit it out. Mayliss said: 'What a load of bullshit. I don't think you should allow yourself to be treated that way.' She sighed, almost smugly, down the phone. 'This is probably a mean thing to say,' she said, 'but when I hear all the stuff you tell me, I'm relieved I did it on my own.'

THROUGHOUT APRIL, the kids were sick pretty much constantly. Colds, conjunctivitis, stomach bugs. Another round of head lice. The thing that must have been Covid, even though the tests were negative. Suppositories, Vaseline, tissues, the laundry loads of vomit-covered bedding that whirred day and night. I didn't speak to Mayliss then. I had enough to deal with getting through caring for the kids and the long, repetitive discussions with Helene about which flooring we should choose before we renovated in the summer, which company we should go for, which of us had the greatest need for sleep. Maybe it was Helene. Helene was utterly shattered. 'Well, you can't work as well on top of everything else,' she said. 'Today I was so tired I almost started drilling the wrong tooth!'

Once, before we had children, we visited a female friend who had recently had a boy and a girl on her own. When, a few harried hours later, we finally left her, we were almost euphorically relieved that her life wasn't ours. 'She's aged a decade, the poor thing,' Helene said, laughing. 'I hardly recognized her!' Now the same thing had happened to Helene's face. And she laughed at that, too, because it was comical, how all the arrogant thoughts about what elegant mothers we would be had been pulverized. 'Just look at us,' we might say, standing there shivering in our pyjamas at six in the morning, with vomit and chocolate-spread stains on our chests and dark circles under our eyes after yet another sleepless night, 'we've turned into two dirty old biddies.' And at those times,

I could feel it, too: the glory in standing there together as two dirty old biddies, who are doing their best, who, even though they might wish they were somewhere else entirely, continue to get up and go to bed and get up and go to bed, and who in the life that plays out within these simple, confined limits, are doing what little they can.

I'M DONE WITH THE BATHROOM. Not a tube of moisturizer or cotton bud or dried-out mascara remains. All the towels lie neatly folded in transparent plastic bags – I've set aside the tattiest ones to shove into the charity recycling bins. The nappies are gone. Helene's straighteners and earrings and the Donald Duck comics Olav likes to flick through while sitting on the toilet – all of it has been packed up. Oh, it's so satisfying! And just think, soon these half-rotten tiles will be chipped away, and the floor taken up, and new pipes will be laid, and new underfloor heating cables, and the new floor will be cast with the right incline so the water doesn't run everywhere when we shower, and the shower curtain will be replaced with glass, and the sink will be minimalistic and elegant, and hexagonal green marble tiles will adorn the floor and walls. It's going to be lovely, truly lovely, and I know that I too have become a superficial middle-class woman, and that the people who will undertake this work for us probably want to be sick at how rich Norwegians are, or at least the Norwegians who hire them, and I'm well aware that it's probably leaving one hell of a carbon footprint to transport the tiles from India, or wherever they're being manufactured nowadays, and who knows what the conditions are like at the factory where they're cut, but I don't care, I don't give a shit about it, I'm just a person, a self-centred person, maybe, but at least I'll soon have a beautiful bathroom. Helene is the one who picked everything out, who researched and found the right suppliers; it's taken time, and I didn't quite understand why it was so fucking important when we were in the middle of it, but now, now I just feel so grateful, I need to text her, imagining the new bathroom quite simply allows me to forget myself, to forget all the shit. *Jesus*, I write, *I'm so looking forward to getting everything done, I'm so looking forward to spending the autumn here in the house with you,* and I mean it, and because I mean it, I feel the rising pressure in my throat, I begin to cry, and I cry because I might not get the chance to share my joy at the new bathroom with her, and probably I cry because I've been drinking gin, and I cry because I almost never look forward to our future plans any more, and it's as if all the joy has been taken from us.

I'VE NEVER SMOKED regularly enough to be able to use ciga-rettes to help me relax. But I try, I sit on the steps outside the house. 'Just imagine how we must look right now,' Joachim would say as we stood outside Copenhagen Business School, smoking. 'Everybody walking past must think: Wow. The two of them are really living the life.'

It's the last cigarette in the pack. I smoke it slowly, it tastes disgusting, I always think that, and that's why it's good, as if what I'm inhaling, and what I am, finally harmonize. The girl from Askøy stubbed out her cigarettes on her forearms in a kind of chic display of self-harm that made me both loathe and admire her. I'd never dream of smoking when I'm with the boys. And preferably not in front of Helene, either, she's seen too many smokers' mouths at work. So I adapt. Healthy through and through; strong, affection-ate and amiable. I can be like that. A lazy binge-eater; blunt and full of contempt. I can be like that, too. Human beings are full of contradictions, as they should be – it's what makes life beautiful, isn't that what they say? But that I have this quality, that it's so easy for me to fluctuate along this spectrum of contradictions, as if I have an army of helpers waiting in the wings to assist me with the slick costume changes required by my ongoing autobio-graphical performance – it can't possibly be good. Who are we, really? What weighs most heavily? If you look at the way I judge my own mother, for example, there's no doubt: one is for ever defined by the acts one performs against those who are unable to defend themselves.

Beyond the garden I catch sight of our neighbour, Bjørg, again. It looks as if she's heading this way, she walks slowly, casting scrutinizing glances at the house. I lift a hand, and then she sees me. It's too late to hide the cigarette now, but I set it in the terracotta saucer I use as an ashtray, a thin column of smoke rising up beside me like a signal no one should decipher.

'So you're out here, are you?' Bjørg says. Without waiting for an answer, she hands me what she's carrying. 'I just finished reading this, and I thought it was just wonderful. Maybe you have time for a bit of reading, now you're on your own?' It's one of those thick, vapid titles liked by women of a certain age. Which novel was it that Fitness Guri lured me back to her place to borrow that night? I smile, thank her, say it's really kind of her to bring me something to read. And it is, truly. The wear to her hip joints causes her terrible pain that makes her move slowly and haltingly; she struggles to sleep on her side and is gravely concerned that the cats in the neighbourhood are catching too many songbirds. But still, she's attentive, she listens to everything Olav has to say about the flowers he's picked, lets him pet her little dog, brings us leftover cinnamon rolls, offers to water the plants every time we go on holiday.

But I think: Get lost. Go away. Look at my face.

And still my mouth continues to speak. I say there's still a lot to do in the house, but I can take the book with me to Trøndelag. I ask whether she has plans for the summer, and how it's going with the drops she's been given to treat her dog's eyes, if she's still waking up earlier and earlier, which she always bemoans. 'Henry is just as bad,' my mouth says, 'he often wakes at four-thirty in the morning.' This is a conversation we've had a million times before.

Often these exchanges make me feel normal, like a friendly neighbour, someone who manages to be liked by the people around her. Who knows how to make allowances for the emotional lives of old ladies, and who can even offer up a few tips for little exercises they can do to reduce the stiffness in their bodies, which I learnt from Janne. Moreover, it's good for the kids. To have a relationship with an older person who's experienced a bit of everything life has to offer, and not just the other fucking middle-class parents, who hardly do so much as say hello when we encounter one another at the kindergarten. Especially since the boys only have one set of grandparents to whom they feel close. But now, right now I just don't want it. And still I say: 'Maybe you'd like to come over for a glass of wine?' 'A glass of wine,' Bjørg says. 'It's a long time since anyone has offered me a glass of wine!' She laughs – confused? 'Can we take a rain check?' I smile, oh how broadly I smile. 'We can have it once we've moved back in again in September,' I say. 'Celebrate the renovations, as it were!' I look down at my cigarette as she leaves, but it has long since burned itself out.

THEY MUST THINK I'M A TERRIBLE PERSON. Everyone who learns that Mamma has only met Henry twice. That Olav no longer wants to call her Grandma, even though she insists: he calls her Britt. That she doesn't get to bake buns for them, or take them to the local swimming pool, or come and look after them when we obviously need help. Thanks to Mamma, I exist. And still I keep him away from her. I don't think she'll grab a handful of his blonde locks and pull if he doesn't do as she says. But nor do I think that she'll manage to hide her true self if she's allowed to be with Olav over time. Or with Henry. If she has them both, there's no way on this green earth that she'll manage to treat them equally.

'Can you give Grandma a goodbye kiss?' Mamma asks. Olav is small. He bends towards the screen and kisses it. Mamma laughs. Today she's in a good mood. Next week, she'll refuse to pick up the phone when we call.

'Listen to this,' Helene said as we lay there on the sofa. We were newly married, but I wasn't doing so well, I was on sick leave. 'How to tell if you've been raised by a narcissist – a checklist: One. You have poor self-esteem. Two. You constantly apologize. Three. You had to compete with your siblings for your parents' favour – one was the golden child, and sometimes you were set against each other. Four. You were often told that you weren't good enough. Five.

You struggle with feelings of guilt. Six. You're afraid of conflict... sound familiar?'

Before, Helene and I would speak about Mamma constantly. Helene supported me through the periods during which I broke off contact. She dismissed all my doubting and self-flagellating talk, and said I owed Mamma nothing, even if she did send me letters and moving texts about how she'd got Olav his very own crib at her house, when he was barely a month old. 'Your mother is very manipulative,' she said, 'surely you can see that?'

Of course I capitulated at times, and I felt like a terrible person for not letting Mamma see Olav more. 'You can see more of her if you like, but all she ever does is make you feel bad,' Helene said. It was hard. But we often laughed, too, like when I remembered things I'd been subjected to, unhinged statements that had fallen from Mamma's lips. The problem with having a mother with narcissistic personality traits is that everything becomes a caricature. A script entirely devoid of believability. You can say to people: She always shows her teeth when she smiles, but her smile never reaches her eyes. Or: She might seem confident and cheerful, but she actually thinks someone's out to get her, and that everything I do that isn't in accordance with her wishes is something I'm doing to mock her. Who would believe a father isn't allowed to wear his Liverpool shirt because his wife thinks red doesn't suit him? Who would believe that a mother, between heaving sobs, could claim that her eldest daughter is breaking her heart because she doesn't smile when she speaks to her, while her little sister simply continues to watch *Home and Away*?

It almost isn't believable, all the terrible names she's called me. Or that she threatened to take her own life if I didn't end my relationship with Helene. People gape, they titter, say, 'Gosh, that's quite the reaction,' but deep down, they can't believe it. At the very least, they suspect I'm exaggerating. But when you're in a narcissist's thrall, everything about life takes on a tragicomic logic.

The only person who really knew what I'd been through with Mamma and believed me, was Helene. Helene was there, she saw how Mamma texted to say she wouldn't be attending my aunt's fiftieth birthday party if I was bringing this HELENE with me. If I was feeling too frayed to look at my phone, she opened the messages from Mamma and my sister for me. She stroked my back and said: 'Of course Olav will never have to be alone with her if you're not comfortable with that.'

Talking about my childhood was its own activity, a kind of hobby that bound us together. But it's not like that any more. Because, of course, it's been going on for so many years, in various phases, and I've finally just about reconciled myself to the fact that it is what it is – it no longer feels so acute. But the main reason is that I've used up my share of goodwill. I, who claim to be the opposite of my mother, am at least just as willing as she is to lie, so as not to lose face.

How much empathy do we actually have for each other now? Love is many things, but it has no chance of surviving without this: a fundamental willingness to inhabit the other's perspective.

After Henry was born, I began to glimpse it in her eyes. First vaguely, like when the light from a distant city colours the night sky above a plain. But it grew stronger. She searched for signs that I was recreating what I'd learnt about being a mother in my childhood home. 'Not so fast,' she would say, if I quickly picked Henry up when he was screaming. 'Do you think that's something to laugh about?' she said, when I chuckled to myself for just a little too long after he'd crashed into a glass door. And one day, just after I'd had an entirely ordinary argument with Olav over getting dressed, she said: 'Do you feel you're carrying a lot of pent-up anger?' I stiffened, as if she'd accused me of something utterly insane, like stealing the kids' pocket money. First, I felt flat and sad. Then I felt angry. Right, I thought, you crossed a line. If you're going to use what you know about my past against me like that, then there'll be no more taking me for granted, mark my words.

I BELIEVE IN LOVE. In spite of everything, I still do. But I think about love as a large, open space, where anything can be said, everything can be shown. I don't believe the people who say I have to reconcile myself to compromises, that nobody can be completely honest in the long run. I don't behave like that, but I want to feel that way long-term. I've felt that way before, when I've been newly in love, and for a short while when I was young, before the self-criticism and neuroses caught up with me. When I went to Denmark, it was precisely that feeling which gave me kick after kick, made me almost manic, triggered the wild, raucous laughter that one day simply fluttered out of me, as if an egg had hatched in my mouth: I realized that from now on I could speak freely and wear and be interested in whatever the hell I wanted.

I wasn't going to put up tents or learn how to tie knots. I wasn't going to work in the stables. I was going to talk, snog the faces off girls and drink beer.

I wasn't ashamed then. Quite the opposite. To finally be open about the fact that it was girls I wanted to kiss, girls I wanted to take home with me, a girl's name I wanted to see beside my own on the tenancy contract, made me feel both more important and more interesting than all the other blonde, ponytailed women in the lecture hall. I created profiles on the queer message boards and apps with a clear image of my face and checked 'women' under 'Interested in'; I sat with my arms folded as the hairdresser passed the electric razor over my temples at the salon in Vesterbro. I watched *The L Word* and *Tipping the Velvet* and wrote a fan letter to Anne Grete Preus. I moved in with Joachim in Drejøgade. I thought having a gay sidekick completed me. We watched queer films. We hung out at the Vela and Cozy clubs. We marched in the parade during Copenhagen Pride. We cried when we saw the images from Oslo Pride, the convertible in which Kim Friele and Wenche Lowzow sat and waved. Over the phone, I told Pappa: 'I don't think I'll ever move back to Norway, and definitely not back home.' It's ironic, actually, that that's where I met Helene, out there in Western Norway, right under their noses. Because back home, I remained chaste. Every time I packed my suitcase to go back for a visit, I left my braces behind in the drawer. My sister said: 'It would be nice for all of us if you could just act normally.' I had no thoughts about having children, how one fine day I would become a mother.

THE OTHER MOTHER IS ALONE IN A HOUSE. She is alone in the big bed. Her body aches. She's worked hard: she drank a slightly-too-strong drink after supper. She stretches, thinks it will be good to rest, hopes she can manage to relax now. From her wife, who is back home with her parents, a text dings in about how their youngest son still hasn't fallen asleep. Her wife actually had plans to meet up with some childhood friends, but now that's fucked. *I'll be there to help you soon*, the other mother replies, *I know it sucks*. They text one another good night. Without adding any hearts. Without a single *I love you*. It doesn't mean they don't love each other.

In the midst of the thickest summer darkness, the other mother wakes to the sound of church bells ringing. She props herself up on the mattress and looks out of the window. Is she mistaken? No, bells are ringing. A quiet, slow, cautious pealing. Then it stops.

From here she can see out across the entire neighbourhood. The houses, the forest, the church spire – the church is situated on the side of the railway line where the detached houses are, not among the tower blocks. There are a few openings in the cover of clouds, but there isn't enough emptiness for her to see the stars. The distant rush of the E6 road. Not a single light on in the rows of houses. But she isn't alone. A fox slinks through the bottom of the garden. It is slender, moving on long legs and with a straggly tail. Her pulse rushes – she feels elated, as one does when watching any wild animal. If only her youngest son, the one-year-old, could see this. He's drawn to all the animals he encounters, those that cross his path.

The fox is interested in something under the hedge. The smell of rats? An old, mouldy crust of bread one of her sons has discarded there? She knows little about foxes, what they search for when the chicken coop is burglar-proofed and they roam the streets at night. She has tried to read Roald Dahl's *Fantastic Mr Fox* to her eldest son, but soon realized she would have to give it up – her son was beside himself with fear. For chapter after chapter, Mr Fox and his wife and small cubs dig deeper and deeper into the earth in pure mortal terror because they're being hunted by some cantankerous farmers who want to chase them out of their den and do away with them.

Why were the church bells ringing? Was it just some youths who broke in? Are the priest and deacon having an affair, are they pushing one another against the wall, causing one of them to accidentally press the button that sets the chiming going? Or is someone else hiding in there, families with small children or young, single men who've sought asylum in the church, and who are close to losing their minds because the uncertainty and waiting is unbearable?

In a flash, something opens up inside the other mother: people other than herself exist. There are countless reasons she should be deeply grateful – for a moment she's like a believer taking stock of everything with which she's been blessed. But it's only an instant. Soon, something tightens around the other mother's heart. Soon, the darkness seeps in again. She taps on the window, but the fox doesn't hear her.

JUST HOW DEEP DOES THE FEAR GO?

All the way here, to the depths of the densest forest.

Here she stands, the other mother, with her two little boys. It is almost pitch dark. The forest is black and damp. She doesn't know the paths; they must have got lost. But they can't stay here. The boys, who are tired and hungry, and whose feet are wet, tug at her coat and whine. She should never have brought them here. 'Can the pair of you stop complaining,' she shouts. The boys immediately fall silent. They are so small, of course they don't understand that anger is code for fear.

They are so small. They don't understand that their mother has been overtaken by a fear she had thought passé. One thing is men in yellow T-shirts. One thing is the people who leave nasty comments online, or who snatch a rainbow flag from some balcony.

What she has come to fear is that more and more people secretly believe that those who hate people like her being able to have a family, may, in fact, have a point.

She's become afraid her sons will one day reply: We actually think having two mothers is fucking dreadful.

She's become afraid of what will happen when people realize what the fertility clinics are actually doing.

That the authorities will change the legislation. And that her boys will grow into young men and realize the way in which they were conceived is no longer legal.

She's grown afraid they will one day say: Mamma, we feel like half-people.

Mass-produced. It won't take many using the term in debates and op-eds before the masses will come to endorse it, and say: 'Children are not mass-produced products. We must think about what's best for the children. It's high time.'

She's afraid of the eyes her boys will feel boring into the backs of their mass-produced necks.

She's afraid of the insults and abuse they'll hear with their mass-produced ears.

She's afraid they will one day accuse her of not loving them equally.

And she's afraid of what will happen afterwards, when they have found their way out of here and reached a clearing in which there is a veritable mob of children with blonde curls, bright blue eyes, identical button noses – all these traits reminiscent of her eldest son, the boy she has brought into the world, and when he catches sight of them, something glimmers in his eyes, and he wants to go to them, and he understands that he belongs among them, and it's so obvious that she loses any right she might have had to take the two little brothers by the hand and hurry back towards the forest and act as if they've gone the wrong way, pretend she has no idea who those strange children are.

*T*HESE TWO HAVE PUT ON A PLAY, Helene texts on Thursday morning. An update provided out of obligation. She never replied to the message in which I said I was looking forward to joining them – is that significant? Was she too busy with Henry yesterday to feel affectionate? Does she assume that I know she's looking forward to seeing me, too? Or… No. I can't bear to think about it. What she has sent is a photo of Olav and the girl who lives on the neighbouring farm. The girl is wearing lipstick and something that looks like a Halloween dress, while Olav has dressed up in a skirt, a flowery ribbon around his head. Helene's father probably had a few choice thoughts when Olav trooped up in a skirt, but in all likelihood didn't say anything, he probably just went out to get some work done. Repair a fence, busy himself with the tractor. There's always something to do. He owns several fields, which he reaps. He puts a portion of what he earns from the round bales into his grandchildren's savings accounts.

It's a relief that the business has been shut down. Helene had an easy upbringing, but that was the only thing that kept her on high alert – the fact that her father was a fur farmer. Most people at her school accepted it, but she was never safe from the comments. Someone might stop her out of the blue, accuse her and her family of enjoying torturing animals. 'It made me so angry,' she said. 'So I marched into school wearing Mamma's mink coat. You can imagine how that went down.' One morning, during the summer holiday, she had sneaked outside with an ice cream from the freezer. That was when she saw them, the people who suddenly crept out of the barn and clambered over the fences with their huge video camera. She sat there, stock-still, they didn't notice her, they ran stoop-shouldered across the field and up towards the copse of trees. Inside the barn there wasn't a single trace, as if the people she'd observed had been ghosts. 'But then, in the winter, some images appeared on NRK of an animal Pappa had taken in for treatment. It was awful. They came and scrawled MURDERER in red paint across the side of the barn; one morning we woke up to find our doorstep had been doused in pig's blood.'

As I make coffee, I realize I want to call her. We haven't had a chance to speak since they left. She picks up straight away. She's sitting on the waterbed, her hair hanging loose, wearing a large shirt I haven't seen before, probably her father's – it suits her. Women in oversized men's shirts… where's that from? Oh, yes – *Wait, Blink* by Gunnhild Øyehaug. I loved that novel. I gave it to Helene when we'd just got together. I thought she was so cute when she said: 'It's incredibly funny, for a novel written in Nynorsk!'

'I just wanted to hear how things are going,' I say. She shrugs, her eyes are colourless. 'Oh, you know.' She gives such curt answers. Makes so little effort for me. Had I been Sunniva, or one of her other friends, she never would have replied like that. But I won't let myself get irritated. 'Look, it's pretty empty here now,' I say, turning the camera so she can see the stripped walls, the full boxes. 'It actually didn't take that long!' 'Great,' she says. 'Thank you for doing all that. And are you planning on doing nothing but work on the house for the next few days, or are you going to find something fun to do?' I hesitate, unsure. 'You should find something fun.' She sounds sullen. She's slept poorly, argued with her mother again, who can't see the problem with Henry being given an ice cream every time he plonks himself in front of the freezer. 'You're the one who wanted me to stay here,' I say. 'I know that,' she says, 'but at least do something you'll enjoy. Go for a swim or something.' 'In goose-shit filled Nøklevann?' 'Nøklevann or Sørenga, whatever.' 'I don't know if I can be bothered,' I reply. 'But Jesus,' Helene says, 'you complain every autumn about how you haven't had a chance to do much swimming.' She might be sulky, but she's absolutely right. It's shameful, that I have so little drive. I change the subject. 'So how's your dad doing?' I ask. 'Okay,' she replies. 'I suppose. He doesn't say much. Mostly just carries on as usual. But he's finding it tough.' 'And you,' I say. 'What about me?' 'What do you think?' 'I don't know.' 'You don't know?' 'I mean, it's weird. Empty. But at least they won't have to put up with all the harassment any more, or have to sit around waiting for it to happen again.' 'Yes,' I say. 'That must be a relief.'

When the decision to close down the business was finally made, my mother-in-law developed a stomach ulcer. My father-in-law wheeled the box into the barn and plucked them from their cages, one by one; he finished gassing the entire mink population to death before Henry was born. It was humiliating and dramatic. A life's work, gone to the dogs. Helene's brother treated them to a trip to Crete to celebrate the start of their retirement, but my mother-in-law's stomach ulcer still returns at regular intervals.

The one who least misses the mink is Olav. The first time we took him out there he began to cry – he was so little, and it smelt strong and strange, he clung to me as if afraid I was going to shut him up in one of the cages and leave. We had tried again several times; wearing thick gloves, my father-in-law held out a mink so Olav could stroke its back, but Olav refused, tears streaming down his face, and he shook his head and whispered: 'I don't want to!' 'He can sense your discomfort,' Helene said. 'Well, at least it's good he's letting us know when he doesn't feel comfortable with something,' I replied.

My parents-in-law didn't tell him off. They might have been disappointed, but they both took it so calmly. 'All in good time,' my father-in-law said. 'Would you like to go in with Grandma instead?' my mother-in-law asked. Nobody gave Olav a dressing-down for being a disappointment. No one stopped speaking to him.

On the telephone, Helene falls silent. I don't like it when she grows quiet like this, it stresses me out. 'There's just one more thing,' she says finally. A knot tightens within me. Yes – here it is. This is it. She's been thinking about how she actually knows very little about this Mayliss person she's so often heard me talk about. She's spoken to that colleague of hers, who Mayliss and I bumped into in Majorstuen that time! Or she's googled Mayliss, found her Instagram account, seen all the photographs of Nicolai, or perhaps there's even a new post that attracted her attention, maybe Mayliss has just posted a photo of Henry and Nicolai and captioned it *Brothers 4-ever* and tagged me? 'What?' I try to sound calm. 'I don't know whether I want to say it,' Helene says. She doesn't know whether she wants to say it? 'Come on,' I say. 'You promise you won't just tell me I'm being silly?'

What's this? This is new. I slap on a fake smile, make my voice lighter, more kind. 'Okay, I think you're being a bit dramatic now. I'm not going to tell you you're being silly.' 'Fine. It's probably nothing. But when I was at the supermarket yesterday, I saw my old Norwegian teacher. And he didn't say hello.' I hesitate. Is that it? Is that what she wanted to tell me? It can't be right – she regrets starting down this path, so now she's making something up. 'Okay? So he probably just didn't recognize you?' 'Oh, he recognized me all right.' 'Is it really that big a deal? Maybe he has dementia. Or he's visually impaired.' 'Maybe. But I think it was because I had the kids with me.'

Even though it's a long time since we did it on impulse and because we simply couldn't help ourselves, I might still hold Helene's hand when we're out and about. But when we have the kids with us, I don't want to. I'm not afraid anything will happen, but I just can't stand the thought of glowering old men, the idea that someone might think: Those poor, innocent children.

But it isn't like Helene to think like this. Not even after the terrorist attack have I ever heard her express concern that our kids won't be supported and accepted. And still I don't take it seriously, it's the relief speaking when I cheerfully reply: 'Well, if that's the case, then he's an idiot. Fuck him.' And then the words blurt out of me: 'Had I been there, I would have snogged your face off. A hot, steamy French kiss, right there in the middle of the supermarket.'

Because again, it dawns on me: I miss her. I often don't, but as long as I can still miss her, remember how I've felt close to her and why, surely there's still hope for us? A deep, deep need. I've spoken to her every day for over nine years, sent thousands of texts, probably had some form of contact with her every other hour, at least. Without her, I'd be like one of those brainwashed fundamentalist Mormon girls who lift the skirts of their prairie dresses and climb over the walls of their sect's fortification in Utah and flee, and afterwards sit in front of a Netflix camera crew, explaining that being outside the walls, moving around America, was like entering a foreign country.

But saying the thing about the snogging – that was clearly going too far. She laughs, a strained laugh, as if I'm gross, as if I'm a stranger coming on to her. 'You don't have to say that.'

And then it's as if all the strength goes out of me. I have no desire to say another word. She should be *happy* when I say things like that, it's something she's said many times too: 'I wish you'd make it a little clearer that it's me you want. Like before.'

What is she doing up there in Trøndelag? What is she saying to her parents, her childhood friends? Are they deliberating, telling her: Now's your chance, you're back on your feet after the birth and the affair, right now Silje Marie is sorting through everything you own, and that's good, a break-up is bad enough without all the extra logistics, but now you have an opportunity, Helene, to get away. Maybe you can even find yourself a woman brave enough to drive a car!

'Well, anyway,' I say. 'I need to get back to work if I'm going to get everything done.'

WE RENT OUR CAR ON A MONTHLY BASIS. It's expensive – at least as expensive as buying and owning one – but on the flipside we don't have to think about insurance or getting it serviced, the rental company takes care of all that. Someone from the company books the car in for its MOT and necessary tyre changes; the only thing we have to do is turn up. 'We've been booked in to get the tyres changed to the summer ones on the third of May at ten o'clock,' Helene said as we were sitting at the dining table one Sunday evening, making a meal plan for the following week and going through bills and other logistics. 'That's on Wednesday.' 'Okay,' I said. 'So does that mean you can move some things around, or?' Of course I knew that this wasn't what she was communicating. But I felt I had to let her know. *You can't just take it for granted that I'll do this. You know how scared I am of driving into central Oslo.* 'Surely you can manage it,' Helene said. 'It's only in Økern! We've driven there loads of times!' I shook my head. 'It would be fine if it was just me,' I said, 'but I'll have to take Henry with me. I don't want to risk driving with him in the car while I'm on my own. If he starts screaming and I'm not sure where I'm going, I'll freak out and crash the car.' 'Jesus Christ,' Helene said. She rolled her eyes, and I understood why – I would have rolled my eyes myself, had I not meant what I said so sincerely. 'You can just use Google Maps,' Helene went on, 'and then you give him a dummy, and you'll have a lovely calm drive, it's not in rush hour, and you manage to drive to the garden centre, don't you?' 'That's just down the road,' I said, 'out here, in the middle of nowhere. It's not the same.' 'Are you actually telling me I have to reschedule my work day because you can't manage a ten-minute drive? That I'll have to ask one of the receptionists to call a whole load of patients and apologize, tell them unfortunately we won't be able to see them that day, so could we please arrange another appointment?' 'Of course I don't want you to have to do that,' I replied. 'But I'd also like it if you actually listened to me for once. Can't you just make the time?'

She didn't make the time. She convinced me. She cajoled, said we could go out and do a practice run together, and she acted tenderly and lovingly and said she understood, but that it really wasn't something to be anxious about, that Henry wasn't going to die or be paralysed or get whiplash, and she said I had to see it as a feminist issue, that I had to think of our grandmothers and all the women in our grandmothers' generation who never got their driving licence and therefore depended on their husbands to get from A to B. 'After all, this isn't Saudi Arabia, Mamma Silje,' she said, and we laughed a little, and it was soothing, and in the moment I thought: Fine. Let it go. This isn't something to make such a big fuss about.

But when the Wednesday rolled around, when it was after eight-thirty and Olav had been dropped off at kindergarten and Helene had run to catch the Metro to the city centre, and I sat there in the living room and looked at Henry, who was amusing himself stacking towers of blocks and knocking them down again, I felt as if I had just hours left to live. My bowels were loose, my pulse rapid; I was on the verge of tears, and I felt so fucking stupid for not having stood my ground. I swiped my way to M in my list of contacts and called her and said: 'I know this is ridiculous and I'm probably asking way too late and it might not even be your day off, but can I ask a favour?'

She had never been to my house. Before illness knocked us sideways in April, I had refrained from inviting her and Nicolai here, perhaps due to the little decency I had left, loyalty to Helene, and towards my children – towards Olav, Henry's actual brother. I hadn't allowed Nicolai to sit in Olav's cobalt-blue high chair. Nicolai hadn't been permitted to play with Olav's toys. And I hadn't wanted to risk them bumping into any of the neighbours, and the neighbours later saying to Helene: 'I saw you had visitors earlier today – family, was it?'

Just text me when you get off the Metro, I wrote, *and I'll meet you by the garages. Okay*, Mayliss replied, but as I knelt in the hallway, trying to force Henry into his mustard-yellow wool babygrow, I suddenly heard a knock at the door. I looked up and out through the oblong window beside it, and there she stood. She waved, and I immediately felt her beaming radiance settle over me, how relieved and happy I was to see her, this big, crazy woman who had dropped everything to help me. When I invited her to come into the hallway and wait, she was beside herself. 'Shit, look at this place!' she said. 'You guys have a *house*! And that garden! It's so nice!' 'Yes,' I replied, anxiously, 'or at least, it will be. Once we've redecorated.' But I didn't say anything about the cheap materials and the previous owners' terrible taste – I had at least that much sense.

'Can I come in and have a look around?' she asked, and I knew, even before I glanced at the clock and said we didn't have time because I was afraid we were going to be late, that she couldn't, not now – she could not enter the house. Fitness Guri had once been in our home, it happened just before we were found out, when I was at my most obsessed, when I was convinced she was some kind of erotic guardian angel who was going to lead me to a new life, a paradise where I had multiple orgasms in a pounding rush and needed no other nourishment than affirmation that I was passionate and exciting and unpredictable. And how I regret it, how wholeheartedly I wish I could take it back. I wish she hadn't seen Helene's jackets hanging in the hallway, the poster of *The Dying Dandy* Helene had bought when we visited Stockholm for the first time, the old Rollerblades she'd brought back from Trøndelag before she was pregnant, not to take up roller derby, but to train so she could take part in a kind of rollerblading race with Sunniva in Berlin. I wish Fitness Guri hadn't seen all the things Helene had stuck on the fridge, like the *Remember to change sim card* note and the ultrasound image of our unborn son – she shouldn't have seen any of it.

'So where's Nicolai?' I asked, when we were sitting in the car and Mayliss reversed out of the parking space with the technique and confidence of a truck driver, turning to look over her shoulder and with one arm over the passenger seat, even though our car had a reversing camera. 'He's with my brother,' she said, and this was the first time she had given that answer, it was usually always her mother who looked after Nicolai. She'd hardly mentioned her little brother, and immediately I felt the pangs of jealousy I always feel when people say they have a close relationship with their siblings, and I thought about my sister, Auntie Camilla, my fucked-up sister who lives under Mamma's spell, and who has lived there so long that I've long since given up trying to save her, or hoping she might become something other than a parrot who repeats everything Mamma says.

From his car seat in the back, Henry made no sound. The heater gradually warmed up. 'Why don't you put some music on?' Mayliss said as we turned onto the main road. 'But no kids' stuff, I can't take any more Cardamom Town.' 'So what do you want to listen to?' I asked, because it was her taste that must be prioritized now, she who must be satisfied, Mayliss, hero of the day, and I noted how I almost felt moved – yes, moved. 'I can't believe you're doing this for me,' I blurted, 'I just can't tell you how much I appreciate it.' 'Oh, stop it,' she said. 'It's really no big deal. It's just nice to be able to help out. I'm in the service industry, as you know!' She smiled, and in that smile – what was it I glimpsed, was there something mournful? Was there something loving? Yes – wasn't there? Yes, might that be why she was here? Had she begun to fall in love with me? No, Jesus Christ, I thought, I really need to pull myself together. Joachim would have told me I was being conceited again.

H OW FAR MIGHT HELENE GO? When I tell her that Mayliss's son isn't just a son. That the brief conversations we've had about Mayliss have been on false grounds, that I've misled her, concealed the most important details, revealed her child's identity without her permission. That I haven't discussed something with her, had the conversation, talked through what it means, that these half-siblings exist, and what we'll say to the kids if we bump into them. How we can reassure our children so they aren't thrown into an existential crisis when they realize what it means to be created in the image of a man who is reckless with his genes – genes that, frozen in containers which must be kept at temperatures below –196°C, are shipped all over Europe?

Of course she'll understand that Henry will be none the worse for having spent time with Nicolai – if we break off contact, both he and Mayliss will soon be forgotten – that isn't what this is about, this is between us, first and foremost it's between us, but who knows what Mayliss might do. Perhaps she won't accept being cut off, maybe she'll continue to send me texts and photos and suggestions for things we might do. Maybe she'll begin stalking us. Make the journey out here in August when Henry has started at kindergarten and hang around outside the playground and wave to him over the fence, or leave a letter for him – *Dear Henry, we miss you so much.* Or maybe she'll tell everyone: Nicolai has a half-brother with two mothers out in Bydel Østensjø, and his other mother is a fucking cunt. It isn't likely, presumably none of this is, but I don't know for certain, because I don't know her, and still I've let her in, still I've given her my address and let her sit in my car and take Henry onto her lap when I've gone to the loo: a stranger. It didn't feel that way in the moment, but to Helene she will be a stranger.

The only person I truly know, the one person I've been with through thick and thin, remained close to in all conceivable situations, is Helene.

And she will want to punch me. She won't. But she'll want to.

Because, sooner or later, violence finds its way in, like when water trickles from a tiny crack in an old pipe deep in a wall. Damp spreads beneath the floorboards and insulation, and slowly, imperceptibly, the house becomes rotten to the core. In recent years Helene has started throwing things in anger, or snatching them from me in a way that makes me disconsolate, not just because it reminds me of being a child, but because it's obvious that she no longer cares about making an effort, because she despises me, and who can blame her? But she can't just leave me, because then she'll not only have to give up the dream of the house the architect has designed for us, with solid oak floors, with built-in furniture, with a garden and wispy apple trees, and not only will all the knowledge we've gained about each other, all the conversations we've had in order to know one another better and solve conflicts and make our love stronger, be for nothing, no: she will lose the children. In our worst moments, we hate each other because the other's existence means that if we don't behave, if we don't follow

224

the rules and uphold the values we so passionately promised to build our life upon when we were young and naïve and stood there before the officiant in the courthouse and looked deep into each other's eyes, we might lose the right to participate in half our children's lives.

So we have to stay, we have to find a solution, we have to stick it out – even when Henry has a stomach bug and diarrhoea, the shit stains seeping through his clothes. She asks me for help, he's screaming, I'm exhausted, I've been up since four-thirty, but I help her, she says she has to give him a shower, asks me to get a clean towel, but the cupboard is empty, nothing gets done if I don't do it, and all at once I'm so angry, I sling the damp bath towel back into the shower cubicle and it falls next to Henry as I storm out to find the laundry, the clean, dry items I've done everything with except put away, they're on the stairs, nothing ever gets done if I don't do it. 'Why did you throw the towel at him?' she says, 'I didn't – do you really think I'd throw something at him?' I shout, 'Then why are you stomping around,' she says. 'You always throw things when you're annoyed,' I bellow, 'now it's your turn to see how it feels.' 'I think you need to shut up,' she says, 'just leave.' I leave. Go out, fold some more laundry, return again. 'You know, it isn't very nice,' I say, 'you telling me to shut up.' Ice cold with scorn, she replies: 'It was for your own good.' And suddenly I realize I want to retaliate, because every time she behaves this way towards me, I want to hit back. What's it going to be next? Alone, I tap my knuckles against my cheekbones in the shower. Think: I can't take any more can't take any more can't take any more. But downstairs sunlight floods the living room, and we have visitors, it's our relatives, Great Aunt Mary, Grandma and Grandpa, my cousins, a cream cake with kiwi on it, and Mamma stands over me, she stands over me and talks and talks and talks and says now you had better behave yourself, and the ceiling lights shine brightly, and the sunlight streams in, and there is nowhere to hide.

E VERY TIME HELENE sits scrolling on my phone, I notice that I grow irritated and uneasy, even though I know she won't find anything. If she opens the text exchange between me and MAYLISS (baby music), she'll discover not a single sign that I'm keeping something from her, there's nothing but practical details: where to meet, minor delays, the odd cancellation because Nicolai or Henry is ill. The photo of the boys in the sandpit I've deleted. And in my camera roll there isn't so much as a shred of evidence that Nicolai and Mayliss even exist.

When Olav was little, I remember Helene sitting on the sofa with my phone, and that her voice was fragile and somehow entirely defenceless when she asked: 'Why do you never take photos of me any more?'

Now she's the one who no longer takes photos of me.

When Janne and her family were here just after we'd moved into the house, and Janne and I were in the kitchen arranging salmon and scrambled eggs on the large glass plates we would soon carry out into the autumnally yellow garden, she could see that I was distraught. 'I think it's possible to love in many ways,' she said. 'The two of you have time to figure all this out. In the meantime, I think you should maximize what actually works between you, all the good stuff. There's no guarantee that either of you would find all that with someone else.'

*

She was right, of course. Like how Helene and I agree that the children shouldn't have an iPad. Like the way we laugh until we cry at *Peep Show* and Louis C.K. We disapprove of people who join online pile-ons without thinking. We agree that the floors and the kitchen need replacing. When we have sushi, we order twice as many of the pieces we both like best. We're not ashamed to go on package holidays, to crowd around the children's performers in their big Lollo and Bernie costumes. We don't speak ill of each other in front of the kids. She reminds me that the kids shouldn't hear me speak ill of myself, either. She doesn't give a damn about social media. She gets me out on my skis when I want to stay home, she always carries Henry's car seat and our heaviest item of luggage. She never says she's noticed that I've put on weight, even though my jeans no longer fit me. She lets me read the *A-magasinet* weekend supplement first. She fishes hair from the drain after she's showered. She makes a bread dough every other night. She's taught Olav how to floss. Encountering opposition doesn't paralyse her. Had I been beaten and robbed after going home with another woman following a night on the town, I think she still would have come and got me.

But the fact that I did what I did, and that she took me back – it's shaken not just how she sees me, but how she sees herself. And how I see her. That she can bear to have me in the house despite my black moods and my lies, not to mention my body – it's as if it's killed off any interest I had in hearing what she thinks about films or books or debates; if she says she thinks I'm smart or gorgeous, I almost feel provoked. When she undresses for the night, I silently turn away.

And she – she no longer snuggles up to me, or offers me an arm to lie on.

IN THE ROMCOMS, there are only two possible outcomes to the infidelity plot. One partner in the relationship betrays the other, but the betrayal is revealed, then they're done, and the partner who was betrayed is freed and thereby promised a happier future. Or – and this happens far more rarely – one party betrays the other, and after much deliberation, said party is forgiven, because the betrayal was an obvious deviation from the original love story, and everything works out for the better, happily ever after. Who stays for fear of losing their life's witness? Who can deny the value of weeknight dinners, or having a mother-in-law who calls you her own daughter, or crowding together in a chaotic quartet, each brandishing a toothbrush, in front of the sink?

I remember I once sat on the Metro, listening to a podcast where people could submit their ethical dilemmas to a panel of psychologists. *My husband shows no interest in me no matter what I do, and I'm so unhappy, but I feel I should stay in the relationship for the sake of our kids,* one listener wrote in. One of the psychologists, a woman with an arrogant, nasal voice, took the floor. 'I myself am happily divorced,' she declared, 'and I've never heard a child say they wished their mother had stayed miserable so they could have a better life.' When I repeated the psychologist's ridiculous lie to Janne, we couldn't help but laugh. 'Maybe she ought to start by having a chat with her own kids,' Janne said. 'Just a little tip from me.'

Who will be happy if we end up divorced, and every Friday afternoon the kids have to troop over to one or the other of our homes, their overstuffed rucksacks on their little backs? Who can claim that while it might be a little awkward at first, it will mostly prove enriching, should we find ourselves new partners and they end up with not just two mother figures, but four?

And not only that. Four mother figures, four women who make demands of them. But no father. Only half-siblings, half-siblings everywhere. To be doomed to a life where they are never able to move through the world at peace, without studying other people's faces, without wondering if they might be related to someone in the room.

AISHA97 WANTS TO BUY the bundle of baby clothes I've advertised for sale online. They're mostly pink and purple, but out of principle I post the ad under the category Unisex. We inherit almost all the clothes that Helene's brother's girls have grown out of, pay nothing for the waterproofs and high-quality wool items in exchange for Helene's brother and his wife not having to sort through them first. Which is why we're also flush with skirts and dresses. Olav loved them when he was younger, and for a long time we let him wear whatever he wanted, of course we did, we were proud he wasn't just interested in fire engines and Captain Sabertooth but also in *The Little Mermaid* and Elsa from *Frozen* – he wanted to listen to 'Let It Go' on repeat, asked us to braid his hair, and stood before the mirror wearing his cousins' old tiara and Disney powder-blue gloves. He still thinks it's fun to wear a dress, I know that, even if he's careful not to say so out loud. But I no longer let him leave the house in them. Not because I think it's inappropriate for four-year-old boys to wear dresses, or because I'm particularly afraid of how the other kids at the kindergarten will react, but because I noticed the looks from all the older neighbours when Olav ran around beneath our apple trees in his Elsa dress last spring. That's what happens, they were thinking, that's what happens to boys who grow up in that kind of house.

H ELENE AND I WERE MADE FOR EACH OTHER. Everyone said so. Even though she was taller than me, we could borrow each other's clothes. We matched. Check shirts, straight-leg jeans – no bra, but eyeliner and the same lipstick. The same hairstyles. Same playlists. We reached towards one another, did everything we could to create a story about us that was impenetrable, solid, multifaceted. I accompanied her wherever she went, turned up in sequins to her work Christmas party, tried CrossFit even though I was about as fit as a guinea pig in a tiny cage. And she would usually join me in what I wanted to do. She came to Copenhagen because it was my city, went to a drag show with Joachim, kissed me in front of the marble statues at the Glyptotek. She accompanied me to a ranch in Wyoming, even though she finds horses far too large and skittish. She sang karaoke with me in a basement in Stockholm, 'Something Stupid'; I was Robbie Williams, she Nicole Kidman. She came with me to Sotra, back home to see Mamma, and smiled through gritted teeth as we ate beef with Béarnaise sauce while Mamma complained about all the conspiracies launched against her; said not a single word about how Mamma had treated me, treated her. She was my partner, my support. And we were beautiful. In the wedding photo we are beautiful, the two wedding dresses pressed against each other there at the bus stop, they are beautiful. You can see we belong together. But then the kids came along. And now, when the children are with us, in the framed and displayed photographs of us and the boys... people can say what they like. But it doesn't look as good.

When Henry was a newborn, when we gained another son, who looked nothing like our first son, it was as if it became clear to me for the first time. The absence. The thing that jarred. I googled growing up without a father but didn't find much other than irrelevant articles about how the sons of American single mothers are at much higher risk of becoming criminals. It was simply by chance that I began to flick through one of the books my GP had recommended to me several years ago, about attachment in young children, and which told how in the 1960s researcher Donald Winnicott wrote not only about the children of violent mothers, but also, I now noticed, about the differences he observed in how men and women interact with their children. The play of fathers is far more unpredictable and physical – fathers joke around, tussle and frighten children with high-spirited roaring and chasing in which children take great delight – all the stuff that somehow never occurs to women as they sit there on their soft textiles, babbling away, singing and playing peekaboo. It's utterly typical for women to play peekaboo.

I have never wanted to be a man. And when we only had Olav, the thought never crossed my mind that two mothers wouldn't be enough.

But when Henry's neck was strong enough for him to hold his head up, I began lifting him as high as I could, and when I no longer had the necessary muscle mass to dare throw him up into the air – since the training group at work had dissolved, I hadn't lifted a single weight – I sent a text to the personal trainer a colleague of Helene's had recommended. I thought and thought about how Henry would have reacted if my voice were deeper, my cheeks prickly with stubble. I observed how a father at the children's clinic put his baby over his shoulder as if he were carrying a little Christmas tree – the baby laughed, and later I tried the same thing with Henry. I bought a football when the garden was deep in snow. I fought the impulse to tell Olav to be careful when climbing or balancing on things. When the personal trainer had whipped me back into shape, I lifted Olav as high as I could above my head and swung him around in the air. Every time I saw Helene playing peekaboo with Henry, I pretended to turn into a ravenous monster.

To us, OLAV WAS the first and only, but for Helene's parents he was number three – Helene's brother already had two girls. I said nothing about it to Helene, but before they came to visit us once we were home from the hospital, I was nervous they wouldn't be able to hide that they didn't know how to relate to a child to whom they had no biological ties, created within a familial form that had only existed for a few decades.

They arrived a quarter of an hour early. From the bed I heard my mother-in-law's low but excited murmurings as they washed their hands; they knocked gently before they came into the bedroom, where Olav had fallen asleep at my breast after feeding. 'My oh my,' my mother-in-law sighed. 'Have you ever seen anything so tiny!' 'Oh, come to Grandpa,' my father-in-law said. He carefully lifted Olav and cradled him in his movingly large hands, rocked him, his third grandchild. The winter sky above Torshov was an intense pink, orange and gold through the window behind him, as if a gigantic lava lamp had exploded out there.

Helene sat beside me in the bed and kissed the top of my head. I don't think we've ever acted so lovingly towards each other as we did in those first days of parenthood. 'We're actually considering naming him Olav,' Helene said. 'After my father?' my mother-in-law asked. 'It's a good, strong name,' I said. I thought about my own grandparents – they too had good, strong names. Why hadn't I insisted that we go for one of them, was I really so afraid that

Helene's side of the family would feel the child was more mine than hers? And Helene – wasn't it for her sake that I had suggested Olav should have both our surnames, hyphenated, but with hers first, so they would appear together on alphabetical lists? Whatever, I thought, it doesn't matter.

Three years later, after Henry had been cut out of her by emergency C-section, I sat in the armchair beside Helene in her hospital bed and watched her parents as they studied our teeny-tiny son. I said nothing on this occasion, either, about how I looked for signs that this time they were even happier. And had I seen such signs – wouldn't it have been understandable? Would I have been able to blame them? The only person to blame for anything was my own mother, who once again was apparently out of range when I sent the first text along with Henry's photo, weight and measurements. It was almost a week before we heard anything back, when a delivery man appeared at the door with a bouquet of flowers so big it could have lain on a coffin. *I sincerely hope I'll get to meet you one day, my dear boy*, the card said. *With love, Grandma.*

OF COURSE, I REALIZED that Mayliss didn't have much money. It was evident in the way she always said she'd pay me back every time I bought our coffees or squeezy pouches of smoothie or bottles of Pepsi Max, but never did until I reminded her. Or how she laughed at the prices in the high-end supermarket. Or how, just after she had given birth, she spent a small fortune getting Nicolai's date of birth tattooed on her calf, instead of buying Nicolai a proper sleeping bag for his pram. She was a fat, Hicksville lesbian in cheap, ugly clothes. She said: 'Nicolai is growing so fast – you don't have any spare clothes, do you? I know you probably want to keep Olav's things for Henry, but if you have anything you can afford to do without!' And I, I took several pairs of size 24 shoes from home, two sizes bigger than Henry's, and said: 'But just to borrow.' I gave Nicolai some of Henry's good-quality wool leggings with anti-slip feet, and acted as if I'd just been waiting for an excuse to clear out his overstuffed drawers. I treated her to Thai food and nappies because she'd forgotten her debit card. I said: 'They say it's going to be over twenty degrees tomorrow. Let's go to the outdoor pool in Frogner. Don't worry about the ticket – I'll get it.'

In May, she said: 'Hey, do you think you could lend me some money so I can buy Nicolai a Constitution Day outfit? I'll pay you back next week, after I've been paid.' I said I could have a look in the loft for Olav's sailor suit – it was too big for Henry at the moment anyway.

I told Helene that Olav's old sailor suit had mysteriously vanished without trace. 'I can go into town and buy something for Henry tomorrow,' I said. Helene replied that that would be nice. Helene suspected nothing. And what was there to suspect? I'd done nothing wrong. I'd done nothing wrong, and yet a tingling rush flooded my body when Mayliss and I were waiting for the Metro in Majorstuen and I saw one of Helene's sleek, eternally single friends from her dentistry course coming towards us. She smiled her bright white smile and bent down over Henry in his pram and talked about how big he'd got and how long it was since she'd seen us; how we simply had to get together soon, go over to her place for dinner or for a drink. 'Yes!' my voice replied 'Oh, yes, absolutely, that would be great!'

My blood bubbled. I felt giddy, dazed. She hardly cast a glance at Mayliss; took no interest in Nicolai. But what if she had? Or what if it had been Helene who had popped up, bumped into us just now? It was as if I'd laced up my skates and set off across a frozen fjord, skated further and further out, and now I no longer knew which direction I needed to go to get back on land, and it was frightening, but in it there was also the promise of change, the crossing of a line, like the insane moment when the boat being sailed by Jim Carrey's character in *The Truman Show* hits the edge of the TV studio in which he's been held captive his entire life, and he sets his hands against the fake sky for the very first time.

When Helene's friend had boarded her train, Mayliss said: 'She seems nice.' For the first time, didn't she seem a bit aloof, embarrassed? Yes – and wasn't that why she tugged at the hem of her sweater a little, pulling it down over her round hips? 'Oh her? She's a friend of Helene's, I don't really like her all that much,' my voice said. 'She's a real snob.'

I think it was right after this that she sent the photograph. Of our boys, playing in the sandpit. It was a completely ordinary evening. Helene and I were sitting on the sofa, trying to find something to watch on HBO, when suddenly my phone vibrated and lit up next to the bowl of Spanish paprika-flavoured crisps. I opened the text without thinking about it, and there they were, those two little boys, those two unsuspecting little boys, and I didn't understand why she had sent it to me – for one thing it wasn't a very good photo, you could hardly see their faces – but the terror, all at once it flooded me, like water forcing its way through a crack in a dam: it was the first photograph of them together I had seen. And I didn't even know that she had taken it. 'What about *Billions*?' Helene said. 'Shall we give it another chance?' 'No – it was so ridiculous when Axelrod and that lawyer joined forces,' my voice replied. 'Check Netflix – maybe we can watch *Real Housewives* or something?' *Nico asked after Henry before he fell asleep*, Mayliss texted.

O N FRIDAY I can finally make a start on the thing I've been most looking forward to: ripping up the floors, tearing up the parquet, the laminate, all the cheap, shitty materials that have been slapped on top of the house's original structure. I shove furniture out of the way, I work quickly. Pappa taught me how to use a crowbar – we pulled down the rotten woodshed together when he was here last year. He stayed for three days, but Olav never dared to sit on his lap.

When I'm done with the TV room upstairs, I open the window and throw out the parquet from up there. The planks hit the grass with a dull thud. There's no need to check whether anyone's down there first. If only Pappa could see me now. And the boys. And my parents-in-law. Just look at how hard she's working, they'd think. Just look at all the effort she's going to for our Helene.

M Y HANDS SHAKE as I set the crowbar against the skirting
board that lines the wall where the sofa usually stands.
I've been working for hours, and there's no question that I need
to get myself some dinner. I wheel my bike out of the garden, not
a neighbour in sight – only the pair of magpies that live in the fir
tree beside the mailboxes. It feels wonderful to cycle. Even out here,
among the apartment blocks and terraced houses entirely devoid
of charm, devoid of nerve, I feel myself grow calm. I feel happier.
I should get out on my bike more often. It's an e-bike, and the bat-
tery power gives me a sense of freedom. The European borders are
within reach, signs for Gothenburg and Stockholm not so far from
here. Before the kids came along, Helene and I cycled to Denmark
via Sweden one long, bright summer. I wish we were still bent over
our handlebars, pumping our feet out there beside the Skagerrak.

Of course I know where Marka is. We've been swimming there
and everything. But only in June, towards the end of my maternity
leave, did I take Henry out to the forest. The sun was baking hot.
He sat in his pushchair, I looked for signs that he was tired, so I
could recline the seat without him noticing – that was our routine.
I walked quickly. He didn't seem tired. Now he pointed at something. 'Eee,' he said, 'eee.' I turned to look in the direction he was
pointing; saw the newly erected electric fence first, then the horses.
There were three of them, two Icelandic horses and a Fjord horse.
A summer pasture. I wanted to stop, to open Henry's lunchbox

and coax them to us using his sandwiches, but I didn't, I simply exclaimed, 'Look at the horses, Henry!' and kept walking. There's a reason horses are used in treatment therapies for the mentally unstable. The calmness and beauty of the horse – there can hardly be a nobler creature. I would so love to introduce horses to the kids' lives. The children's farm offers pony rides – I once took a photo of Olav riding a black pony and sent it to Mamma; she sent me a heart emoji in reply. And right then, I felt it. I felt it like a divine presence – her motherly love, her longing, the fear she has carried with her for her entire life, and which has made her into a person who lies and tramples over all boundaries because she'll do anything to avoid others catching so much as a glimpse of it. I had an intense desire to text her something heartfelt, *Dear Mamma, I'm sorry things are the way they are between us*, something like that, but before I could think any more about how I might formulate the message, the photos began to ding in, of my sister, and of my sister's son, on the terrace at my mother's house, in the snow with a huge Easter egg in his hands, all topped off with a passive-aggressive message: *Luckily Grandma has SOMEBODY who bothers to come and visit her, have a nice day*.

THERE'S THIS PREVAILING NOTION that lesbians were never mad about horses when they were little. It was the first girl I ever kissed, the one from Askøy, who introduced me to this theory. I told her I'd come to the cinema straight from the stables. 'Are you sure you like girls?' she asked. This first date of ours felt like one single, long evaluation, in which she was the experienced high-ranking officer who was sceptically observing me in order to reveal that I was just a confused fifteen-year-old, who thought I liked girls because none of the boys at school thought I was pretty. What do I know, I thought, maybe she's right. But when we sat under the bus shelter at Bystasjonen, she began to laugh. 'No, just look at you!' she exclaimed. 'What?' I replied. She pointed at the heel of my shoe, resting atop my opposite thigh. 'Clearly I was wrong,' she said, 'no straight girl sits like that!'

Pappa was the one who was opposed to me getting involved with horses. I don't think it was the horses he was afraid of, but rather Mamma's reaction to me thinking I'd outgrown the Scouts. But Mamma let me quit. To think that she did that, entirely free of any sanctions. Without speaking, she drove me to the stables every Thursday and came and picked me up again two hours later. I got a riding helmet for Christmas. For many years, it was these images that caused me to feel the most guilt, and which still make me feel guilty: she picked me up every week. And, even though I broke her heart, as she used to put it, she gave me a riding helmet.

I HAD ACTUALLY INTENDED on cycling all the way into the city centre, but as I rush down the main road, which has a turnoff for a McDonald's, I change my mind. The McDonald's has a drive-through – I love it, I've been here many times since we moved, in the car with Helene, two medium Big Mac meals, no pickle, Coke Zero for me, an apple juice for Helene.

I cycle in behind a red car and wait until the driver has made his order before I wheel my bike up to the speaker system located beneath the blown-up menu with its retouched close-ups of junk food. When the car has driven to the next window, I catch the eye of the teenage boy who, ten metres ahead of me and inside the building, is taking the orders. I wave at him, laugh a little, I must look like a total idiot, cycling into a drive-through, what a ridiculous situation this is. 'Yes, hello,' I say into the microphone, waiting for him to say, 'Welcome to McDonald's,' but no sound emerges from the speaker. I wave again – the teenager really is looking straight at me, but he doesn't react, he doesn't even throw up his arms or send me any other form of signal, and I get it, I get that it's my bike that breaks with his job description.

Oh, how Helene would have laughed if she could see me now. She'd say: 'That's so typical of you! They should see you at work, where you're the one who's known for being a stickler for the rules.'

*

Of course I ought to keep going, bike into town, pick up an Indian takeaway in Grønland or a bánh mì baguette in Løkka, eat it on a bench during a pause in the rain, watch the summer tourists, the dealers, the pigeons – it's the afternoon, I'm alone, she can't see what I'm doing, she said it herself, that I ought to treat myself, take a break. Maybe I could go to the cinema, or to a concert, if there's anyone performing in the middle of the summer, or I could just cycle around, past the Opera House, around Vippetangen, just be there beside the fjord in the damp summer light, because that's when I tend to think that, in spite of everything, I love Oslo after all.

Or I could have stopped by Glasmagasinet, found a gift for Mamma and sent it by tracked post in the morning, so she'll receive a text that something is on its way from me to her, even though it will take a while before the gift is delivered, and it'll probably be way past her birthday by the time she's able to open it. Still, it's the thought that counts.

Instead, I'm sitting here, in suburbia, inside McDonald's, my bike helmet and a tower of French fries on the table before me, my fingers sticky with sauce. Before we moved out of the city, I never would have thought we'd be able to regularly eat McDonald's without being drunk. Nor would Helene – she'd studied nutrition for an entire year, and only recently gave up her membership of Friends of the Earth. What happened to my principles? Do I even have any? When I interviewed for my job, my boss had said: 'It's all well and good an applicant having exceptional grades. But I don't actually care much about that. Someone who got a C can be just as good as someone who got an A or a B. What I'm looking for is someone down to earth and honest.'

At the time, I'd actually thought this was a perfect description of me.

I don't understand people who manage to be consistent, who without exception act in accordance with the values they hold dear. While I, well, often it doesn't take much – after a couple of glasses of wine I'm tipsy enough to stop by the Narvesen newsagents and buy a bacon hotdog made from tortured pigs with no qualms at all. When I see a beggar rattling his cup, I reject him far more easily when I'm alone than if I'm in the company of a friend. But there's no point in judging myself too harshly, as if my actions weigh more heavily than anyone else's. Because who among us manages to hold onto our ideals, when nobody sees us or life gets tough? When Danish pork is on special offer at a quarter of the price of the organically farmed stuff? The couples therapist closes the curtains and tells his wife to shut up or else. Exhausted after a long day, the feminist activist flops down in front of her computer, opens a private browser window and types: *Pornhub*. The pregnant dentist learns that her marriage might be about to unravel and stops flossing, even though she knows how easily her gums become inflamed. The first evening after Helene moved back in with me, I saw that she finished brushing her teeth by wiping tiny flecks of blood off the sink.

B ECAUSE MAINTENANCE is being done on the Metro lines, there's a replacement bus service during the summer. At the bus stop outside McDonald's, the old people sit huddled together. They don't speak to one another. They look so dismal. How many of them are grandparents? How many of them have no contact with their grandchildren?

Sometimes I think of the donors' parents, who presumably go about their lives without the slightest inkling that their sons have given away the family's valuable genetic inheritance. I imagine them walking around – perhaps they're on a weekend trip to Barcelona or Paris, or simply in their home village in the Danish countryside – and then, on the street or in a restaurant, they catch sight of a child or teenager with facial features that fill them with warmth and nostalgia, without them understanding why.

The fact that Mamma isn't going to get to know Olav. That's what eats me up. I hardly ever think about the fact that she doesn't know Henry either. Because Olav looks like my uncle. Olav looks like me. And I look like my mother.

In the time before I became pregnant, even when Mamma had early-stage cancer in her left breast, our relationship grew ever more strained, with several periods in which she and I alternately cut contact. The lead-up to each break in contact was demanding – when the toxic texts streamed in, I could hardly concentrate at work, couldn't reach orgasm, couldn't eat sugar without glimpsing Mamma on the other side of the table.

My homophobic GP looked at me sympathetically and said: 'You need to practise tolerating this pain. Because it isn't dangerous, even if it feels that way.'

Most of my friends knew how things were – I'd spent countless hours analysing and recounting and despairing – but still the most common reaction to my pregnancy was for a kind of hopeful light to flicker in their eyes. 'Don't you think things will become much better between the two of you,' they said, 'when your mother becomes a grandmother?' People acted as if there was only one solution, a single ideal – as if the only thing I wanted was reconciliation, for us to put the past behind us and embrace. That I would give birth to this child, and a new era would begin. But I had no fantasies of reconciliation. I didn't even want to tell her I was pregnant. 'Never in its life,' I said to Joachim, 'is this kid going to call her Grandma.' 'I mean, that's what she is, though,' Joachim replied. 'And even if you get to be a grandmother, that doesn't mean you're released from all culpability. There are all kinds of grandmothers and grandfathers. I'm sure Hitler would have been a fantastic grandfather, too.' 'Oh knock it off,' I said, 'I'm not in the mood.'

Of course the doubts crept in. Of course I knew I couldn't keep it secret. But I wanted to tell her myself. I was a little over five months pregnant and on my way home from the office when I noticed the missed calls on my phone: MAMMA (9). I stopped. I felt as if I was sinking and receiving an electric shock at the same time, as if I was trussed up at the bottom of the sea somewhere with electric eels sewn into my growing belly. But the person who had divulged my secret was, of course, my sister.

I HAVE TO TELL HER MYSELF. I can't allow anyone else to reveal any of this. I'll beat Mayliss to it. I'll protect myself. There is a way to do this – why haven't I thought of it before? I feel lighter already. So light, as I float on my bike beside Østensjøvannet, where the swans glide around in the green mulch. How bad can it be? Like, bring it on. It's about my approach, the way I say it. Yes – I can simply tone it down a bit! You know, something occurred to me earlier when I was with that woman from baby music – her son, Nicolai, he really looks like Henry. Just think if they're brothers! And if she reacts in the way I know she can react, Helene, then she might simply begin to laugh, simply laugh at the absurd thought: Ha ha, yeah, just think, if that's true we'll have to start inviting them to family gatherings with your mother and everything! Ha ha!

I PULL UP THE REST OF THE FLOOR. Around the wood burner and the kitchen cabinets, in the dining area. It's like child's play. I've put on Pappa's Creedence LP at full blast. I'm high on my own decision. I can just play the whole thing down a bit! Embellish the truth a little! It doesn't have to be any harder than that – what have I been getting so paranoid about? Oh hi, how's it going? All the flooring is up now, the concrete is bare! Look, here I am in the middle of this huge, naked space!

I can still taste the McDonald's as I tug clothes from the drying rack in the laundry room. I pack. A flannel shirt. Three T-shirts, socks, underwear. Which jacket – my anorak? Or maybe I can borrow the blue Patagonia fleece I gave Helene for Christmas, the one she said she wanted but hardly ever wears.

I'll beat Mayliss to the punch. I'm going to come out of this just fine – I'll mention it as if it's the most insignificant thing in the world, and Helene will be slightly taken aback, perhaps ruminate on it a little afterwards, and she might ask what Nicolai is like, and what it is that makes me think they're so similar, and if I think it changes anything. She might wonder if it's actually a little strange, the fact that we've never properly spoken about the possibility of bumping into biological half-siblings, but she'll be nowhere close to falling into certain other chasms, and she'll feel no need to get in touch with Mayliss, because should Mayliss contact her and repeat any of the things I've told her, or say anything about the relationship between Henry and Nicolai, which I've ruined by cutting contact with her, then Helene will roll her eyes to herself and think, okay, that woman is *slightly* crazy, and she'll feel safe – almost superior. She'll feel she knows all there is to know, because I'll already have prepared her for both the possibility that Henry and Nicolai might be half-siblings, and that Mayliss isn't of entirely sound mind, and yes, perhaps even jealous of what Helene and I have together, and that's why I've decided to phase out this maternity-leave friendship of ours.

When should I do it – now? Or on Sunday?

I imagine how it will go. I'll have a good energy about me. Maybe even have put on some make-up. I'll walk towards Helene there in the arrivals hall with my wheeled suitcase and be outgoing and on the alert. I'll lean over the handbrake and give her a spontaneous kiss on the cheek as she takes the exit towards Stjørdal; laugh and wave towards my in-laws, who are waiting out on the front step; praise my mother-in-law's newly bleached hair. I'll hug my boys. Say that I love them. If they're not too occupied with showing me everything they've been playing with, that is. I'll get involved in their games. I'll build Lego and towers of blocks, listen to what Olav has to tell me, pull Henry onto my lap and patiently read him a picture book. Wipe the corners of Henry's mouth. Remind both of them to wash their hands. Take the shortcut from the farm and saunter through the forest with them to the local supermarket, where they can each choose an ice cream. If it's too far to walk, Henry can sit on my shoulders. If Olav whinges that it isn't fair, I'll do my best to not get irritated. If Henry throws a tantrum and casts himself onto his stomach in the middle of the path because he's finished his ice cream while Olav is only halfway down his cone, I won't threaten to leave him. Even if no small white stones illuminate the forest floor, I'll know which way we need to go. And afterwards, when we come back, I'll look at Helene in a sort of trustworthy way and say I have a funny thing to tell her.

Or – no. I'll ask Helene to come with us to the supermarket, so we can take the long way round past the neighbour's place and see his harness-racing horses. And while we're standing there under the open sky and feeding the horses grass through the electric fence, and when I'm sure the boys can't overhear, I'll start by saying that I've once again let down a friend. Yes, I'll actually call her a friend, the other mother, the woman from baby music. I will look Helene in the eye as I speak. I won't jump straight to the defensive if Helene's expression frightens me. I will stand there straight-backed and calm and take responsibility. It will be fine. It will be easy!

But the boys, when I FaceTime them, are arguing. Both of them want to hold the phone, and since Olav is loudest and strongest, he's usually the one to get his way. The image trembles and flickers – I can't see them, but I can hear them. 'I want to hold it,' Olav shouts. 'It's my turn!' Henry screams – he's furious. 'Mamma, we went blueberry picking,' Olav cries to make himself heard over his little brother's rage. 'Mamma can't hear you,' I say. Helene appears on the screen: 'If the pair of you can't behave, we're hanging up right now!'

It takes several minutes before she calls back. She's gone outside and is sitting on the front steps. 'Jesus,' she says, 'they're completely rabid today.' 'Uff,' I say, 'I know how it is.' She sighs. 'I'm already looking forward to the kindergarten opening again,' she says, 'this is going to be a long summer. But anyway. How are things going at the house?' 'Good,' I reply. 'Really good. I made a start on the floors today, and I've nearly finished them already.' Silence. For a moment I think the image is frozen, but then I see that her hair is moving, that the breeze is pulling a few locks of it across her face. She looks tired. Pale, as if it's winter. Her expression makes me nervous. 'The flooring was thin as cardboard and the glue was pretty bad, so I just ripped it up,' I continue. 'And the furniture is being picked up tomorrow. But I forgot to buy paint for the boys' room today, so I'll have to do that in the morning, and then I suppose I'll need to get the second coat done on Sunday, before I catch my flight.' 'Before you catch your flight,' Helene says.

Why is she saying it like that?

'Why are you saying it like that?' I ask. She doesn't reply, but she smiles in the sad, dejected way she smiles whenever she wants me to figure out the subtext for myself. She waits for me to go on. She waits, even though she knows I can't tolerate silence. That it triggers me, that it takes no more than this to make me start arguing like a teenage girl. 'What's up with you?' I ask. 'Are you in a bad mood? Have I done something wrong?' 'I don't know,' she replies, 'have you?' 'You must realize you're making me nervous now,' I say. 'About what?' Helene says. 'Do you even want me to come?' 'Do *I* want *you* to come? What I think,' she says, slowly, 'is that you're actually talking about yourself now.' 'What do you mean?' 'Well, what do you think I mean, Silje? Do *you* want to come? In all honesty?'

It's so strange. You long to be seen, you send out signals, like small, floating lanterns made of tissue paper, you want nothing more than to be found, fumbling around there in the forest with your despair and unbearable secrets, but when it happens, when the way out shows itself, you make a U-turn, you do everything within your power to remain concealed. 'How can you even say that?' I blurt out. 'I think that's a pretty fucking mean thing to say. Do I *want* to come? I've sacrificed this week for the sake of our family. I've spent this entire week here, working on the house to make it nice, to satisfy you so you can be *happy* here, so it will be up to your *standard*.'

I just can't help myself. My manipulative voice goes straight on the defensive, rattling off one pathetic thing after another. 'Yes, you have,' Helene replies. She looks off into the distance, away from the screen. 'And I have a bad feeling about it. Have you really spent all this week working on the house?' 'What else would I have been doing?' 'Well, you say you only just ripped up the floors today.' What the hell, I think. What is this? 'You're kidding, right?' I say. 'I've been working like a maniac ever since the three of you left. Do you have any idea how much stuff we own? Do you have any clue how long it took just to sort the clothes?' 'It isn't just this week. I've been thinking about it for a long time. Don't think I haven't noticed. You've been so distant. At the airport you didn't even want to kiss me goodbye. And then you're suddenly sending sweet messages, completely out of the blue, just like that. Is it the distance between us that makes you say you *miss me* and that you're *looking forward to seeing me*? Because you know what? I just don't buy it.'

I can't work out how to respond. I can't think, reflect, do anything at all. Her eyes – they flash. 'Is it her again?' 'Her?' I ask stupidly. 'Don't make me say her name. Ingrid. Ingvild. Or whatever the hell her name is.' 'Um, hello,' I say, 'have we really not moved on at all from this?' 'I don't know, Silje Marie, I just don't know. You tell me.'

Okay. Fine. If *that's* what she thinks of me. If she really thinks I've sunk so low.

I tell her I don't want to speak with her any more, not while she's in this mood. I tell her if she's going to be like that, then I may as well just call Norwegian Airlines and rebook my ticket and go somewhere else entirely. Then I hang up. Like a furious one-year-old I stomp aimlessly through the house, I want to go up into the loft, I want to open all the boxes and tip their contents across the floor up there, so the mouse traps snap shut over forks and cables and blankets, and the royal-blue ceramic cups from Lisbon, I'll bring them downstairs with me, I'll crack them and break them, I'll smash them to smithereens on the tiles that cover the bathroom floor, the stupid, worthless pieces of crap.

THE RUSH OF THE E6 FALLS SILENT AT NIGHT. I lie with my eyes wide open, as if my eyeballs have swollen and the lids grown too tight; they're pulled up of their own accord. I could just call Helene and come straight out with it. Right now. It's no more difficult than that. Presuming she doesn't have her phone on silent. But I'm angry. Who does she think she is? That she could even think I've got back in touch with Inghild. That I might do something like that again, after all we've been through.

I'm angry. But the self-inflicted sadness is worse. At the fact that Helene no longer sees me. That she doesn't want to see. And that she won't stand for it, should she actually open her eyes.

After lying there tossing and turning for a while, I get up and go pee without turning on the light. I glimpse my reflection in the darkness. The broad jaw, the low forehead – I fit right into the data collected by those researchers at Stanford and the AI program they developed to recognize gay and lesbian facial features. The program's accuracy is astonishing. I often wonder how long it'll be before it ends up in the hands of a regime that wants to persecute us.

If people only knew. If people only knew how I behave. How long would they keep on saying: Of course two women can be parents?

My hair isn't white. It's unkempt and dark blonde, grey at the temples. My eyes. That fucking mournful gaze. I see someone who never tells the truth. I see my mother. I see someone who is incapable of loving both her children.

I T'S A SATURDAY IN JULY. The girl is small. Maybe seven years old? Her father isn't home, he's offshore, in the North Sea. The girl and her mother and sister are going to the Sartor shopping centre. They go there every Saturday. The mother stands in front of the cupboard where they keep the sweets, and tells the girl to come here. The girl feels a shock of ice run through her. And she also feels hot. Because she's eaten everything in the bag, all the Daim – she's thrown the tiny wrappers in the waste bin in the bathroom. And her mother knows. She knows everything. She can see right through her. She can see through walls. She can see back in time. 'Do you know what we call people like you?' Her sister watches the scene play out. Her little sister. 'Go to your room,' the mother says. 'Sit there and think about what you've done.' The girl goes to her room. She feels ashamed. She feels so ashamed. She yearns. Her heart yearns and yearns. She hopes her mother will come into her room. So she can apologize, and then they can go to the shopping centre and everything can be as it was before. The girl loves her mother. She hates herself for disappointing her mother. Poor, poor, Mamma, the girl thinks. Then she hears the car start. She waits for her mother to come and get her. Her mother doesn't come. The girl runs to the window and sees the red car reversing out of the driveway. The girl is afraid. The girl needs to pee. The girl mustn't pee herself, but the girl cannot leave the room. The girl lies frozen still on her bed, for many hours, many years. When the girl hears the car, she lies there as if paralysed. She prays to God that her mother will hug her. Her mother opens the door. She smiles. The girl must come out now; she has to come and slice herself some cucumber, which she must sit and eat beside her little sister on the sofa, her little sister who is eating her Saturday sweets. When their mother is in the kitchen, the girl's little sister gives her a chocolate from the bag in secret. They are so stupid. They don't realize their mother can smell the chocolate on her breath. It's the girl's own fault. Her bottom stings. The girl pulls up her knickers and creeps into the ivy. Hears her father's footsteps out there. Apparently he isn't in the North Sea after all. Her father, who coaxes and then drags her out. 'Go and say you're sorry,' he says, softly, as if to a terrified horse in a burning stable. 'Now go and say you're sorry to Mamma.'

I T'S HER OWN FAULT: her mother says they can't feed the emaciated kitten that hangs around, howling, outside the house. And still she gives it liver pâté and milk. It has diarrhoea. Still she hides it in her room.

SATURDAY MORNING. The house is packed up. Out in the garden the construction-waste bag is overflowing, torn-up skirting board and parquet sticking up from the tall grass. I have bruises on my shins. I have to wear shoes indoors now, the naked concrete is rough. The Latvian decorator stops by to take a quick look while I'm trying to shovel down a crispbread; he says no thank you to coffee, goes from room to room to inspect and take measurements. The floor will be delivered as early as next week, he says, 'So that's very good for us.' There is an echo when he speaks. I wonder whether he has kids, I'm sure he does, a wife and children he's left behind in order to work here. I follow him, stop behind him in the boys' empty room. 'How about paint in this room?' I shake my head. 'I'm going to get that done today.'

It isn't Eastern Europeans, but two Swedes who come to pick up the furniture. They are young, cocky and muscular, but one of them has one of those belts around his waist that looks like the kind weightlifters use. They stick labels featuring QR codes onto everything, then scan them. Carry everything outside at breakneck pace, even though the guy with the belt is almost limping. I sit in the garden and watch them. I don't offer to help them with the carrying. It's raining, but no water droplets hit me.

EARLY IN JUNE, Henry and I went to see a puppet show for young children at the Oslo Public Library with Mayliss and Nicolai. Afterwards, we stopped by a playground. I was the only one who had brought along a packed lunch; I divided the food between them, a slice of bread spread with liver pâté and a segment of orange each. Nicolai gobbled down the orange. 'More,' he demanded, 'more!'

It was a completely ordinary day. The cherry trees were in bloom. Dogs on leads peed on lamp posts. Kindergarten children were ushered through the park in their little reflective vests. Mayliss sat on a bench checking Snapchat, while Nicolai balanced on a low kerb. I pushed Henry on the swings – he squealed with delight. All at once, I saw Nicolai trip. He didn't manage to put out his hands to break his fall. His mouth smashed straight into the concrete. He screamed and came towards me, bloody-mouthed, blood on his chin. I let go of the swing and crouched down; embraced him as if he were my own child. 'Mayliss!' I shouted. She was already on her feet – she came and knelt in front of us, stuck her fingers into his mouth. 'Shit,' she said, 'they're loose!' 'I'm sure he'll be fine,' I said, 'kids bash their teeth all the time!' 'But what should I do? What if they fall out! Oh Jesus, it's so gross! What do I do now? Can you ask your wife?' 'You want me to ask Helene?' 'Yes, can't you just ask her what I ought to do?'

This was what she asked of me. This impossibility, which she uttered as her only wish. 'Don't worry,' I said, 'don't be scared, I'm sure it looks worse than it is.' I googled the number for the local public dental clinic while I said that Helene works at a private clinic for adults, not with children. I took wet wipes from Henry's nappy bag to dab the snot and blood from Nicolai's face. I examined the kerb for splinters of tooth. I distracted Henry by pointing to a Dalmatian, and when Nicolai had calmed down, I offered him more orange. I used the Ruter app to find out which bus Mayliss should take to reach the dental clinic. I reassuringly stroked her back. And as soon as we had parted ways, when we had gone in opposite directions with our pushchairs, I hurried to pull off my thin, bloodstained sweater.

H ELENE HAS TRIED TO CALL ME. She's texted *I'm sorry.* Sorry for making accusations against me. For having things she needs to work through. *Maybe I'm a little paranoid.* A little? If Mayliss were here now, I would have said: Ugh, sometimes she can be such a fucking bitch.

Of course I understand that she's suspicious. Of course I understand that some sort of backlash was inevitable. 'You failed her when she needed you most,' Janne once said to me. 'A relationship can't survive without repair.' I wish I could just meet up with Janne now. Blurt everything out. Receive some comfort. But she'd have said: 'This is your own fault.' Because I've pushed Helene's trust too far, because my lies have now done irreparable damage.

I text: *You've disappointed me.*

If Mamma finds out about this… without Helene, I won't stand a chance. I'll end up trapped in her net again. Take the boys over to visit. Sit there next to my sister and her son at the table, praising her food, praising her life, praising the presents she's bought the kids, before I have to excuse myself and leave the table, because nodding and smiling and pretending everything is fine gives me sudden-onset diarrhoea.

The boys' room. I fill holes and sand down the filler and apply masking tape. It's actually idiotic, all this to save the 8,000 kroner the decorators wanted for the job, it's small change in the overall budget, which we're financing with a loan, I should have just let them do the lot. But this was the agreement. I'm keeping my side of the deal. I apply the first coat of paint without taking a break. Sky blue at the top, purple at the bottom. These are the colours Olav chose – Henry's too small to be asked. The day simply passes. I wait for the paint to dry. I don't eat. I hope I've grown a little thinner. I open the boxes containing the children's toys, the ones I still haven't carried up to the loft. I tip them out onto the concrete and sort them into various categories, put pretend food and Duplo and plastic animals into transparent plastic bags before I throw them all back into the boxes. But maybe I ought to just label them with MAMMA SILJE and MAMMA HELENE, respectively. So later in the autumn, the boys can unpack the boxes in their two new homes.

TWICE I DRAFT A TEXT TO MAYLISS. But I don't send the messages. I have no idea how she's doing, how she would react, should she hear from me now. But if she saw me, face to face. Only that would mollify her.

OUTSIDE THE GARAGES stands the young guy whose name I can never remember, but who always remembers mine. He's cleaning out the boot of his car and is more smartly dressed than usual. He's going to visit his mother in Bærum, he says. Where am I off to? He tells me I don't need to get the bus, it takes for ever in the summer, he can drop me off at Oslo Central Station.

Soon I'm sitting there in the passenger seat, acting as if everything is normal, nothing amiss. I make small talk. About how nice it is to have moved out here. About how lovely the house will be when we come back in September. I even say I'm pretty sure the children couldn't grow up in a better place. Where on earth did I get that from? I seem so normal. The fact that my mouth can simply continue to rattle off these sentences, it's unnerving. I'm wearing one of Helene's old running T-shirts and a pair of shorts, both flecked with paint. My thighs are pale and huge, but I know that he's looking at them.

THE AREA OUTSIDE the train station is teeming with people. By moving away from suburbia's 130 metres above sea level, it's as if I've travelled to another climate zone. The heat and noise are intense, as if Oslo city centre is trapped beneath a bell jar. I just don't get how so many people can want to meet here. Accordion players and the gliding of the trams, electric scooters on the pavements, teenagers shoving each other around. The groups of grown women staggering about shitfaced in summer dresses that are far too short, and who all erupt into harsh hysterics simultaneously, as if someone is playing a laugh track. All the chain stores and restaurants, the shitty places. If Mamma or my sister were in town, they'd be sitting there now, upstairs in the Byporten shopping centre, grabbing a bite to eat in Egon.

I walk up Karl Johan. Among the crowds of tourists, the street is teeming with young Roma women. 'Excuse me, may I ask you a question?' They have young bodies and black teeth. Poverty devours one's dignity, decency, sincere amiability: you're willing to do anything, to practically step over corpses, and the privileged are too naïve to even imagine it is possible.

An entwined young couple comes towards me. Because the street is so crowded, they have to let go of each other's hands for a few seconds and walk one behind the other. The young girl hurries along a few steps behind the boy, and the shining, happy expression on her face lingers as her gaze meets mine, and I'm allowed for just a moment to stare straight into it: it is sick with love.

The hotel Mayliss works at isn't far from my office. I know that she's got a shift this evening. She always works Saturday nights. I stand outside, peering in. Is she there?

The junkies swarm around me. Like intoxicated animals, animals that have drunk from a poisoned lake. One of them, a kind of raggedy, toothless David Bowie, asks me for money. I say that unfortunately, I don't have any cash on me. 'Then can you buy me a bun?' the junkie asks. 'Just one bun?'

Any willpower or sense that I have the right to say no in good conscience was used up by the Roma women. I accompany him across the street and into the 7-Eleven. 'Which kind would you like?' I ask. 'Chocolate,' he replies. 'And then I need two hundred kroner. Can you take out two hundred kroner?' I look at the guy behind the till. He rolls his eyes. But I want to be a good person. I am a good person. 'And I'd like to take out two hundred kroner in cash, too,' I say to the cashier. The junkie snatches the note from my hand and strides away. He doesn't thank me. I don't even get a fucking thank you. I want to run after him. Set my boot on him, hear his skull crack against the ground.

Pride pennants still hang in the window of the bar next to the 7-Eleven, they must have forgotten to take them down after the parade. I can just leave now. I don't need to be here. But I cross the street and walk back to the hotel. Through the windows, I can see that the reception area is empty. But Mayliss is sitting there, behind the counter, wearing a black shirt, her name on a little badge pinned to her chest.

I am calm. Utterly calm. All the fear, all the thoughts I've had this week. And then there is simply this. A woman behind a hotel reception desk. It feels as if many years have passed since our last meeting, in her apartment. She stares at the computer screen before her. Is she thinking about me? Is she planning her next move? Or is she simply sad? No, this is too idiotic. Because what am I going to do? Threaten her into silence? Tell her she holds my life in her hands?

I catch sight of my reflection in the window. The paint-spattered T-shirt, the short shorts. What do I look like? Joachim would die if he saw me out in public looking like this. And although I cast a glance at the hotel's revolving door, I know that I won't go in. Because it isn't Mayliss that's the problem. She isn't the mother with attachment issues. I am.

I T'S ONLY TWO WEEKS since we last saw each other. The week
before Helene took the kids to Trøndelag, Mayliss texted: *Lunch
at my place, Tuesday 1 p.m.?* How could I not accept? I felt guilty about
the situation with Nicolai's teeth – I had to reassure her I hadn't
meant to seem uncaring. Just this once, I thought. Just one more
meet-up, and then I can slowly vanish into thin air. *Should I bring
anything?* I asked. *Just little Henry :) :)*, she replied.

It could have been a nice day. It was a nice day. I strolled part of
the way, before I got on the Metro at Økern. Henry slept in his
pushchair, on top of the lambskin, wearing chequered shorts and
a vest, his little chubby arms flung above his head. It was hot. We
had Skyped the architect that same morning. He'd sent us drawings
for the kitchen, which he had adjusted in accordance with our suggestions. 'Oh, this is going to be just wonderful,' Helene said. Her
eyes shone. She was happy. And I thought: This isn't just about the
new house, but also about her wanting to live in that house with me.

I'd never been to Rødtvedt before. My suburbia was postcard-
perfect compared to this. Industrial buildings and car parks and
tower blocks, the roar of Trondheimsveien's traffic. Girls in hijabs.
Large clusters of restless teenage boys, left to their own devices for
the summer. All the things people back home on Sotra speak ill of
and feel afraid of when they watch the evening news or accompany
their kids to Norway Cup youth football games.

Her apartment block was on Rødtvedtveien. 706. On the seventh floor. I rang the bell, the intercom crackled, 'It's Silje Marie,' I said. Nobody replied, but I was buzzed in. It was one of those typical, characterless buildings. White-painted concrete walls, a long row of green mailboxes just inside the entrance. Hers was in the middle. I parked Henry's pushchair under the stairs. Then I stroked Henry's eyebrows. 'Are you awake, sweetie?'

He hung heavy in my arms when I picked him up, but he wasn't irritated at being woken. He peered around at the new surroundings, shifting focus in the perplexed way only small children can. 'We're going to visit Nicolai,' I said. 'We're going to take the lift.'

I used to be afraid of lifts when I was younger, but alongside his studies at Copenhagen Business School, Joachim had a part-time job at the switchboard of a Scandinavian lift operator. They were an entire group of Norwegian students and artists who chatted amiably with panic-stricken Norwegians stuck in Norwegian lifts, day and night, live from Copenhagen. 'So you can just relax,' Joachim said. 'We always get you out.'

The lift doors closed behind us. 'That?' Henry asked. 'Lift,' I said. 'Do you want to press the button?' I bent down and guided Henry's hand towards the number seven. He gave a start when the lift began to move, then began to laugh. I laughed, too, validated his laughter. 'Does it feel funny in your tummy?' I said, and we looked at ourselves in the wall-to-wall mirror. He was still tired, he rested his forehead against mine, and our noses touched, and silky-soft tenderness slowly drifted through me, it was the kind of touch that makes you think: from now on, I'll endure anything.

The lift stopped and the doors opened. Mayliss stood outside her front door, waiting. At first, I almost didn't recognize her. She was wearing a tight, low-cut dress and her arms were bare, revealing a

271

chaos of black-and-white tattoos; she'd flattened her hair against her scalp in a kind of slicked-back style. And on top of her head, above her bleached-blonde fringe: a party hat, purple and glinting, like the most absurd stage prop.

'Hi, Henry!' she shouted. Henry gave an open-mouthed smile. 'Nice hat,' I said, as I frantically thought: Surely this can't be for Nicolai? He doesn't turn two until the autumn. 'It's my birthday,' she said. 'Come in.' 'It's your birthday?' I said. 'How come you didn't say anything?' 'Nah, it's not a big deal. Come in, come in. I have an Oreo cake.' 'So how old are you?' 'Forty.' 'Forty!' I repeated. 'But Mayliss, I haven't brought you anything!' 'Oh no, don't worry about that,' she said. 'The most important thing to me is that you're here.'

Yes. She actually said that. And of course it was nice, and not only was I relieved that she clearly wasn't mad at me and didn't intend to confront me about how I'd behaved when I refused to call Helene from the playground, I was also happy she wanted to celebrate her fortieth birthday with me, or, well, maybe happy isn't quite the right word, but I was flattered, at any rate. At the same time, however, I felt a vague discomfort, because wasn't this a bit depressing, the fact that she'd got dressed up on her own birthday just to sit here in her apartment with SILJE MARIE (baby music), and did I really want to be a central figure in such a dreary life event? But I was here now. The only thing to do was go in. And despite thinking I'd soon have to cut all contact, I'd also been looking forward to chatting with her, sharing my latest news: Things have actually been pretty good between Helene and I lately, we're looking forward to getting the house sorted out, and yesterday we found her old KORG, yeah, it's a synth, she tried to learn to play piano on it a few years ago, although she didn't get much further than memorizing the notes, but yesterday she said she'd like to take it up again, if for no other reason than to be able to show off by playing a bit of synth at parties.

How full her hallway usually was I didn't know, so I didn't react to all the shoes that were there, not even the little glittery ballet flats. The air smelt familiar. Cheap hairspray. Melted cheese. 'I can hold him,' she said as I bent down to take off my sandals. 'Come on, Henry,' she said, 'shall we go see if we can find Nicolai?' I followed them down the dark hallway, deeper into the apartment, towards the light and the cool breeze from the open balcony doors, and the first thing I saw when I entered the living room was that there was a striking panorama view over Groruddalen and Oslo, and I noticed that she had a Pride flag hanging out on the balcony. Along one wall stood the aquarium, which she had mentioned several times. It was huge, with enormous yellow fish swimming around in it – she had taught me that they adapt to how much space they have, that all those teeny-tiny goldfish you see in smaller tanks should actually be big as trout. On the drying rack in the middle of the living room hung one of Olav's old, small T-shirts, with a faded print of a lion on it. And back there, to the right of the drying rack, beside the coffee table, stood Nicolai, with a plaster on his chin. And he wasn't alone.

Squeezed together on the sofa sat four people: an older woman, a guy of around my age, an older man, and a chubby girl of around twelve in a short pink dress. So many people, in the middle of the day on a Tuesday, and everyone except the little girl sat in complete silence and stared at us as we came in, and the similarities were unmistakable – true, the old man might be lanky, but the woman and the younger man were huge, huge and trashy and in possession of Mayliss's features, the same small ears, the same unnaturally long faces, and the older woman grinned in exactly the same way Mayliss sometimes grinned. 'Well I never!' she exclaimed, and she needn't have bothered introducing herself, I knew immediately: this was Mayliss's mother. Her mother, her brother, her niece and her stepfather. And I understood, all at once I understood why we were there, and I heard her say it: 'This is Silje Marie, and this here is Henry, who might be Nicolai's little brother.' 'Well, I don't think there's any doubt, is there?' Mayliss's mother cried, and she got up, and strode straight towards Mayliss, who still had Henry on her arm, 'Hi, Henry!' she squealed. 'What a handsome little boy you are!'

What should I do? It felt like being invited back to someone's place without realizing that the person wants sex, like an ambush in a dead-end street, and I was outnumbered, I could do nothing but give myself over, let it happen. I shook their hands, one after the other, Mayliss's brother had dirty nails, her mother smelt strongly of perfume, and I smiled, and I sat there with them, sat there as we bent over the coffee table and ate Oreo cake and cheap no-brand ice cream, and my heart pounded as if possessed, and I stared at Henry, the whole time I stared at Henry: Start crying, I thought, become hysterical, fall and hurt yourself so we can excuse ourselves and leave. But Henry didn't cry – unlike Olav, he isn't wary of new people and new places. Henry was on top form, Henry ran around the apartment with Nicolai, Henry knelt down and said choo-choo as he pushed a little train back and forth, Henry clambered all over the sofa, Henry slapped his palms against the aquarium glass, Henry ate three portions of ice cream.

I answered all their questions comparing Henry's interests and abilities with Nicolai's. I nodded and agreed that only two boys with the same father could have such similar eyes and faces. And when she pulled Henry onto her lap, when Mayliss's mother pulled him up onto her huge lap, with him on one thigh and Nicolai on the other, and shook her head as if to make those long, dyed-black tangles into flowing tresses, as she asked someone to bring a camera and take a picture, I just sat there, on the verge of tears, my hands folded in my lap, as if I were secretly thanking God.

THE EVENING BEFORE Helene and the boys left, I texted Mayliss and told her I'd call her after dinner. I could have waited until after they'd gone, until I was alone; that would have been easier, more practical, I would have had more time then, would have really been able to think about how to best express myself, but I couldn't take it any more, I couldn't breathe. I heard the voice of Mayliss's mother in my head; in my mind's eye I rummaged around in Mayliss's apartment as I helped Helene to pack. Outside the garage I put down the bag of supplies I'd bought for the boys for the flight. First, I thanked her for inviting us to her party. 'You have such a wonderful family,' I said. 'A really friendly and inclusive bunch. I'm really sorry I didn't bring you a present.' She laughed. 'Oh, stop it, honestly,' she replied. 'You're so worried about keeping up appearances!'

I leant against the green box from which we collect grit in the winter. The magpies cackled in the fir tree. The evening sun beat down upon my face. I rubbed my free hand against my cheekbone, hard. 'It's just… there's something I need to talk to you about.' 'Oh? That sounds serious.' 'I'm so grateful that we've been able to spend so much time together this spring. And it's been lovely. But…' I hesitated. I felt stupid, like a stupid, reckless idiot. 'But?' 'But I think we have to call it a day.' She laughed again. 'Call it a day?' 'I don't think we should meet up any more. Get things muddled. Confuse the kids.' 'How are we confusing the kids? We're not confusing the kids.' 'Not now, maybe. But they're getting bigger. And… it isn't just that. It isn't right. That I haven't told Helene.' 'Told her what?' Yet again, she laughed. But now she sounded unsure. 'What is it you think I want from you, exactly?' 'Nothing, nothing. I've just started mulling things over, that's all.'

My shame. My shamelessness. Of course I felt it. But I didn't care, I just kept going, once I'd started, it was actually easy. 'I'd like to ask you not to say anything to anybody else. Nor to Nicolai. About Henry. That Nicolai has a biological relative you know of.' 'But Silje,' she said, 'honestly, are you really going around thinking about that?' 'For all we know, they might not even be related,' I went on. 'It isn't as if we've taken a DNA test.'

She fell silent. I stood there, waiting. My heart was hammering, I started to feel queasy again. 'Hello?' I said. 'Are you still there?' 'I'm here,' she said. 'But surely you can understand why I might be feeling a bit put out right now.'

Then came the accusations, the ugly, invasive allegations. 'Well, I suppose I shouldn't be surprised. You're not exactly overflowing with love for Henry, either.' 'Where on earth did you get that from?' I replied. 'That's totally uncalled for!' 'I'm only repeating what I've heard,' she went on, 'I'm only saying what I've seen. And Mamma completely agrees.' 'Your mother?' She didn't reply. 'So, what exactly does your mother think?' She gave a snort. 'You've got a nerve,' she said. 'Calling me up and talking to me like this.' 'I don't mean to be rude,' I said, 'I really am concerned with what's best for the kids.' 'You can't tell me what to say or not say. You're not the only mother in the world, you know.' 'We're not your family,' I said. 'Henry and Nicolai are not family.' 'Have I ever said that?' 'Then why did you invite us to meet your family? Why did you invite us?' 'They stopped by, on a surprise visit. And anyway, what's the problem? Are you really *that* fucking ashamed?'

Is she lying? I don't know. It doesn't matter. Because the visit did happen. Henry's identity has been made known. And the next things she says are indeed said. 'You know what, Silje Marie? You have problems. You really have some work to do on yourself. It's clear that you're struggling. I feel sorry for your kids, yeah, I really do. And I feel sorry for your poor wife. If she only knew what you've been going around doing, the secrets you've been spilling. If she only knew what you've said about Henry.'

THE DAY IS BURIED IN DARKNESS. The sky has collapsed, the light plunged to earth. We are down on our knees, digging. Henry is born, it's an emergency C-section, but I'm allowed to be present. He is bloody and healthy. 'Congratulations,' the doctor says, 'you have a big, beautiful boy!' I stare at the child. I feel nothing. I am black and empty. They ask me to cut the umbilical cord. What good will that do, I think, but I cut it.

A few days later, when we have come home from the hospital, I lie in bed beside Helene and Henry. It is night. Olav is in his room at the other end of the apartment. He's asleep. But I can't stand the thought that he's alone, that he might wake up and be afraid and alone. I want to go to him. All my instincts demand that I go to him. But I can't. I have to stay here and change Henry's tiny nappies and help Helene to breastfeed him and keep an eye on the stitches in her abdomen and show that I'm there for her. Olav's other mother has had a child, and this child prevents me from going to my own.

WHEN OLAV WAS LITTLE, I WAS SO CAUTIOUS. Everything was new. I was a sensitive, first-time mother. But when Henry came along, I grew careless. I drank coffee while I carried him in the baby carrier at my chest. I did this, despite knowing that far too many babies are admitted to hospital with scalds and burns. How often is it suspected that these injuries are intentionally inflicted? I thought about adoptive parents and step-parents, I couldn't stop thinking about stepfathers, about how there's nothing that makes a child more vulnerable than growing up with a stand-in for its biological father.

THE CHILD'S FACE was smaller than the flat of my hand. I pulled him close to me, he lay still, and then he started up again. His hand, with its single, sharp fingernail – he clawed at my neck, it made me livid. I tore his hand away, hard, and then I kissed him, sort of hoping he hadn't noticed anything untoward. It was night. He had woken up, I had laid him down next to me, he stroked my boob. I let him do it. But then he pinched me. 'Stop it,' I said, 'no!' He pinched harder, dug his nail in – it was so painful, sharp, like the tip of a knife. I grabbed him quick as a flash, I was distant, and wasn't that only right, wasn't it a reflex? I was gentle immediately afterwards, explained, said that it hurt, but I noticed he was acting strangely, that he was eighteen months old and fighting not to show how he wanted to cry.

You can grab a child, hard, by the arm. You can be alone with the child and grow angry and hit something, snatch something, to demonstrate your power. But afterwards, it will return to you. Day after day it will return, the hope that from now on, we can act as if nothing is wrong.

O LAV IS BUILDING A DUPLO CASTLE. Henry keeps knocking it down. 'Don't,' Olav says. He builds a Duplo castle. Henry knocks it down. 'Don't,' Olav says, 'stop!' 'Cut it out!' I shout. Olav says: 'Mamma, don't be mean to Henry!'

We're standing beside the E6. There is heavy traffic. If both boys run out into the road, I know which one of them I'm going to run after.

Did I really say that? It slipped out of me, but of course I didn't mean it, I don't mean it. 'It's a thought I sometimes have,' I added, and Mayliss lay there on her stomach wearing only her bra and shorts and trustingly closed her eyes, as if I hadn't said a single thing that might be the slightest bit shocking on this glorious May day beneath the baking-hot sun at Frognerbadet swimming pool. 'I get it,' she said. 'It's a pretty strong force, this maternal instinct.'

I don't mean it. But Helene won't believe me. And now that I've thought these thoughts, cultivated this sense of distance? Can I be his mother? I haven't betrayed Helene. I have betrayed my own child.

THE CATHEDRAL IS OPEN both evenings and nights, says the sign outside. I stop. I can almost feel the cool air flowing from the wide-open doors. Should I go in? Is there a priest on duty? Is there someone I can kneel before, ask for absolution? Olav isn't the only one who's attracted to churches, you'd almost think it was genetic. The first time I went to Trøndelag with Helene, we drove from her parents' farm and into Trondheim. She showed me the bars she used to sneak into when she was in high school, the cute houses in Bakklandet, the romantic bridges, the view of Munkholmen. But I – all I wanted was to go back to Nidaros Cathedral. I stood there and stared, mesmerized by the sculptures, the sheer dimensions of the place, the enormous volume of cut stone. I just couldn't get over it. That such a church had been built there, in the middle of nowhere. Something so holy, in the middle of medieval Norway. 'I'm afraid I'm going to have to disappoint you,' Helene said, chuckling as I shared my fairy-tale fantasies. 'The whole thing burned down in the seventeen hundreds, so this is just a reconstruction.'

I try to call her. She declines the call. *Putting Olav to bed*, she texts. But I know my son. I know he must have fallen asleep ages ago. *My dear better half*, I write. *What's going on?* I send the message. Then add: *We have to talk*.

She's there – she replies straight away. *I know. But I don't think I have the strength for it tonight.*

It's actually not what you think, I write. *Can I call you?*

Not tonight.

But do you even want me to come up there tomorrow?

Yes. Probably. I don't know.

She doesn't know. The sorrow of this: she doesn't know. Doubt has taken her. Doubt has overwhelmed her once again, brought her down. Now I'm going to get what I deserve. My true face will be unveiled. It's a little over twelve hours until the flight departs, until it becomes clear to everyone that I no longer have the right to show up and flop down on the sofa there among them.

I SHOULD HAVE KNOWN how Mamma would react when I told her about Helene. I should have been prepared, because I hadn't forgotten what she had demanded of me when she read my diary, and I remembered how she changed the channel if that lesbo Kim Friele was on TV, and I remembered how she spoke about the effeminate, single young man who lived next door to Grandpa, and how Pappa didn't dare disagree with her, especially since he'd often eaten apple cake at the neighbour's house when he was little. I knew she had been brought up in a time and society in which homosexuality was forbidden and an abomination, and that she herself was alternately subjected to affection and slaps and rejection if she forgot herself, forgot the rules that applied. And still I came to her, nervous but bolstered by love's arrogance, in the belief that I occupied such a special position in her life that it would force her to overcome all these notions and realize that times were different now. That she would feel relief, yes, and perhaps even be glad, when she saw that she had raised a child who may not have chosen the easiest path, who may not have done exactly as her mother had wished or imagined, but who, at long last, felt happy and free.

M Y PHONE'S MESSAGE notification dings again. I don't want to look. Has Helene come up with something else to add to her long line of reasoning about what a treacherous, deceitful wife I am? Or maybe it's Mayliss – did she see me through the window, as I stood there like a goddamn stalker?

No. It's just a text from Joachim. He's at a *totally epic party*. *WHEN are you coming to visit?*

The contrast to this – the fact that I'm standing here now – it's ridiculous. I simply can't help but laugh. I laugh loudly – I stand here outside the cathedral like a crazy person and laugh. Nobody hears me. Nobody cares. Oslo is full of crazy people. *I wish*, I write. I write that everything is now so fucked up that I have no idea how I'm going to carry on. *It's done*, I write. Everything I thought I had under control is lost.

O N THE WAY HOME, I have to take a bus replacement service. I feel vague, distant, as if I'm floating outside my body, as if I'm the reflection of myself I used to glimpse out there in the winter darkness when I sat on the number 20 bus from Torshov to work. The bus is full. A family gets on. It's late. Far too late to be out with small children. A father, a mother, a sleeping baby in a pram, and a child of around two or three. The bus maintains a high speed. I want to get up, try to signal to the father that they can come back here, that there's space. The little boy and his father are flung around the bus. The father doesn't take hold of his son. The boy falls, just once at first; I look away, then I hear another thump, the boy has fallen again, he starts to cry. 'Jesus, you have to hold him!' I shout, but the man doesn't even look in my direction. Smiling and unaffected, he drags the boy over towards the mother, the mother who's just sitting there with the sleeping little brother in the pram. The man smiles and slings the wailing boy towards the mother, like a sack, then bends over the sleeping little brother, pulls out his dummy and shoves it into the little boy's mouth. The boy writhes and cries even more loudly; the mother plucks out the dummy and says: 'He doesn't like it.' The man smiles, the boy sniffles and looks at his mother and puts a hand to his forehead. 'Leon hit his head,' he says. Nobody on the bus says anything. I stare at them. Hope that the mother will catch my eye. Look. I can help you. But at the next stop, they get off.

I RETURN TO OUR EMPTY HOUSE. The bag of building waste is overflowing beneath the apple trees. The family's three bicycles – Henry doesn't have one of his own yet – stand in the garden; the code to the lock on Helene's bike is my birthday. The sun has set. The summer darkness seeps in and settles around the house like bluish gas.

So this is how it's going to end. An empty house. A fucking renovation.

When I let myself in and go into the living room, where the last boxes I haven't yet carried up to the loft are stacked, I just know it: we will never move back here. And my kids will come to blame me for inflicting this lambasted, unethical life upon them.

S OMEWHERE FAR AWAY I CAN HEAR A KNOCKING. Now they're coming, I think. They know that I'm alone, and now they've come for me. The knocking is coming from downstairs. Hard raps. What should I do? I get stiffly to my knees on the mattress. Lean cautiously towards the windowpane and look down into the garden.

But then I start to laugh. There he is, like a stray ghost. Joachim. In white trousers, a white vest, light brown loafers. With a moustache! He sees that I've seen him, and I'm not thinking clearly as I tumble down the stairs, over the dusty, stripped concrete floor and towards the terrace door, which I tug at like a desperado and slide open. 'What the hell…?' I exclaim. 'What on earth are you doing here?'

He doesn't answer at first. He just smiles and looks at me, his gaze partly affectionate, partly astonished, presumably at the sight of how I've come barging out to him, half-naked and pale and puffy-eyed, and partly smug – he has done this, surprised me, come here, not just to a bar or café in the centre of Oslo, but to this suburb, to Kringkollen, to the house where I live with my family. 'Oh, honey,' he says. 'Come here.' And he holds out his arms, like a soldier returned from war, and I hesitate for a moment, as if I'm a child and can't quite believe that this soldier is the father he claims to be, or as if I'm a fugitive who's been living alone in the forest and who is now seeing another person for the first time in years. But I soon surrender, there is nothing I want more than to surrender. I walk straight into Joachim's embrace, into those bare, gym-toned arms, to the solid chest, the smooth hollow of his neck. His skin is clammy and cold. 'You'll catch your death,' I mumble. 'No comments about how sweaty I smell, thank you very much,' he says. 'I've spent all night sitting on a FlixBus. And I am never, ever doing that again.'

My phone's screen is packed with missed calls, unread texts. One from Helene – that one I leave unopened. Nothing from Mayliss. But from Janne. She's called twice. *Are you okay?* And Joachim. He's the one who has called the most, sent the most messages. *Stay where you are. I'M COMING!* I feel my insides soften. It's as if I become a person again. A person somebody will leave a party for, a person who can make someone jump onto a stinking, international-border-crossing bus. I may not be that person. But maybe it's good enough that he thinks I am. Because if he believes it, then I can believe it too.

He doesn't close the door to the hallway toilet when he pees. When we lived together it didn't irritate me, it didn't feel transgressive, more like a symbol of our trust in each other, of everything that was different from the rules of the house in which I'd grown up. I stand there and watch as he washes his hands and face in the small sink. His fringe is still thick, still dark. His face as smooth as it ever was. I know that people encountering him for the first time often think he's happy-go-lucky. But the things he struggles with were there long before his mother went insane. Only this new Murray Bartlett moustache makes him look older. Much more rugged. And beautiful. I want to tell him he's beautiful! 'What are you looking at, hmm?' he asks. I shake my head. 'It's just so absurd that you're here.'

What else is there to do, other than show him around? The emptied rooms, the naked walls, the sanitized, vaguely drain-smelling bathroom upstairs. Only the odd trace of the boys remains. The changing table. The cot, without its mattress. The big, heavy hobby table in Olav's room, which the decorators have said it's no problem to work around. Right there, in front of the window, with a view of the railway line and apartment blocks, is where he usually sits. With his beads and shells and stickers. Often while Henry stands beside him, clinging to his thigh, wanting to climb up next to him, and Olav shakes his head: 'No!' And the harder he refuses, the more Henry wants to climb up, and in the end Olav often relents and allows Henry to sit next to him on the red bench, and it's a special moment, right until Henry empties the tray of beads across the tabletop or tugs the booklet of stickers towards him and Olav begins to scream.

Had Joachim come a week ago, he could have seen it for himself. But now it's almost as if they don't exist. When I'm with Joachim, I can still pretend I'm not a mother. Or act as if it's a subcategory of my life, something temporary I simply have to get done, and which I will get done, if he can just give me a moment and wait.

In the living room, our voices echo. The vapid novel Bjørg brought over lies in the middle of the floor. 'Well, this is certainly… cosy,' Joachim says. 'I know it's awful,' I say. 'But once we've redecorated, it will be ours, at least.' He looks at me askance, as if he isn't sure whether I'm lying. 'But it has potential,' he replies, 'with the garden and everything? It's a thousand times better than I was expecting.'

I've left the coffee things out on the kitchen counter. I grind beans, fill the coffee machine with water. Four level spoonfuls. A splash of milk. He likes his coffee exactly the same way Helene does. Every morning for almost ten years I've drunk coffee with Helene. 'I only have paper cups,' I say. Joachim pushes himself up to sit on the end of the kitchen counter. In his tight white clothes he looks like some preposterous angel. 'So,' he says. 'Qué pasa?' 'Qué pasa what?' I reply. 'Well, first off – what have you done with them?' 'Helene and the boys? They're on holiday with her parents. Didn't you read my messages?' 'Didn't I read your messages? I thought Helene had left you, I thought you were on the verge of suicide.' 'And so you came all the way out here to save me?' 'I was planning on coming home for the summer anyway, I just brought it forward a bit.' He grins. I know how he's actually feeling when he grins like that. I go over to him, stop in front of him, sitting there on the counter, and he leans forward and takes my face in his hands, kisses the top of my head. The tenderness. It's almost unbearable. 'Joachim,' I say, 'I've really messed things up this time.' 'Tell me something I don't know,' he replies. 'And clearly it's been a little too long since you last saw a hairdresser, too.'

A T THE BACK OF THE HOUSE IS THE MORNING SUN. The rattan furniture is all askew. There's bird shit on the terrace boards; soil and withered plants stick up from frost-cracked pots. The traffic along the E6 can be heard as a low rumble. In the final week before the summer holiday, before we headed to the kindergarten, the boys would sit out here, each drinking their cup of breakfast chocolate milk. Both wearing handed-down pyjamas from their cousins, worn cotton and sagging bottoms with patterns of ponies, rabbits, flowers. One big. One small. One with blonde curls. One whose hair is thin and dark. The blonde one with the Cardamom Town cup, and the dark-haired one with the Forest of Huckybucky cup. The blonde one wants to use a spoon. Then the dark-haired one also wants to use a spoon. The blonde one asks for more. Then the dark-haired one asks for more, too.

Joachim and I sit at either end of the garden sofa, which I've moved around to the back of the house to free up space for the decorators. I pick at the skin around my fingernails. I don't know where to start. The cherry tree hangs heavy above the fence. The clouds stand still against the sky. I look at my watch. Are they eating breakfast now, in the kitchen? Is my father-in-law frying eggs, are the boys groggy and content?

*

I don't know where to start, but soon I blurt it all out. I release all my grimy, inner darkness, I withhold nothing from this person who has been sent to me. I admit that I almost sought out Mayliss yesterday. I even say: 'When I tell people I have two children, two sons, it feels as if I'm lying.'

My cheeks are hot. I have a stomach-ache. But I hear it, of course I hear how he responds to me.

The way he says: 'Seriously? Haven't people fought so we don't have to think like that any more?'

The way he says: 'Jesus Christ. You women. Honestly! How hard can it be? Do you feed him? Do you change his nappies? Do you tell him you love him? Stop yourself from hitting him? Do you treat them pretty much the same?'

The way he says: 'At least you can have kids. We have to take advantage of poor women in India if we want to do that.'

The way he says: 'When Olav was just as little as Henry is now, you were having a total crisis. Back when you were messing around with that young girl. You even said you'd thought of leaving Helene for her. Remember that? And you didn't go around thinking you were a bad mother to Olav then, did you? No!'

The way he says: 'Of course you love him. All you ever do is talk about those goddamned kids. You send me photos all the time. LOOK, Henry's eating ice cream. LOOK, Henry and Olav are holding hands. LOOK, Henry and I are out for a walk and now we're petting this horse.'

The way he says: 'Okay, so maybe there's like a whole fifty people out of eight billion who wouldn't have had the opportunity to exist without that guy wanking off a few times.'

The way he says: 'Maybe they just won't care. Or maybe they'll get hung up on it and turn into super-angry panellists on the *News at Six* and join the religious far right. Who can say?'

The way he says: 'If you keep thinking this way, it's going to have a negative impact on your kids.'

The way he says: 'Your kids are growing up in a different gay reality. They're not living in our childhood, Mamma Silje.'

The way he says: 'Helene must be going crazy. I don't know anybody as conflict-avoidant as you.'

WHEN JOACHIM SPEAKS, everything seems so easy. When Joachim speaks, I'm almost convinced. I should have recorded our conversation, cut out my own voice and simply listened to his arguments. Listened to them daily, like a kind of indoctrination. Maybe it would have helped. Maybe, if I only listened to the recording often enough, it would have caused the hard shell of my thoughts to crack and split.

But I know how things will feel when I'm left alone again.

I know how cowardly I become when I encounter resistance.

Joachim leans his head back against the garden sofa and yawns. Poor thing, he's hardly slept. From the sky above us comes a rumbling sound. The aeroplane must be just behind the clouds. 'I'll make some more coffee,' I say.

In the downstairs toilet I reluctantly open the message from Helene. But – there is no accusation. It's a video. Sent at 05:23 this morning. Henry standing there in nothing but his nappy, groggy-eyed and big-bellied. He's holding something in his hands. Our wedding photo. My mother-in-law framed it, of course – it usually stands on the telephone table in the hallway, surrounded by tea lights in heart-shaped holders which she lights whenever they have guests. 'Who's that?' Helene asks from behind the camera. He points at her, quick and forthright. 'Mamma!' 'And then who's that?' Helene's voice asks, 'who's that there?' 'Mamma Sise!' He doesn't point this time. He leans forward and kisses the photo, he closes his eyes, he says: 'Mmmmm.' 'Do you miss Mamma Sise?' Helene asks, 'Mamma Sise is coming today, won't that be lovely?' 'Mmmmm,' Henry says. Again and again he kisses the face of the bride in the whitest dress, with the shortest hair, with the shiniest eyes, and this is something I wasn't prepared for, because who would have thought it was possible, who would have thought it wasn't too late, but – I recognize her. If I put down my phone right now and look into the mirror above the sink: I think she's still there.

The scenes from the farm belonging to Silje Marie's in-laws are partly taken from a piece I wrote for *Dag og Tid* in 2012.

The text naturally features traces of a number of authors whose works I have read and who mean a lot to me – among them Stig Sæterbakken, Kristin Berget and Anne Helene Guddal.

Warm thanks to Ida K, Tine S and Lisa W.

This book wouldn't exist without Øyvind E, Hege Susanne B, Kristin B, Ronja SB or Christine S.

LOVE & PRIDE
4EVER

WHEN WE CEASE TO UNDERSTAND THE WORLD
THE MANIAC
BENJAMÍN LABATUT

NO PLACE TO LAY ONE'S HEAD
FRANÇOISE FRENKEL

FORBIDDEN NOTEBOOK
ALBA DE CÉSPEDES

COLLECTED WORKS: A NOVEL
LYDIA SANDGREN

MY MEN
VICTORIA KIELLAND

AS RICH AS THE KING
ABIGAIL ASSOR

LAND OF SNOW AND ASHES
PETRA RAUTIAINEN

LUCKY BREAKS
YEVGENIA BELORUSETS

THE WOLF HUNT
AYELET GUNDAR-GOSHEN

MISS ICELAND
AUDUR AVA ÓLAFSDÓTTIR

MIRROR, SHOULDER, SIGNAL
DORTHE NORS

THE WONDERS
ELENA MEDEL

GROWN UPS
MARIE AUBERT

LEARNING TO TALK TO PLANTS
MARTA ORRIOLS

THE RABBIT BACK LITERATURE SOCIETY
PASI ILMARI JÄÄSKELÄINEN

BINOCULAR VISION
EDITH PEARLMAN

MY BROTHER
KARIN SMIRNOFF

ISLAND
SIRI RANVA HJELM JACOBSEN

ARTURO'S ISLAND
ELSA MORANTE

PYRE
PERUMAL MURUGAN

RED DOG
WILLEM ANKER

AN UNTOUCHED HOUSE
WILLEM FREDERIK HERMANS

WILL
JEROEN OLYSLAEGERS

MY CAT YUGOSLAVIA
PAJTIM STATOVCI

BEAUTY IS A WOUND
EKA KURNIAWAN

BONITA AVENUE
PETER BUWALDA

IN THE BEGINNING WAS THE SEA
TOMÁS GONZÁLEZ